Jeremy Kline
and the
Invisible Village

A Modern Fantasy

Book 1

To Betsy,
Enjoy this wild
magical adventure.

Ray Wenck

Ray Wenck
Glory Days Press
Columbus, Ohio

Ray Wenck

Glory Days Press
Columbus, Ohio

Book Layout © 2016 BookDesignTemplates.com

Jeremy Kline and the Invisible Village/ Ray Wenck. -- 1st ed.
ISBN 978-1-7360350-5-4

Dedication

This work is dedicated to dreamers. Without you, this world is a duller place.

Acknowledgement

Someone recently asked me, "Another series? How do you keep up with them all?"

Good questions. I like series. I enjoy reading as the characters develop from each subsequent storyline. I wanted to offer the same thing with my own writing. After all, I spend all that time developing characters, and I want them to stick around for a while.

Never at a shortage for story ideas, one of my first thoughts is if the story can be developed into a series. Most of the time, the answer is yes. However, series have their own built-in problems. If readers enjoy the story and the characters, they want to read more, which puts pressure on the author to deliver at least one story per series per year.

I currently have five active series and am working on the sixth. That means six of the stories I write each year must be an advancement of those stories. Do the math. Currently, I write six novels a year. That doesn't leave any room for solo or new projects. Consequently, something has to give.

Don't panic. I'm not sure which series may go into hibernation for a while. For the moment, I am sustaining. Each series has a new release due this year.

None of this could happen without you. I'm grateful to all my readers and vow to keep them coming as long as I have your support. Thank you all.

I want to thank Jodi McDermitt for her wonderful work in bringing this story to life with her editing.

Until next time, read all you want. I'll write more.

Ray Wenck

CHAPTER ONE

With the Master's warning reverberating in her head, Daria ran harder than she'd ever run before. Motivated by fear, her endurance and speed were greater than ever. Her slight frame almost soared on the warm breeze that rustled the leaves on the trees as she flew past. Or perhaps she had created the wind.

She dodged and weaved through the dense woods, whipped often by the branches she pushed through rather than ducked under. A warm trickle tracked down her face from one of them. Her foot connected with an upraised root. She stumbled and continued, keeping her balance but losing much of her speed.

Forced to slow or fall, she grabbed at a branch. Once on balance, she burst forward again, sucking air down her raspy throat. She pushed harder, testing the limits of her endurance. She leaped a small stream and wished she had time to stop for a cool drink. Ahead there was an opening. Not good. Daria slowed as she reached the tree line. Eighty yards of open field stretched before her. Not good at all. But it didn't matter. She had to reach the village. Lives depended on her. They'd been found, and it was up to her to warn the others.

She'd been forced to memorize the directions. The Headmaster feared if she was captured, she'd give away the secret location, thus ending the war before it started. She couldn't allow that to happen; however, if she was being honest, the fear of being captured added to her speed as much as her own capability.

With a glance toward the sky, Daria broke from the cover of the trees and sprinted toward the far woods. Her long stride ate up the ground fast. She grew hopeful as she closed in on the safety of the woods. A sudden gust of wind hit her like a detonation concussion, throwing her weight forward and off balance. She tripped, fell, and rolled, the uneven ground and thistles tearing at her clothes and skin. Daria knew the gust was as unnatural as the being that had created the beast.

She rose and cast a worried look toward the white clouds, scanning the blue sky in the gaps. She pushed to her knees and wiped the blood from her palms, but before she could stand, a shadow crossed over her. It was so dark in its nature and ripped all warmth from the affected area. She searched the sky again and spotted what she feared. A Harpy. They had sent a Harpy after her.

Wasting no precious time, Daria was sprinting before she reached her full height. The distance to the safety of the woods was shortening in a hurry. If she could just reach them, the Harpy would be forced to either circle above or land. She could no longer go to the village for fear of leading the horrid creature to those she was sworn to protect, but perhaps she could lead it away and double back. If the Harpy landed, it was far too formidable a beast for her to confront by herself. Her speed would be her salvation.

The wind gusts gave her warning. She dove to the ground as the Harpy swooped low. It missed snatching her from the ground, but managed to scrape one of its long, sharp talons along her back and carve a furrow into her flesh that elicited a scream. Fire ignited down her back. She had to get up. Run to safety. Get word back to the village before it was too late. With strength and energy quickly depleting, she pushed to her feet, unable to box up the agony flooding her brain. Warm blood ran down her back, plastering her torn shirt to her skin.

Her speed had been cut in half. Each step was followed by an agonized cry or moan, but she kept moving. To stop was to die, or worse--to get others killed. How long could she hold out against torture before she gave up the village? She didn't want to find out. Daria forced more speed, yet she wasn't fast enough. A mere ten yards from the tree line, the foul wind buffeted her again.

She fell more than dove this time. The Harpy hovered over her. A screech of victory pierced Daria's soul as its putrid breath washed over her, which was an attack of its own. It lowered to her, talons spread and ready to grab. Daria scrambled backward, never taking her eyes from the creature. She didn't fear death. It wouldn't kill her, but there were things worse than death. It watched her; its long, muscular wings beating in slight, rapid strokes. Was it toying with her?

It made no move to corral her. Daria took advantage of the delay. She spun on the ground and bear crawled to the trees. A whispered prayer played across her lips.

Eight yards. What was it waiting for?

Five yards. The shadow hovered over her. It was playing with her. Teasing her. Giving her hope. She was out of time, yet still she moved faster, straining every muscle, pushing every limit.

Three yards. Two. The talons dug deep into her sides; the pain so intense, her mind shut down to protect it from self-imploding.

Her body was wrenched from the earth as she dug fingers into the ground, hoping to at least slow the inevitable. The field retreated beneath her as the Harpy beat its wings in powerful strokes now. It let out another victorious screech and turned back toward her escape route.

Daria had only one chance to get free, but it meant breaking the first rule. *Do not use magic.* Did that matter if she was dead? Did magic even work in this world? She forced all pain and fear from her mind, clearing it to concentrate on her task. With what was at stake, the Headmaster would forgive her.

She extended her arm to draw in energy and panicked when she could find no source. Off the ground she could only draw on air. Perhaps this world did not have energy sources. Acrid bile began to climb her throat as the fear and panic bit deeper into her core. Then as if in answer to a prayer her flailing fingers touched an energy stream.

She drew it in as desperate as if it were lifesaving air then lifted an arm toward the beast's belly, mumbled the words she shouldn't know, and snapped her fingers. Nothing happened.

No! She tried again. Same result. The frustration weakened the walls erected in her mind. The pain seeped through, followed closely by escalating fear. Hadn't she read somewhere in her studies that Harpies had a natural resistance to magic?

She could not allow failure. With all her will, she shut down her brain, allowing only a narrow channel for what she needed. Again, she lifted her arm. The words flowed from her clearer and stronger. She felt the power come. She snapped her fingers once, creating a spark. Hopeful, but not enough. She was still young and mostly untrained, but it felt like her limited magic was weaker than normal. She tried again, this time shouting the words that would activate the spell. This time the snap of fingers gave the expected result.

"Firyanatus!"

Small fires, birthday candle-size, flared at her fingertips; their red-yellow flame dancing as the air rushed past. She touched the flame to the Harpy's belly with no immediate result. She forced all her internal energy into the spell. The flame grew more intense. Feathers smoked. It was working but showed no effect. She strained her body, every taut muscle straining to the point of tearing. Seconds before her strength and her life were extinguished, the feathers began to smolder. The Harpy slowed, aware something was happening. When the flame caught and grew, the creature bellowed. It fought to stay aloft as it struggled to put out the fire with its breath and flapping wings. As the fire lapped upward around its torso, the Harpy went into a spiral, brushing the treetops, the impact knocking Daria from its grip. She plummeted, bouncing off branches with bone-jarring impact. They slowed her descent. She clutched at a limb as she fell, but her weight ripped her hands free. She continued her plummet.

Her body hit a thicker branch twenty feet from the ground. A blinding lance of pain shot through her side. The impact catapulted her head over heels. She tore through the branches of a tall pine and smacked into the trunk, knocking her unconscious. She slid down the trunk a few feet before hitting another branch. For several seconds she hung, bent in half. Then in slow but increasing increments, her body tilted. Once the balance had tipped enough, she fell the final ten feet to the ground. Daria never felt the final impact.

CHAPTER TWO

"Happy birthday to me. Happy Birthday to me. Happy birthday—" He paused to examine his face closer in the mirror. He sighed. "To me. Happy birthday, you old fart. Happy Birthday—ah, who cares?"

Jeremy Kline pushed back from the bathroom sink. His vibrant blue eyes, perhaps the only body part left not displaying his age, still focused on his image. "Sixty-six. Where have the years gone?" He put a hand under his chin and pulled his cheeks back. "Still, the years haven't been too harsh on you. You look pretty good for a fossil."

He left the bathroom and entered his bedroom. It was true. His body had aged well. He was still trim and well-toned. He had a good head of fifty-fifty hair that was half brown and half an annoying white. Though thinning, he was proud to have kept from going bald. He had no real medical conditions to hinder him and wasn't on any prescribed medications. He didn't even need glasses except for cheaters. But despite his good health, he cringed at the thought of turning sixty-six. To him, it was the beginning of the end.

It wasn't even so much the years that made him depressed. It was knowing he'd attained that age without achieving anything important over that span. Not so long ago, he'd been a young man with dreams to accomplish and goals to achieve. Well, maybe it had been longer than he thought, but he'd never really come close to reaching his dreams. He wasn't sure he even remembered what they were. That depressed him further.

He looked at the clothes he'd laid out to wear. His daughter and the grandkids were taking him out for a birthday dinner. Although he appreciated the gesture, his mood dictated he should stay home and away from people to avoid dragging them down too. He called Chandra to beg off, but before he could speak, Chandra was onto him.

"Nope, you're coming. End of discussion." Then she hung up. Where had she learned to become so rude? Must be from her mother, God rest her soul. He glanced upward. *Just kidding, Miranda.*

He missed her. She'd been gone for...what? Almost two years now. Dead from some strange disorder the doctors had never seen or heard of. Despite all their collective skill, knowledge, and pompous arrogance, Miranda had passed right from under them as they argued about the best treatment. It was just like his precious Miranda to be stricken by some disease as unique in death as she had been in life.

He stopped to pick up a photo of Miranda taken on her last birthday. She sat at the kitchen table with Chandra and their son Nick. It was the last time they were all together when she was alive. Nick attended the funeral, but Jeremy had not seen his son since. He got a phone call on his birthday last year, but the caller did not speak until just before hanging up. He heard a quick, "I'm sorry," and the call ended. Though the voice was strained, Jeremy was sure it had been Nick.

Miranda sat behind a cake. *Happy Birthday* was written in cursive in green icing. Green was her favorite color. She had made the cake herself. Never one for extravagant celebrations, she refused to be taken out for a fancy birthday dinner, preferring to make it herself. God, she was so beautiful. His hand shook as he set the photo down.

Eyes misty, he turned away. Then he stopped, placed two fingers to his lips, and pressed them to the photo. If he spent too long thinking about Miranda, he'd never leave the house. He didn't need Chandra upset with him.

He dressed in black pants, a pullover shirt, and slip-on Docksiders. Causal, but dressy enough to pass Chandra's inspection. Jeremy wondered if Cliff was coming. Cliff was

Chandra's husband. He was a big shot financial adviser and was usually too busy to be involved in the basics, like raising a family. Jeremy had never warmed to the man, but he tried to keep his opinions to himself for Chandra's sake. He was sure he'd failed.

He checked the time. Thirty minutes to spare. He debated watching some television but knew if he sat down, he might not want to get back up. To Chandra, birthdays were to be celebrated. To him, it was another reminder of time passing without accomplishing the dreams of his youth. Thoughts of his birthday depressed him enough, but after thinking about Miranda...well, he'd better get in the car and leave now, or he would shut down for an extended period.

He stopped at the outer door, gave the room one last sweep for anything that might burn down the house, then exited. He got into the car, started the engine, and stared at the house. A strange feeling came over him, like he'd forgotten something important. Forgetting was becoming more commonplace. He searched his memory but could not find the source of the feeling.

He shrugged and mumbled, "Must not have been that important." He shifted into reverse. "But probably is."

The sky was a reenactment of a Civil War battle, with the gray surrounding the small patches of blue and working them toward surrender. Rain was coming. *Hope it holds off until I'm back home,* he thought. It was another sign of his increasing age. He no longer saw well at night and it was even worse during a storm. It didn't help that he lived outside the city in a hilly area with twisting roads and no streetlights.

The drive to the restaurant was thirty minutes, which meant he'd arrive early. He slowed his speed. He hated driving so long for a meal. He hated that his daughter had guilted him into going out. He hated that he had to make the drive alone. He hated getting older. But the thing he hated above all else was not attaining any of his dreams. That had been an ongoing theme since Miranda's passing.

He only had himself to blame for his lifelong failure. He had never worked hard enough at any one thing to achieve success. He just expected that an opportunity would fall into his lap and everything would be great. Whenever he reflected on his life, regret was the one thing that always surfaced.

He remembered when Chandra came to him with a career dilemma. Though she had studied interior design, she'd been given an opportunity to intern at a local TV station. The job was unpaid, but she'd always wanted to be a reporter. The twinkle that lit her eyes told of her excitement and desire. He told her, "Opportunities like this don't come around often. Don't live your life in regret. Don't get to be my age and look back on your life and wish you would have done it."

Over the objections of the more practical Miranda, Chandra took the job and did so well that she was hired as a reporter when her internship ended. Then Chandra worked her way up to news anchor. She loved the work and was good at it. Then she met a man, and everything changed.

Such good advice. If only he'd taken it himself. He'd always felt he was destined for something big. He didn't know what it was, but he was a dreamer, and dreamers only dreamed big. Now it was too late. His time had come and gone and here he was, still managing a small bookstore. He wasn't even the owner, just an employee. Oh, it was a good job, but it just didn't pay well. The owner was always on the verge of going under. At least that was the excuse he gave every time Jeremy mentioned a raise.

Twenty-two years he'd worked there. He was always able to provide for his family, but it was never enough to do the extras, like family vacations. There was another source of regret.

He came to a stop sign and could not make himself go farther. His mind went into a trance thinking about the time they'd planned a vacation to Disney World with the kids, and then when he had to tell Miranda they couldn't afford it. She had showed no emotion. Her eyes were blank. It was then he understood she wasn't upset because she already knew they wouldn't be going and never were going to go in the first place. That knowledge crushed him.

A horn blared behind him. A glance in the mirror was blurred. He wiped his eyes and made the turn. All he could think about the rest of the way to the restaurant was all the times he'd let his family down over the years. He was a failure to himself, to his children, and Miranda.

"Forgive me, Miranda."

CHAPTER THREE

Chandra and the kids were already at the restaurant when he arrived. As he approached the table, five-year-old Connor, named after Chandra's father-in-law at her husband's insistence, ran to him. He called out, "Pe-Pop!" and leapt into his arms. It was their name for him and he loved it. Connor's teacher told him the proper name was Grandpa. Jeremy was annoyed when Connor used the term and told the boy he was still Pe-Pop. He was tempted to go to the school and tell the teacher to leave Connor alone. Connor kept calling him Pe-Pop, though, and he dropped it. Three-year-old Harper called out, "Pe-Pop!" but her attempt to copy her brother's leap into his arms was halted by Chandra. The girl squirmed and squealed as Jeremy made his way to the table.

"Here I am, little one." He put Connor down and lifted Harper from her mother's arms. He hugged her and she wrapped her small arms around his neck and squeezed. He gave her a peck on the cheek and set her down.

She wiped at the kiss spot and said, "Mommy, Pe-Pop slobbered on me."

"No, he didn't, silly girl. He gave you a kiss."

"A slobber kiss," Connor said.

Chandra rolled her eyes. "Connor, sit and behave." She stood and embraced her father. "Hi, Dad. Happy birthday."

"Thanks, Hon." They released and sat. Jeremy noticed circles under her eyes. She was a beautiful young woman. The image of her mother. She looked more than tired. She looked rundown. "How's everything?" It was his way of asking how her home life was.

"Just fine." She beamed a smile that was put on.

He knew better and she knew he knew better. Life with Cliff was not easy, and Jeremy believed that had the man been home more often, life might actually be worse. Not for the first time, Jeremy thought about taking the snob someplace secluded and beating some sense into him. He had a beautiful wife and wonderful children, but he barely acknowledged their existence. Some things were more important than making money. Jeremy should know, having had a great family and no money. At least he had spent time with his children.

"Where's Mister Wonderful?"

Chandra rolled her eyes. "Dad, don't start."

He held his hands up in surrender.

"You're Mister Wonnerful, Pe-Pop," Harper said, pointing at him.

"Why, thank you, Harper."

Chandra called the waitress over and they ordered, even though Jeremy hadn't had a chance to open the menu. He knew the drill. The kids could only maintain a certain amount of good behavior in a short time. Once they lost control, the meal was over, and Chandra would be out the door. He looked at Chandra, who spoke with mild exasperation.

"Dad, you know you always get the same thing every time we come here."

Yeah, he thought, because I've never had a chance to crack the menu. He shrugged, handed the menu to the waitress, and said, "I'll have the pot roast."

While Chandra prepared the kids for their meal, she said, "So, what's new?"

"New?" He snorted. "What could possibly be new? I'm old and getting older."

"Oh, stop that, Dad. You are not that old. It's not like you can't do things."

"What is there to do?"

"Why don't you take a vacation? When was the last time you took a few days off and did something for yourself?"

He didn't even have to think about it. The answer was never. With the kids grown and gone, he had the extra money now to do something, but the truth was, he carried so much guilt over never taking Miranda on a real vacation that he couldn't bring himself to do it now.

"What about female companionship? There has to be someone you'd like to take to dinner or a movie."

He shook his head. They'd had this discussion before. "No. There's no one."

"Come on, Dad. You can't just sit around the house and do nothing for the rest of your life."

"Why not? Is there some law against it?"

Chandra gave him the look, the same one Miranda gave him when he was being stubborn. "Dad, I worry about you. It's not good to be alone all the time."

"I'm not alone. I have you and these wonderful grandkids." He reached over and ruffled Connor's hair.

"Hey, Pe-Pop!"

He smiled at the boy, busy coloring in a book Chandra had brought for him. When he glanced back at Chandra, she still displayed the look.

"Mom wouldn't want you to waste away."

He sighed. "Maybe someday, but I'm just not ready yet. Besides, I still have my job and lots of projects to do around the house to keep me busy. And every once in a while, I get to see my grandkids."

"You could see them a lot more if you stopped over now and then."

Now it was his turn to give a look.

"Come on, Dad. You have to lighten up on Cliff. He works hard to provide for us. He can feel your disdain for him."

"Who has a stain, Mommy?" Connor asked.

"No one, honey."

The waitress arrived with the drinks. Chandra was busy helping the kids. Jeremy watched her. She was a good mother, just like her mother.

Chandra shifted her attention back to him and noticed his gaze. "What?"

He shook his head. "You're good with the kids. Just like your mom."

She reached a hand across the table and gave his hand a squeeze. "Thanks, Dad. That means a lot."

"But I think it's you who needs a break."

Now she sighed.

The food came and Jeremy helped Connor cut his chicken breast. Then he studied his own plate. It was full of overcooked carrots and potatoes and hunks of chewy, fatty meat. He would have to remember to take a carryout menu home to find a new choice.

After the meal, Jeremy helped clean the kids up and walked them to Chandra's minivan. He gave each one a kiss and a hug, then embraced Chandra.

"I'm going to look into a senior cruise for you," she said.

"No. I—"

"Yes. Let me do this for you. I'll make it a short one to a nice, warm place. That's my birthday gift to you."

He didn't offer any objections and resigned himself to her whims. She'd made the offer before, but once she got home and involved with the kids, she'd forget. He didn't want to provoke her so she wouldn't remember.

She gave him a quick kiss and slid into the van.

"Bye, Connor. Bye, Harper. Thanks, Chandra. I love you."

"Love you too, Dad. Say goodbye to Pe-Pop, kids."

The kids waved as the van pulled out of the lot. He watched them go, then made for his car.

As he walked, he thought about going on a cruise. For a moment, it excited him. Then he thought about Miranda. No. He'd never go on a cruise or anywhere else. He didn't deserve to go. His mistake—well, one of the many—was thinking there'd always be time.

"I wish I had it to do over again, Miranda. I'd take you on a cruise. I really would."

CHAPTER FOUR

Daria came to with a groan. A cacophony of insects played a forest symphony. Damp, musty air filled her nostrils. The memory of the Harpy and her fall returned to her in bits and pieces. She opened her eyes. For a moment, she thought the fall had blinded her. Then she realized it was night. With slow, deliberate movements, she attempted to sit up. A sharp pain lanced her arm. She felt a stitch in her side. Her back was on fire, the shirt plastered to the dried blood. Her head pulsed and nausea assailed her. She cried out and dropped prone again faster than intended, and ignited pain from all over her body.

She lay still for a while until the aches and pains quieted. Then she took inventory. Likely broken arm. Possible broken ribs. A concussion for sure. Maybe a fractured ankle…no, not fractured. It hurt bad and was swollen, but she could put a little weight on it. A long laceration down her back. Minor scrapes and bruises everywhere. All in all, a small price to pay for escape. That thought sent her anxiety to its peak.

Had she escaped, or was the Harpy still above her somewhere, hunting? Regardless of her pain, Daria had to move. She had to reach the village and warn them about what might be coming. They had sent a Harpy for her, but what they would send for the rest of them was much worse. That was motivation enough for her to rise again.

She slid up and rolled to her knees. With her good hand, she reached out and grabbed a branch, pulling herself to her feet. Any attempt to lift her head brought pain, nausea, and dizziness, so she remained hunched over. How would she get to the village? Maybe she shouldn't even go there. The Harpy could still be hovering. She couldn't take that chance, not with the lives of her friends and classmates at stake.

She thought about the directions and made an alternate plan. She would take a circuitous route and come in from the west instead of the south. She glanced skyward to get her bearings. The quarter moon was almost directly overhead. She turned left.

With her broken arm pressed to her chest for support, she moved, still bent at the waist. Using the trees to keep her upright, she moved slowly. Sharp, excruciating pain shot through her body and reinforced her belief that at least one rib was broken. She stopped for a minute to catch her breath and steel her resolve. She had to reach the village. Nothing else mattered.

Daria sucked in a deep breath and released it as she moved.

* * *

Night had fallen. The sky came to life once he was away from the bright lights of the city. The luminescent stars lit the sky like the opening scene of a space movie. If not for the twists and turns of the road, Jeremy would have kept his gaze focused up in search of the brightest star, the one he figured was Miranda looking down to keep an eye on him.

He found a bright star out the side window. "Hi, my love. Thanks for watching over for me."

He turned around another curve and the car angled upward as he reached the first in a series of hills. Though beautiful during the day, this was his main stretch of concern when driving at night. One false turn and he could plummet down the side of the hill.

As the road swung back to the left, he caught sight of the star again. It warmed him to think of it as Miranda. The star was obscured as he came to the top of the first hill, but then he saw it again in the side mirror.

As he started down the hill, his eyes bugged from his head. A person—a woman, he thought—was standing in the middle of the road. She tossed an arm up against the headlights.

Jeremy braked so hard and fast that a wave of pain shot through his knee. Not sure he could stop in time, he swerved to the left toward the slope of the hill. He worked the wheel hard to bring the car back on level ground, but the front tires had already gone over the side. His breathing came in short gasps as he feared he was about to topple and roll down the hill. Images of Chandra and the grandkids flashed before his eyes. Miranda.

Then the car stopped. With a flood of relief, he released the death grip on the wheel and lifted his shaking hands to his face.

"That was a close one."

He placed his forehead against the side window and searched for the star. He found it high overhead. "Thank you, Miranda." Then he remembered the young woman. He unbuckled his seat belt and opened the door. It was dark, but the glow of the interior light showed the first step was a bit farther down than anticipated.

"Huh. Best I crawl over the console and get out on the passenger side."

He lifted his leg as headlights shone up the hill from the opposite direction. Whether the driver couldn't see him or because he was distracted, the vehicle kept coming at full speed until almost on top of his car. Expecting a collision, Jeremy dove prone over the console. The truck braked. The sound of screeching tires tore through the quiet night. Jeremy scrunched his eyes shut, as if not seeing the impact would prevent it. The truck smashed into his car's rear quarter panel, slamming it sideways and over the edge.

The car tilted in slow motion. Jeremy screamed and clung to the seat. The car rolled and Jeremy was pitched to the windshield, then back down on the seat. Against one door, then the opposite one. He lost track of how many flips he did and was not awake when the car stopped falling.

* * *

Daria went from bone-numbing fear to all-out relief, then to sheer horror as the oncoming car bore down on her, managed to swerve to avoid hitting her, then was knocked over the edge and down the slope by a truck. The driver of the truck had lost control after the impact and bounced off the inner side of the hill before coming to a rolling stop in the middle of the road.

The driver got out and Daria hastened to hide behind a tree. The man cursed, examined the damage to his truck, and cursed louder. Only then did he make a move to find where the car had disappeared. He looked down the hill, slapped a hand to his forehead, and swore again. Then he turned and ran to the truck. He got in and sped away, leaving the scene and the other driver down the hill and in need of assistance that she was unable to offer, both because of her condition and her mission.

Still, she felt guilt over leaving the driver. She moved to the edge of the slope and peered down. It was too dark to see much. She glanced up and down the road and seeing both directions clear for the moment, she pushed aside the pain and moved both hands together in a motion like packing and forming a snowball.

"Illuminous!"

A small globe of light sat in her palms. She held it out over the edge. It showed the car's path but did not light down far enough to see anything else. She lifted, moving her hand like pitching a softball, and the globe lifted off her palm and floated downward.

The wreck came into view. It was perched against a tree about thirty feet down the hill. She saw no movement. Daria wanted to slide down the slope and see if the driver was all right but knew her injuries wouldn't allow it.

Lights tracked up the road. She had to move. With the flick of her good hand and a single word, the globe winked out. She moved on down the road, offering the only help and hope she could give. A prayer.

CHAPTER FIVE

Jeremy's eyes fluttered open. Pain and confusion surrounded him. He tried to move but couldn't make his body respond. He scanned outside the car. A ball of light drifted downward toward him. Was it a flashlight? Was someone coming to rescue him? The ball seemed to hover overhead. Then it blinked off.

"No," Jeremy tried to say, but his voice was thick with pain. He closed his eyes. He drifted in and out of consciousness.

Something shook the car. It was enough to stir him awake. A dark shadow deeper than the night settled over the car. Was that a face looking in the window? As his sight cleared, the visage came into focus, sending an alarming scream from him. A wild beast like nothing he'd ever seen stared down at him. It let out a bone-chilling shriek and vanished.

When Jeremy came to again, he was in a hospital surrounded by white-clad masked figures in constant motion. One of them gazed down at him.

"He's awake," she said to the others. "Mr. Kline, do you know where you are?"

He had a good idea but shook his head anyway. His movement was restricted, which gave him a sense of panic.

"Do you remember what happened to you?"

To this, he nodded, still feeling the restriction. His heart pounded in his chest.

"Just relax, Mr. Kline. Don't try to move your head. You're at Mercy Hospital. You were in a car accident. We have your head immobilized until we can determine if there's spinal column damage. Can you speak?"

Jeremy was about to nod again, but swallowed and croaked, "Yes."

"Good. Do you have any severe pain anywhere?"

"Some."

"Can you tell me where?"

"My head." He tried to point, but his hands were secured.

"Okay. You have a laceration there that was cleaned and bandaged at the scene. Anywhere else?"

"My left leg and my right wrist."

"Okay. What about your torso? Your abdomen, chest, back?"

He took a mental inventory. "I-I don't know. Maybe, some but not as much as the other places."

"Okay. We're taking you for an MRI. Do you have any metal in your body? Any replacement parts, piercings, shrapnel?"

"No." To his embarrassment, tears welled.

The masked woman leaned down and said in a soothing tone, "You're all right, Mr. Kline. You are in the best hands. So far, we don't see anything that is life-threatening. The MRI will tell us more. Just relax as best you can. We've got you." She patted his arm and faded from his sight as he was passed along to a tech.

He slept through most of the tests. When he woke again, soft voices filtered through the haze. He tried to focus, recognizing his daughter's voice before his vision cleared enough to confirm it was her.

A woman in a long white coat with a clipboard in her hands said, "His wrist is broken, and he has a mild concussion. Other than a few scrapes and bruises, I don't see anything else of concern. We'll watch him tonight, but if nothing else presents, he should be able to go home tomorrow. Does he live with someone?"

"No. Since my mother passed, he's been on his own."

"He really should have someone stay with him for the next few days. Head injuries need to be monitored."

"Okay. I'll take him home with me."

"That'd be best."

"Anything else?" Chandra asked, glancing at Jeremy.

"No. Considering the extent of the damage to the car, your father was very fortunate. The angle of his body gave us concerns of neck or spine damage, however, nothing showed on the scans." She paused for a moment, then said, "We did find a strange anomaly in his blood. I've never seen or heard of anything quite like it. Is there something in your family history that might explain it?"

"Not that I'm aware of. Is it a disease?

"I can't say. The lab is analyzing it now. I should know more later today."

"Could it have something to do with the crash? Like causing him to black out?"

"I wish I had an answer. For the moment, we'll have to wait for the lab results. Is he on any medications or taking any drugs...legal or otherwise?"

"What are you asking?" Chandra's voice raised. "If my father's a drug addict?"

"We have to know if we are to treat him properly."

"No!" The word had force behind it. "My father is not an addict, nor is he on any medication. As far back as I can remember, he's always been healthy."

"Okay. I had to ask. I'll let you know what I find."

The doctor left the room and Chandra came to his side. "Hi, Dad. How are you feeling?"

"Tired."

"I'll bet. Did you hear what the doctor said?"

"Yes."

"You were very lucky."

"Don't feel so lucky."

She smiled, then turned serious. "I called to make sure you got home all right, but you didn't answer. I thought maybe you forgot to charge your phone. When I didn't get you in the morning, I got worried. I called the police. They called back two hours later and said they found your car down the side of a hill. Apparently you'd been there all night. What happened, Dad?"

An image of the young woman came to him. Her bloody, injured body. Her large eyes round with fear.

He cleared his throat. "A girl...a young woman...was in the middle of the road as I came around a bend. I braked and swerved to avoid her. Then another vehicle came down the hill from the opposite direction and slammed into me, knocking me over the edge and down the hill." He thought about mentioning the floating light and the strange creature but decided that would only make her worry more.

"And the other driver never stopped to help?"

"I don't know. I never saw anyone."

"You were very lucky. Your injuries are minor compared to what they might have been."

He held up his arm with the cast. "So other than a broken wrist, I'm all right?"

"A broken wrist and a concussion. That's the most serious injury. You'll have to stay here tonight. I'll take you to my house tomorrow."

"Oh, Chandra. I don't want to be a burden to you and your family. You have enough to do with handling the kids. You don't need to add me to your trouble."

"Nonsense. That's what's going to happen, so get used to it. You need to have someone with you for a few days in case the concussion proves to be more severe than they thought. After that, well...we'll talk about it. You shouldn't be driving up those hills anymore. They're too dangerous."

"For an old man, you mean."

"Stop that. You're not old. But it might be something for us to think about in the future."

He turned his head to gaze out the window. He knew exactly what that meant. Cliff would not want him at their house longer than necessary. The only other solution was to put him in a home for seniors. He wouldn't argue now, but no way would he allow that to happen.

Chandra changed the subject to ease some of the stress and they chatted for a while until Jeremy grew sleepy.

"I'll let you rest now. I'll check back later tonight." She leaned over him and planted a kiss on his forehead. "I love you, Dad."

"Love you too, Chandra."

She smiled and left him to his thoughts.

CHAPTER SIX

Though he slept, it was not restful. First came the endless tumbling. Then when the world outside the window stopped spinning, the creature came and settled on top of the car. Its horrid face and hungry maw pressed against the windows, straining to get in. He screamed and tried to scramble away but there was not much space. The beast locked eyes with Jeremy, then rocked the car, sending it spiraling downward.

A ball of light appeared near the side window, and the face of a young woman looked in at him. "Help me!" he cried, but the woman glanced behind her, took on an expression of sheer terror, and vanished. Soon, the creature was there again, clawing wildly at the car and swatting it back and forth like a ball between its mighty paws.

The car split open, leaving him unprotected. As the beast brought its yawning, dripping maw toward him, Jeremy screamed.

Light filtered through his lids and someone shook him gently. "Mr. Kline? Mr. Kline, wake up."

His eyes fluttered open. He lifted his arms across his face as a last defense against the creature. A bright flash behind his eyes blinded him and sent shards of pain through his body. He was no longer in the creature's grasp.

A voice reached him. "Jenny. My God, Jenny! Are you all right?"

"He was having a nightmare."

A nightmare? He fought to open his eyes but the pain enshrouding his head would not allow it. As the pain slowly withdrew, his body relaxed. He was drained. He slept, this time, dreamlessly.

Consciousness returned with slow clarity. Cautiously he opened his eyes, first as a slit; then, when the pain did not assail him, wide open. Sunlight was pouring into the room. He tried to lift a hand to block the rays but found something restrained the motion. He glanced to the side to find his arm secured to the railing with a leather strap.

He checked the other arm and found it too had been restrained. What was going on? Was this some precaution against him getting out of bed? He reached for the call button, but it had been placed on the rolling cart and moved from his reach. The idea of having his hands strapped down angered him.

"Nurse! Nurse! Some assistance here, please."

No one came. He called several more times before a voice startled him.

"What can I do for you, Mr. Kline?"

"Huh? Who's that?"

"I'm a nurse. What do you need?" Her voice was icy.

He realized the voice was coming through the call button speaker.

"How about unstrapping me?"

"That will have to wait until there are two of us available."

"What? Why? What's going on here? Am I a prisoner?"

"For the moment, yes."

"What? Let me out of here. Now!" he shouted.

"It sounds like it's better to keep you strapped down. Are you in pain?"

"Yes."

"Very well. I'll bring you something to help with that, but I will not release you."

"I don't understand."

The hissing of the small speaker ceased. She was no longer listening. This was crazy. Why would they strap him down and only come into the room in pairs?

He stewed for a while, losing the battle with staying calm. Five minutes later the door opened, and a scowling nurse and a male tech entered. The tech rolled in a monitor.

"Why am I strapped down?" Jeremy asked, annoyance evident in his tone and demeanor.

"Because you attacked one of the nurses last night."

The statement was like a physical blow. "Attacked? Why would I do that?"

"Good question, but I'm not giving you the chance to attack me."

"I would never—"

"Luke, please hold his arms down. I'll give him the pain pill and some water."

"You don't need to hold me down."

"I do if you want this pill."

"Forget the pill. I want my hands free."

"Are you refusing the pain pill you requested?"

"I don't want the pill. I want to be able to move my hands."

She turned to Luke. "You heard him. He doesn't want the pill. I'm going to note that in the chart. I need you to initial the notation as a witness. I'm also going to note that he is extremely agitated."

"What is going on here?"

All heads turned to see Chandra enter the room with Connor and Harper in tow. "Why is he secured to the bed? What kind of hospital is this?'

The nurse squared up to Chandra. "The type that does not take kindly to having their employees assaulted by a patient."

"Assaulted? My father? You have to be mistaken."

"No mistake. A report has been filed."

"You will release him this second or I will be filing my own report, followed by charges and a lawsuit."

"Go right ahead. The hospital administration is considering charges against him."

Chandra was not one to mess with. She pushed past the nurse and began unbuckling the straps.

"His arms are to stay secured until further notice. If you continue, I'll be forced to call security."

"Call whoever you want." She freed one arm and started around the bed to undo the other. "But they better bring an army, 'cause I will not allow you to continue to abuse him."

The nurse started to speak.

"Get out." Chandra unbuckled the second strap. In a huff, she leaned on the bed and repeated, "Get out. Now!"

Flustered, the nurse whirled and stormed out of the room. The tech, caught in the middle, looked from the nurse to Chandra, then followed the nurse.

Chandra walked to the door and shut it hard.

"That was awesome, Mom," Connor said.

"Yeah. Aweshum," said Harper.

Chandra took a calming breath. "You two be quiet for a moment. I need to speak to Pe-Pop." She came to the bed. "What is going on?"

"I wish I knew. I woke up with my arms tied down. When the nurse came in, she said I attacked one of the nurses last night."

"I wish I would've been here."

"I thought you were coming."

"That was the plan, but Cliff didn't get home until late, and the kids were already in bed. I left you a message."

"I have no idea where my phone is."

"I should have made sure you had it before I left. How do you feel?"

"Right now, angry. I'm ready to get out of here."

"I'm ready to take you. Let's see what the doctor says first."

The door opened and the nurse and two security men entered. She stepped aside and pointed. "She set him free. He attacked a nurse last night and is supposed to remain secured."

The older of the two men said, "Step aside please."

"Not happening. Call the doctor and have her release my father. I will not allow this sort of abuse to happen."

"He is to remain secured until the doctor makes her rounds. That won't be until sometime this afternoon."

Chandra reached into her purse and pulled out her phone. She punched in a number and quickly stepped in front of the two men.

"I want to report the abuse of my father by the medical staff of Mercy Hospital...Yes, that's right. The names are Butterman, Schorling, and Nurse Ratchet is Linda something."

The security officers stopped and looked at each other, then at the nurse. Chandra covered the phone and said to them, "And I'll be naming both of you as well as her and the hospital in the lawsuit that follows. Use some better judgment than her." Back into the phone, she said, "They are physically abusing him and strapping him down. He was in a severe car accident yesterday and is in no condition to get out of the bed, let alone be a threat to anyone. It seems to be perpetrated by the hostile nurse...Yes. Room three fourteen. I'll be here."

She pocketed her phone and looked at the two men before settling a challenging glare on the nurse. "You better pray the hospital will have your back, because with the amount of negative publicity they'll get over this, they're just as likely to fire you."

The nurse paled.

"You better run and contact your administration before the police get here."

The nurse backed from the room.

Chandra turned her attention to the security men. "I know you're just doing your job, but you can see he's no threat to anyone. Besides, I'll be here with him. If one of you wants to station outside the door, that's fine, but for now, we'd like to be left alone."

"I'm not sure what's going on here," said the older man, "but no matter who you call or what you threaten, we will not allow anyone to harm the staff."

"Understood."

"I'll leave Schorling here outside the door."

"Thank you."

CHAPTER SEVEN

Dorothy Canby, a hospital administrator, came to the room and listened to Jeremy and Chandra. When they had finished, Dorothy said, "I questioned the nurse from last night. She admitted she entered the room because you were having a nightmare. Evidently, she tried to wake you. Though she swears she never saw you lift a hand, she was thrown backwards and fell. She insists she's all right and is willing to let the matter rest."

"Then I shall, as well," Chandra said. At her insistence, the doctor was called. Instructions were given over the phone regarding Jeremy's release, and by eleven, they were in her minivan driving away from the hospital.

"Strange that the police still haven't arrived," Jeremy said.

"Stranger if they would have, since I never called them."

Jeremy looked at his daughter with surprise. "You faked that entire call?"

"Yep."

"How'd you get so devious?"

"Family secret."

They drove to Jeremy's house to get some clothes, but once there, Jeremy had other thoughts.

"I know you're worried about me, but honestly, I feel fine. I'm going to stay here. You can call me on an hourly basis if you like, but we both know me staying at your place will only cause problems with Cliff."

"Dad, I don't care what he says. You're my father. If he doesn't like it, he can stay at a hotel."

"See? That's what I mean. No sense getting everyone stirred up. You know it's for the best, if only to keep the peace. I'll stay right here. I can't go anywhere. My car's wrecked."

"You still have Mom's car."

"That tiny thing? I was never comfortable in it. I think she bought it because she knew I'd never want to drive it."

Chandra smiled. "That wasn't the main reason, but it was one of them."

They laughed and went round and round for the better part of an hour. In the end, she cooked lunch, cleaned up, and took the kids home.

Jeremy settled into the lounge chair in the family room and stared out the rear window. It was a nice view. Though the house sat on a stretch of level ground, fifty yards behind it, the land dropped into a sloping green valley. In the distance, taller hills surrounded the valley, making for a scenic panorama. He and Miranda loved to sit on the back deck and watch the sunset.

"It had been a good life, hadn't it, Miranda?"

He wanted to believe it with all his heart, but he knew better. It might have been an all right life, but it wasn't great, and maybe not even good. Once more he wished he could do it over.

His thoughts returned to the girl in the road. Maybe she was a young woman. He'd caught such a quick look that he couldn't be sure. Had he really seen her, or had his night vision played tricks on him? He turned the TV to the local news. There was no mention of a girl or anyone found injured on that road. He thought for a moment, then got up and went to his desk. He turned on his computer, waited for the old piece of technology to boot up, and began scrolling through news stories from two days ago. Still nothing. Hopefully, that meant she was all right, whoever she was.

A short time later, the phone rang. It was his insurance agent. The car was a total loss. They'd be sending a check for the value of the car, which was an amount much lower than Jeremy believed to be the true amount. After complaining about it, the agent agreed to up it a bit. Still lower than it should have been, Jeremy agreed, and it was settled. At least the car was paid off. The downside was that now he'd have loan payments. Nothing he could do about it unless he found an older car, but that would have its own set of problems. He convinced himself he was lucky to be alive to have this problem and forgot about it for the moment. He laid down to take a nap. His dozing was disturbed a short time later by Chandra's check-in call.

"You okay?"

"Yes. Fine. I'm trying to take a nap."

"Oh. Well, I won't keep you from it. I'll call later after I put the kids to bed."

To his annoyance, Jeremy could not get back to sleep. He watched TV, then tried to read for a while, but neither brought him closer to sleep. After a while he gave up, thinking a nap at this time would only prevent him from sleeping that night.

By six o'clock, Jeremy was feeling antsy. His body ached. He'd been warned to expect it. He took a pain pill and searched the kitchen for something to eat. Nothing he had was appealing or would take too much work to prepare. Chinese food sounded good. There was a little place that he and Miranda used to go to once a month after the children had grown and moved out. It wasn't far, and they walked over when the weather was good.

He couldn't walk there now, and it would be dark by the time he started back. He looked at the key rack next to the garage door. Miranda's keys were still there. Her car hadn't been driven in a long time. It might not even start. He walked toward the door and reached for the keys. He wasn't kidding when he told Chandra he didn't like driving the car, but it was a way to get around until he bought a new one.

Chandra. He promised her he'd stay home. What if she called while he was away? She wouldn't; she said she'd call after the kids went to bed. He still had at least two hours. But the girl was devious. She might check early just to test him.

He was hungry. He opened the door and stepped into the garage.

Who was he kidding? This trip had nothing to do with Chinese food. He wanted to find that girl. Needed to find her to prove to himself he wasn't crazy or seeing things. Besides, out here if she had fallen off the road somewhere, it might be a long time before anyone found her. What if she was seriously hurt? She might still be out here like he had been, undiscovered for days.

He got into the tiny Mini Cooper, then got out and adjusted the seat to its farthest point. Even then it felt tight. The engine cranked and didn't want to turn over. He tried several times before it coughed to life. Jeremy pressed the remote clipped to the visor to open the garage door and let the engine run for a few minutes.

He backed out of the garage and turned around in the driveway. He liked to pull out going forward; not trusting himself to back into the sometimes busy street. He worked his way to the main road that ran up and down the hill.

His house sat about three quarters of the way up the hill. He turned right and drove downhill, slowing as he neared the crash site. There, he scanned it from the car, then stopped and pulled to the side of the road. He walked toward the road's edge and peered down. Sunlight drifted through the canopy of leaves and seemed to focus on the site like a spotlight. A lot of leftover debris from his car remained down the slope. A tree was bent at an odd angle and there was a bare place on the trunk where the bark had been torn away.

He shuddered at the spot of his near-death experience and stepped back. Jeremy turned and scanned the road where he'd seen the woman. Where would she have gone from here? The closest house or closest anything was a half-mile up the road. Would she have gone that way, or risked going cross country down the hill and into the valley?

Guess it all depends, he thought. But depends on what? Whether she's...

"Being chased," he finished aloud. His mind jumped back to seeing the horrible face staring at him through the window. He thought he'd dreamed that. But what if she was real?

His mind clicked to an image of the female. He now believed her to be younger than he'd first thought. She appeared injured and weak, like she'd been in an accident herself, or perhaps a fight. What if some crazed person was chasing her? Or if something was? Why had he thought that?

Jeremy spent another ten minutes walking and searching the road's edge, but whatever he'd hoped to find was either long gone or had never existed.

Discouraged, he got back in the Mini and drove down the hill for his Chinese food.

CHAPTER EIGHT

Daria woke with a start. Eyes wide, forced open by fear, she scanned the small shed where she was hiding and listened for approaching footsteps. She sensed she was alone, but what had awakened her? How long had she been there? At least overnight, since it was daylight now.

After leaving the scene of the crash, Daria had moved up the hill at a slow and labored pace. Then she heard the Harpy's cry and forced her tortured body to go faster. She cursed herself for using the globe of light. The creature could surely sense magic. That was why she had been sent on the mission to find Daria. It was as much a mythical being as she was, at least in this world.

She had done the best she could with the wounds inflicted by the Harpy's talons and her fall, but it was not her gift, and Daria had not been trained in the healing arts. Besides, she was only a first-year student and wouldn't learn those skills until her third year. If she survived this ordeal, she vowed to study the art harder. Though she managed to stop the bleeding, the pain was still intense, and she suspected the gouge marks were infected. If she did not reach the village soon, she would surely die.

In the shed, she found a strap and figured out how to cinch it around her chest to immobilize her broken arm. Sharp pain shot through her and she couldn't prevent her audible gasp. For a moment she feared her reaction might bring the shed's owner out to check on the sound, but after a tense few minutes she relaxed.

She slept for a while, woke, and dozed off again, but her anxiety at being discovered or failing her mission—which would be worse—did not allow for a restful respite.

A sound from outside had her on full alert. She pushed into a corner and covered herself with an orange tarp. Under cover, she worked up an offensive spell in case she needed to fight.

The shed's door swung open. Light filtered around the tarp's edges. She tensed, ready to spring, although she doubted she could move with any speed. Someone entered humming a tune she was unfamiliar with, and then it sounded like something was being dragged outside. Seconds later, the roar of a motor drowned out the pounding of her heartbeat.

Though the sunlight continued to fill the interior of the shed, the sound of the motor decreased as it moved away. Slipping out from the tarp, Daria crept toward the side window and risked a peek. A man was pushing a motorized machine along the grass. As she watched, he turned around and started back toward the shed. She ducked, fearing he'd seen her. In a crouch, she waited for him to confront her, but as the machine roared closer and she readied to launch, it made a sudden turn and again moved away.

Her sigh of relief was louder than intended. Again, the machine reached a certain distance, then grew louder. As it came closer to the shed, she saw tiny blades of grass fly past the open door. The man was trimming the grass. She had never witnessed the task before. No one ever bothered to shorten grass where she was from.

Realizing the pattern, Daria waited for the man to make the turn and head away, and then she made her move from the shed. Hastened steps to the side of the house gave her cover enough to slow down. She reached the walkway in front of the house and limped down the street. As she passed other houses, the locals gave her strange looks. Her appearance was conspicuous and drew more attention than she wanted.

One man performing a similar act on his grass stopped his pattern and asked, "Young lady, are you all right? Do you need me to call someone?"

Daria offered a smile and shook her head. "No, thank you." As she continued past, she glanced over her shoulder and found him watching her. She scanned her clothing and realized it was torn and bloody. With her arm still cinched to her chest, she looked like she'd been in a fight and lost.

She had to get off the main road and get her bearings. Between the Harpy grabbing her and the confusion of night, she had no idea where she was or where to find the village. She needed to stop and think and search for landmarks.

The road ended up ahead. Trees blocked any farther travel by car. It would be a perfect place for her to lose herself until she figured out where she needed to go. As she reached the end, she stepped over a long metal railing and moved between two pine trees. The long needles scraped at her skin and caught on a tear in the sleeve of her shirt. A quick look back showed the man still watching her. Not good, but nothing she could do about it.

The ground dropped away, almost taking her down, but she grabbed a branch for balance at a painful cost to her already ravaged body. Using the trees for support, she worked her way down the steep slope until she reached the bottom. There she was forced to sit and take a breath, which angered her. Too much time had passed since she was dispatched from her world to bring warning to the refugees. She had to push aside her injuries and quicken her pace.

Determined, Daria stood and pushed through the thick growth. The going was slow. Several times she rolled an ankle on raised roots, but she continued though she had no idea where she was heading. The overhead canopy of branches and leaves did not offer a line of sight for her to get her bearings.

With growing frustration and weakening muscles, tears began streaming down her face. She wanted to scream and thrash something into pulp, but even if she gave in to the desire, she had little strength or energy for it. She continued, praying something would happen to give her a sign or direction.

Her foot splashed into cool water. She stopped to look. Hadn't there been a stream like this in the woods before the Harpy found her? Buoyed by the discovery, she bent and splashed water on her face. Not sure how safe the water was to swallow, she cupped some in her hands, sipped, and swished it around her mouth, then spit it out.

Daria moved on, a new release of adrenaline fueling her. *Oh, please let this be the right stream.*

An hour later, she still didn't have an answer. The ground had leveled and the trees were no longer as dense, making moving easier. Still, her reserves were depleted and the last of the adrenaline had burned off a while ago, leaving her more exhausted than before. Her legs moved mechanically as if on their own, carrying her swaying body onward. She followed the stream for what felt like miles.

Before she realized it, there were no more trees and she was walking across deep weeds toward a rise in the ground. She doubted the Harpy would be in the air during the daylight, but that didn't mean Bradenbaugh hadn't sent others to hunt her. Behind her, she heard a strange squeal. She whirled and scanned the woods. Something moved along the tree line.

Daria dove to the ground to hide in the high weeds. She froze for a minute and listened for the sound again. When it came, it was farther to her right. An answering call echoed somewhere to her left. At least two beings were following her. Did they already know where she was? Did they have her scent?

Fear spiked another adrenaline rush. She wanted to bolt for the rise ahead, but that would surely give away her position. Instead, she forced herself to creep through the weeds, making every effort to limit the disturbance. At a slow but steady pace and hindered by the strapped-down arm, she made her way toward the rise, hoping that if she got over the top, it would offer cover on the other side.

Her chest hurt from the heavy thudding of her heart. With a sudden jolt, she realized she had wandered away from the stream. Another angst-filled thought assailed her. If there was a rise in the land, what had happened to the stream? Had she been following it all this way for nothing?

She looked over the weeds and panned the rise. To her relief, she spotted a large metal pipe cutting through the elevated ground. It had to be where the stream went through. She angled toward it. Before she moved five feet, a high-pitched squeal rose behind her. It was joined by a second one. She spun around and spotted a beast standing at the edge of the open ground. It was a tusked hunting boar. Native to her homeland, they were used by the wealthy and evil to hunt humans. Entranced by spells, the powerful and tireless beasts could sniff out their human prey and run them down. Their double corkscrewed tails had sharp barbs on the ends to whip and strike at their prey. The barbs had a paralyzing agent within them that made it easier to gore and eat their prey.

The sight caused a numbing terror to strike at her core, freezing her in place. Her body shook violently. The beasts were slow, but once on her scent, they would never stop. She had no hope of outrunning them.

Above on the rise, a large, motorized vehicle that she recognized as a truck moved from right to left on a road. Maybe she still had hope. If she could get to the road and wave down a car, she might convince the driver to take her to safety. With hope fueling her, she broke through the immobilizing dread and hastened her efforts toward the rise.

Behind her, the squeals steadily grew excited. Without looking back, Daria knew they had her scent. She pushed to her feet and ran as hard as she could toward what she prayed would be salvation. But even as she ran, Daria realized it was the first vehicle she had noticed on the road since she'd been in the field. What were the odds another would come along when she needed it?

CHAPTER NINE

Jeremy had the Chinese food for breakfast. Once back home, he was too exhausted to eat and went straight to bed. Not surprising, the dreams he remembered centered around the girl and the horrible visage that had looked down into the car. Had it been the same person?

As he cleaned up after eating, the phone rang. It was the towing company asking if he wanted to go through the car and take out any personal items before they sold it for scrap. He couldn't remember if there was anything worth keeping but decided he'd go check. After getting directions to the lot, he hung up, showered, and dressed.

Before he made it out the door, Chandra called.

"Did you survive the night?"

"Obviously."

"Just checking. What are your plans for today?"

"Nothing. I'm on a doctor's and a daughter's orders to rest."

"Good answer. Do you need anything? You want me to bring lunch?"

"No thanks. I'm good. I've got some leftover Chinese I can heat up."

"Chinese? When did you get that?"

"A few days ago."

"Define a few days. How old is it?"

"It was the day before I met you for dinner."

"Okay. I don't want you to get food poisoning on top of everything else."

"It's fine. Thanks for worrying about me."

"No problem. Love you, Dad."

"Love you too, Chandra."

He breathed a sigh of relief that he'd been home to answer. Otherwise, Chandra would have driven across town to check on him. Then he'd really be in trouble.

He got in the Mini and drove toward the tow lot. It was a beautiful day. The sun sat in a clear blue sky and there was a cool breeze. Jeremy drove with the window down to enjoy the fresh air. When he inhaled, he thought the air smelled like fall, even though the official start was weeks away.

He turned on the radio. The lively bouncing rhythm of an Irish song came through the speakers. The fiddle player made the piece come alive. Although he didn't usually listen to this type of music, it reminded him of Miranda. He let it play.

At the top of the hill, he stopped at an intersection. To his surprise, he realized he had turned the wrong way out of his driveway. The quicker route was down the hill. Why had he chosen to go this way?

"Another sign of your old age, Jeremy, my boy."

No matter. It was a pleasant day for a drive and would be as long as Chandra never found out. He could still reach his destination from here. It would just take longer.

He turned left and wound his way down the hill to the north. After a series of twisty curves along the hill, he came out on a long stretch of road that led through the woods. An Irish tenor sang a soft ballad that eased him on his journey.

Jeremy hummed along with the classic tune, so thoroughly enjoying himself that he almost didn't catch the movement in the fields to the left and ten feet below the road. Someone was running and waving an arm wildly in the air. He slowed, watching.

It occurred to him the person wasn't swatting at biting insects or bees but was waving at him. Or waving him down. He slowed down even more and thought he heard a voice. He leaned out the window and listened. Though he couldn't see the person clearly, he felt certain it was a girl. But it could have been because he still had the other girl on his mind.

Other girl?

He braked and stared at the figure. He thought she was saying something, but it was not so much a word as a sound. She was calling to him. He checked the mirror. No cars coming. He pushed the gear shift into park and leaned out farther. Was she saying hey? Then it hit him. Help. She was yelling help.

He opened the door and stood, watching as she reached the base of the rise. A squealing snort drew his attention. Crashing through the weeds were two large creatures with massive, tusked heads. They appeared to be chasing the girl. No wonder she was running and looked frantic. He'd be running too.

The head poked up over the rise. Jeremy moved toward her. A frightened girl looked up. He guessed she was about twelve.

"Help me! Please."

He reached down and grabbed her hand. He pulled but the grip wasn't secure enough. She slipped and fell. The beasts moved closer. His heart climbed into his throat.

"Hurry," he croaked.

The girl had one hand strapped to her chest, making her climb all the more difficult. Her head cleared the rise again. This time, Jeremy stepped closer to the edge and wrapped his good hand around her wrist. The beasts were close enough to smell. Their foul, musky odor spiked his adrenaline. He pulled hard. His feet slipped on the grass, threatening to send him over the edge.

He dropped to his seat, dug in his heels, and pulled harder. The girl rose, feet digging for traction. She cleared. Her momentum sent her sprawling and Jeremy toppling over backwards, pain shooting through his body. The beasts reached the rise and squealed ear-piercing cries as they tried to scale it. Though steep, Jeremy didn't doubt they'd make the climb somehow. He rolled to his knees and pushed to his feet. Grabbing the girl around her waist, he propelled her toward the car. He opened his door and unlocked the back door with the buttons on the door panel. He yanked the rear door open and the girl dove in headfirst.

Jeremy shut the door and hopped in the driver's seat as the hooves of the first boar broke the top of the rise. He shifted and pressed the pedal down and the small car lunged forward. The Mini showed great guts as it reached sixty in mere seconds. A glance in the mirror showed one of the boars standing on the rise as the other one scrambled for purchase.

He wiped his casted wrist across his sweaty brow. His hand shook and blood raced through his veins at a dizzying speed. He felt faint. He leaned his head out the window and sucked in huge gulps of air and a small insect. He coughed and hacked to bring it back up.

The boars out of sight, Jeremy slowed. A head poked up from behind the seat. He watched her watch the road through the rearview mirror.

"It was you, wasn't it?"

She gave him a quizzical look; eyebrows raised and lips tight.

"The other night. On the road. It was you that ran in front of me."

Her eyes widened as his words registered.

"Yeah, I thought so."

A look of panic filled her face. She slid toward the far door and moved to open it.

"No. Don't."

She hesitated.

"You need help. Let me help."

She didn't respond or open the door.

"What's your name?"

No answer.

"I'm Jeremy. I've been looking for you."

Again, the look of terror.

"You look like you need a doctor. You want me to take you to the hospital?"

She shook her head.

"What were those things chasing you?" Jeremy was getting frustrated with the lack of answers. He wanted to pull to the side of the road and face her, but if he did, she might bolt.

He slowed. "Someone is chasing you."

She sighed. "Yes. Look, I appreciate that you want to help and I'm thankful you were there to save me, but I have to get to my people. It's urgent. Please. Can you just drive me?"

Jeremy studied her. She was worried about something.

"Okay. Where am I going?"

"I, uh, I don't know."

"You don't know where you live?"

"We, uh, just moved. We live in a cabin in the woods. I'm just a little confused where it is."

Now Jeremy pulled over and shifted into park. He turned, staring at her, trying to ascertain how much truth was in her words.

"Will you recognize the place when you see it?"

"I-I think so. There is a landmark. A dead tree in the middle of several live ones. I'll know it when I see it."

"Do you have any idea how many trees are on this hill alone? The entire area is one big forest, and you are trying to find one tree?"

She opened the door. "I'm sorry to have bothered you. I'd best search on my own. Thank you for picking me up."

"Now hold on a minute, young lady. I didn't say I wouldn't take you. I just wanted you to know how difficult it would be if you don't know where you're going."

She paused with one foot out the door.

"Come on. I'll take you."

She looked outside, then down the road behind her before pulling her leg in and closing the door.

"Daria," she said.

"Ah. De nada."

"What?"

"Huh?"

"My name is Daria."

"Oh. Ha. I thought you were saying thank you in a foreign language."

A smile flickered across her face and disappeared an instant later. Jeremy turned around and put the car in drive.

CHAPTER TEN

For the better part of an hour, they searched with nothing to show for it. He eyed her off and on through the rearview mirror. She looked around the interior of the car with awe as if she'd never been in one before.

"Daria, we've been driving for a while. Why don't we take a break and get something to eat? Are you hungry?"

She sunk in on herself as if not wanting to admit she was hungry, then nodded.

"Okay. I have to make a stop and there's a place to get some burgers next door. You're not a vegetarian or a vegan or something, are you?"

She thought for a moment as if unsure what she was, then shrugged. "I don't think so."

"You eat meat?"

She gave a tentative nod. "Sure, depending on what type."

"Well, this place will have a choice. Either chicken or beef. I suppose they'll have fish too. That okay?"

She nodded with more enthusiasm.

They entered the fast-food chain restaurant parking lot. Jeremy looked at Daria. "You feel all right?"

She nodded unconvincingly.

"I think we'll go through the drive-thru. The blood on your clothes might scare a few people. How's your arm?"

She looked down at it. Her fingers twitched. The motion caused a grimace.

"I know you don't want to, and I don't blame you since your parents aren't present, but you need to get that checked out. It may be broken." He lifted his arm and showed the cast. "Like mine." He got in line behind three other vehicles. "What do you want?"

"To find my home."

"To eat."

"Oh." Her cheeks colored. "I-I don't know. I've never had the food here."

"Really? I thought everyone had tried this stuff. You must not be one of the millions served, huh?"

She shrugged and took on the sunken look again.

"You like beef? Or would you prefer chicken?"

"Chicken."

"What about to drink? Coke? Seven-up? I'm not sure what brand they carry. I usually get an iced tea."

"Tea is good."

"Sweetened or un?"

"Ah, sweetened."

He placed the order, paid, and pulled to the next window to collect the food. The aroma filled the little car. A grumbling came from the back seat.

"Was that your stomach? Wow! You must be hungry."

She nodded and her tongue flicked out and circled her lips.

"Give me a minute to get parked and you can start eating."

Jeremy pulled across the street and stopped in the tow parking lot. He rummaged through the bag and handed over Daria's food and drink. "You dig in. I have to go inside and pick up a few things. I should only be a few minutes. You okay?"

The girl gave a quick nod as she ripped open her chicken sandwich. She tore off a bite bigger than her mouth and shoved what stuck out inside. Her cheeks expanded with the huge bite. Her eyes rolled up and a soft moan of delight escaped her. Jeremy smiled and got out of the car.

Inside, he spoke to a man in grease-smeared coveralls and was directed out the back door into the salvage yard. From there, another man led him to what was left of his car. An involuntary shiver raced the length of his spine. The car's roof was crumpled. Most of the glass was gone. The hood and the trunk were smashed.

On the roof, he spotted four puncture holes, each bigger than the width of his thumb.

"Did that happen when you guys hauled it up the hill?"

"No sir," said the skinny young man in coveralls that were even more grease-coated than the first man's. He wore a baseball cap with the logo covered in grime and unrecognizable. "They was already there when we arrived. I was the one who scooted down the hill first and I remember seeing them. Got four more just like them on the other side. Like something poked holes in the roof like they's gonna rip it off or something. Maybe it was the firemen using that jaws of life contraption."

"Yeah, maybe."

But a horrifying thought swept over him. That was the place in the shattered windshield where he'd seen the woman's face staring down at him. Had she done that damage? No. Impossible.

He went through the car grabbing what he wanted, which wasn't much, and shoved it into a plastic bag the attendant found for him. He was back outside in less than ten minutes. He didn't see Daria's head in the back seat of the car.

He rushed to the car, wondering if she was laying down. She wasn't. With a sinking heart, he scanned the area and did not catch sight of the young woman. He sighed and slid into the car. He tossed the bag onto the passenger seat and started the car. He gave one last look. Not finding her, slipped the car into gear.

He had just pressed the accelerator when he heard, "Wait!"

He braked hard as the door opened. Daria slipped in with a groan. Jeremy whirled around.

"Are you okay?"

"Yes." She clenched her teeth to fight back the pain. "Just bumped my arm getting in."

"Daria, you really need to see a doctor."

"Get me home. There's a healer there."

A healer? Was she one of those people who didn't believe in modern medicine and used old-world remedies? He hoped not.

"I got worried when you were gone."

"I saw people at the burger place throwing their bags into that can, so I did the same."

"You ate so fast. You must have been starving."

"Yes. It was good."

"He glanced at his bag. "There's more if you're still hungry."

Her eyes widened and lit like sparklers. She nodded with enthusiasm. He passed the bag back and she dove into it.

While she ate, Jeremy said, "I've been thinking. The first night I saw you, you were up Hillside Road. You remember that?"

She took a bite of burger and nodded.

"Is that the area where your home is? Because that's miles away from where we were searching."

She said something with her mouth full that sounded like, "I think so."

"I'll drive up that way. Maybe something will look familiar."

Jeremy drove the main road back to Hillside. He made the turn and the Mini began to climb. Daria was finished wolfing down the food and she grabbed the back of the passenger seat and pulled forward to look through the space between the seats.

"I remember coming down that hill. That's when I saw you and you swerved off the road."

"Yeah. You caused my accident. You realize that, don't you?" He didn't know what he expected her reaction to be, but if guilt or sorrow registered, it didn't show on her face. She ignored the statement altogether.

Up close, he saw the grime, blood, and bruises on her young face. She did need to go to a hospital. If they found her home, he'd have to impress on her parents the need for medical services. Though her wrist was still secured to her chest, the discoloration was clear. The wrist was swollen and there appeared to be a small impression on her skin from the inside. Possibly a broken bone. It had to hurt like crazy. He knew his did.

Daria said, "Yes. I came down from there. I was up on top. Up there."

"Okay. There's a road that leads up there, but much of it is unattainable by car."

He made the turns that brought them to the top of the hill. With no traffic, it was easier to drive slowly.

She pointed. "That direction."

"You sure?"

She closed her eyes. With her good hand, she traced a line in the air, perhaps recalling her path. "Yes. That way. I'm sure."

As Jeremy maneuvered the turns, he said, "I want to ask you something. After I crashed, did you climb down and get on the roof of the car?"

She gave him a furtive glance and shook her head.

"Did you see anyone or any...ah, thing?"

She visibly blanched and shook her head again.

"But you know what I'm talking about, don't you?"

With a sudden move, she shot her hand out and pointed. "There. I was over there." She reached for the door.

"Hold on. Let me stop the car first."

"Yes, this is the spot. I remember entering the woods here. I came out on the other side and saw the tree. I was almost across when—" She stopped.

"When what?"

"I, ah, got sidetracked and then got lost." The words spilled from her mouth so fast, they sounded like one long word. Jeremy was sure she was lying.

Daria opened the door and was out before he could speak. Just before she shut it, she said, "Thank you, Jeremy."

The door slammed and she was gone.

CHAPTER ELEVEN

Ecstatic she had found the path, Daria darted into the trees without a backward glance, ignoring the pain in her ankle. She was grateful to Jeremy, but she didn't want to answer any more of his questions. She was sure he knew she was lying, but it was for his own good. He didn't need to know what had followed her into his world. She could never tell Jno, Gianna, or Rowan about her interaction with a New Worlder. Any contact was strictly forbidden and held severe punishment. Only a select few were trained in New Worlder ways and allowed to mingle, and she wasn't one of them.

She worked her way through the trees, traveling almost the same steps as her first crossing. She felt a moment of regret. She should never have told Jeremy which direction she had taken. Not that she thought he would follow her, but it was another breach she dared not confide to anyone in the village. But even if he did follow her, the village was protected against discovery. Precautions were taken in case a New Worlder accidently wandered into their midst. Only those of her world and with basic magic training and ability could see the home they'd created. Anyone else would either be enticed to deviate from the course by magical suggestion, or if they did make it through the barrier, they would walk through without seeing anything.

Though buoyed by the food, Daria was still weak from her injuries and blood loss. By the time she reached the edge of the forest where she had stood before, she was exhausted and breathing hard. She leaned against a tree and studied the open ground. Across the way and to the right was the dead pine tree.

She searched the sky for signs of the Harpy. It was daylight, so the beast was probably not in the sky. However, knowing Daria had come this way before, she might be perched in a treetop, scanning with her sharp vision for Daria to make the crossing again. Unfortunately, Daria had no choice. This was the only way to the village. She had to enter on this side, or the entrance would not appear.

She swallowed hard and pushed aside her fatigue. She needed all her skills and strength to make this crossing. Lives depended on her. She could not afford to let them down. Steeling herself, she stepped from the tree cover and walked. She wanted to save her energy in case she needed to run. If she started off running, she'd fade before reaching halfway.

Ten steps from cover and all looked good. She kept her head turning, scanning both the sky and the tree line for pursuit.

She was only a quarter of the way across when she heard the Harpy's soul-piercing screech.

Her knees threatened to fold beneath her. Terror engulfed her worse than the first time she'd heard the cry. She did not have the strength or possess the skill to ward it off. Though her instructors said she had enormous potential, she was but a novice. They were forced to leave their home world before she had completed her first year.

She snapped her fright and took off hobbling as fast as her ankle allowed. She already felt her strength waning. Her usual sure-footed stride faltered. She stumbled and without thinking, put her hands down to keep from falling. The reflex action sent fiery, blinding pain up her broken arm. She gasped. Her lone arm collapsed and she fell.

Daria made an effort to roll and keep her broken limb from impacting the ground, but even doing so jarred the arm. More pain ripped through her, bringing tears. She struggled to her feet, sure the Harpy was upon her. She ran in a crouch, as if she'd be farther from the lancing talons. She was barely halfway across when she felt the downstroke wind of the wings.

She dove to avoid the talons, but the beast was prepared for the maneuver. It hovered above her, then slowly descended, ready to move wherever Daria did.

Quickly she conjured up the lone offensive spell she knew, but without the use of both hands and under the pressure of releasing the spell before the Harpy could grab her, it fizzled and failed.

A scream erupted from her core as the beast closed in. She rolled up on her back and lifted her legs, kicking at the talons. She evaded the initial grasp, but the creature had snared one foot and began to rise.

Then the beast let out a scream that was different from its normal cry. This one sounded like it was in pain. As she looked up from her dangling position, a still-smoldering blackened spot shone on the breast. Singed feathers gave off an unfamiliar odor.

A bright light stretched across the field and struck the Harpy. It screamed again and was propelled backwards, but still it held on to its prey. Wings beat harder and they began to rise. Daria kicked and kicked at the one talon holding her leg. The second claw swung toward her, but before it pierced her, another bolt of light slammed into it; this time with such force that its wings were blown back. They began to plummet.

Before crashing, the powerful wings stroked furiously. Her hand struck the ground. Desperately she clutched at the grass, hoping to snatch something to yank her free from the Harpy's grasp. It clutched her tighter, causing new waves of severe pain to sprint up her leg.

The light blast was joined by a long tongue of flame. Feathers ignited. Foul air wafted downward, filling her lungs and making her want to heave up her lunch. She hacked and swung her arms wildly to wave the stench away, but it had little effect.

The creature screamed as flames licked up its body. Suddenly she was falling. Though the distance wasn't great, in her current condition, the pain was overwhelming. Her last conscious sight was of a flaming bird like a Phoenix rising into the sky. Then everything went dark.

The sound of voices woke her. Though her mind and vision remained hazy, she knew she was being carried. She didn't understand the words, but the one thought that worked through the fog was that the tone of the voices sounded concerned. Daria tried to speak and let them know she was all right, but she could not tell if she was making a sound. Her body bounced and seemed to float. Whoever was carrying her was in a hurry. She fought to break through the ever-swirling mists that encompassed her mind, but nothing worked.

Tired. So tired. She gave in to the call of her body and let sleep take her again.

A warm, pleasant sensation washed over her body like waves. Her eyes cracked open enough to see a woman standing over her. She was familiar, but her name escaped Daria. A bluish cone emanated from the woman's extended hands and hovered over Daria's body. The woman's eyes were closed and her lips were moving. Though Daria could not hear the words, she imagined they were part of a beautiful song that was being sung for her benefit. It was nice. She closed her eyes and drifted on the calming musical phrases.

Yes, beautiful. So beautiful and warm. Like being rocked to sleep in her mother's arms. That made her sad. Her mother. Warm. Comfort. The sad thought faded from her memory. All she could think about was the lovely melody the woman was singing. She hoped it never ended.

Then the dreams came. She was walking along a beach holding someone's hand. She looked up to see the smiling face of her mother looking down at her. The sad thought tried to work through the magic of the memory. She looked at her bare feet as they left impressions in the wet sand. A foamy blanket of water caressed her feet. It made her smile. She looked up again, but this time her mother was not there. Instead it was an older man with a bald head, nice eyes, and a strange smile like he had a secret.

Then abruptly, his face was gone. Not just gone. The flesh from his face melted away, dripped down his arm, and slithered toward her hand. She tried with all her might to pull away, but the grip tightened. An acrid odor assailed her. The person or thing holding her hand was on fire. The smell of burned flesh made her eyes water, but the flesh smelled good, like cooked meat. Like a chicken sandwich. *A chicken sandwich?*

Her eyes fluttered open. She was lying on a bed. Her eyes scanned the space. She recognized it as one of the cabins in the village. Her body was covered in bandages.

The door opened and in walked Biatta, the healer and one of her professors from the academy. She beamed a wide smile. "Ah, you're awake, little one. You had us quite worried for a while. Your body took a lot of punishment, but you'll be all right. You just relax and rest. You're safe now."

"But, but—"

She reached toward Daria's face and wiped away strands of hair. Her long soft fingers stroked Daria's face and stopped at her temples.

"I have to warn—"

Biatta smiled and said, "Yes, child, we know." Her fingers traced light circles around Daria's temple. "Sleep."

And she did.

CHAPTER TWELVE

Jeremy watched Daria disappear into the woods. It bothered him to see her go, but not because she was company and he was a lonely old man. It bothered him because he knew she was injured, and without medical care—correction...without *proper* medical care—she might be in severe danger. The entire encounter bothered him. From the moment he saw her on the street up to now, something was off about her. She'd lied to him about this being her home, and he had a feeling certain aspects of her story were false. He could see it in her eyes each time she lied.

But it was her decision and he wasn't her father. He shrugged it off and drove on, yet he couldn't dismiss his unease. Something troubled him. The girl had been chased by those two beasts, but there was something more. She was in trouble and someone was after her. No, he couldn't let it go. He had no idea what he was going to do, but he turned the car around and headed back.

From this way, he missed the spot and had to turn around again. He slowed in front of the section of trees Daria had disappeared into, but nothing was in sight. A car horn honked, making him jump in his seat. The two-lane road offered no place to pull over. He was forced to drive another mile before an opening appeared on the side of the road. He pulled in, allowing the car behind to pass, then shut the engine down and locked the car.

The hike back did not take long. Jeremy studied the trees. He remembered the sapling near where Daria had entered the woods and angled toward it. He stopped before going in, wondering about the intelligence of traipsing through the woods alone; without any equipment or anyone knowing where he was. The thought dampened his enthusiasm and he turned away.

"That's right. You're just an old man. You couldn't handle a little excitement anyway."

The words poured from his lips. He stopped, suddenly angry with himself. *A young girl might be in danger and you're the only one who knows where she is. You can't walk away from this, even if you think you're too old.* He turned an about-face, moved the sapling aside with his cast, and stepped into the woods.

The going was slow. The denseness of the trees and undergrowth surprised him. How could this much greenery grow in so little sunlight? He looked up. The canopy was thick, only allowing slivers of rays to shine through. It was cooler under the trees. The air smelled different too, damp and somewhat musty. Yet he walked on invigorated, whether from being in the forest or the idea of being on an adventure, he didn't know nor care. It felt good to do something, especially if it was to help another person.

He walked ahead, not having a clue where Daria might have gone. He checked his phone to keep track of time, estimating he'd been walking for about twenty minutes. He paused to get his bearings and locate landmarks in case he needed help finding his way back. Ten minutes later, he reached a clearing.

"Now what?"

He studied the tree line on both sides, then remembered Daria had said there was a dead tree on the opposite side. He did not see one. With no clue where to go next, Jeremy walked out into the middle of the clearing and turned a circle, scanning the trees. He turned a second one, looking at the treetops, hoping to see smoke. Nothing.

The idea of searching began to lose its appeal, but he knew Daria had to be here somewhere. She didn't just disappear. He kicked at the overgrown grass. Maybe she lived underground. He looked to the right, back the way he came, then left, then at his phone. It was still early. He didn't want to be out there at night, but he could afford another hour. He turned and headed for the next section of trees. *At least I'm getting some exercise.*

The second section of forest was much the same except for having a greater scent of pine. He wondered if someone many years ago had planted this forest with a certain purpose in mind. He wondered who it might have been and why anyone would take the time before deciding it was just folly and his mind was turning to jelly.

Through the branches ahead he saw sunlight. He hurried to the tree line and stopped to catch his breath. He'd been moving fast and taking in so much brisk air. As he rested, he panned the next section. With a spear of excitement, he stopped on a dead pine tree to the right across the open ground. To his surprise, he found his heart racing. Could that be the tree Daria had spoken of? Only one way to find out.

Jeremy stepped into the open field. His step quickened with anticipation of finding Daria. Then a new thought struck him. What would he give as an explanation for following her? Would her parents be upset? They might think he was stalking her. If he found where she lived, perhaps it would be best to just observe. If he saw she was all right, he'd turn around and go back. What more could he do anyway? If she was with her parents, he had no right to interfere.

A breeze drifted across the field and bent the tall grass, weeds, and assorted wildflowers. It brought with it a foul burnt smell. He stopped to see if there was smoke anywhere. He looked to the far corner of the woods where he just came from. From this distance, he could only see it was something large and quite blackened. Thin wisps of smoke lifted into the air over the trees and drifted away on the breeze.

Jeremy had an inkling to investigate, if only out of curiosity, but decided one mission at a time was enough. If he found Daria, he could explore the blackened husk on the way back. He continued toward the third section of trees with the growing expectation of finding his quarry.

He stopped at the tree line, a sudden chill settling into his bones like a portent of some dire event on the horizon. He hesitated, then glanced over his shoulder at the smoking hulk. Was it a carcass? If so, what could have brought down a creature of that size? Again, he looked at the trees an arm's length before him. With deliberate slowness, wary of what was beyond, Jeremy lifted his hand toward the tree to break the barrier with his fingers first to make sure nothing untoward occurred. He yanked his hand back at the last moment and exchanged it for the hand in the cast that was already injured.

He eased it closer. Had all the usual forest sounds ceased? Sweat popped like rivets along his forehead and felt just as hot on his skin. His hand broke the plane and he jerked it back. Annoyed with his fear and angry at his cowardice, Jeremy thrust his hand up to his elbow past the front line. Nothing happened. To his disgust, he realized he had closed his eyes in fear of what he might see or feel.

Exasperated at his behavior, he stepped inside the trees. It felt the same as it had in the last two sections. Wait. Did the air feel colder, or was it his imagination reacting to his angst? He blew out a breath and strode forward. He listened intently to the sounds of the forest, seeking those which did not belong.

Fifteen minutes later, nothing had changed. Not the sounds, the sights, the air, or the smell. It was just another forest. To the right a squirrel raced up a tree, its claws tapping on the bark. An insect buzzed past his ear. Birds chirped somewhere overhead. He decided if he didn't find any sign of Daria by the time he reached the break in the trees, he was turning back. He'd made the effort; that's what counted to ease his conscience.

Ahead something flickered, caught in a thin ray of sun. Jeremy focused on the area. Though he saw the reflected light twice more, if something was there, he couldn't see what it was. In a crouch he advanced with caution, not wanting to spook anyone who might be there. He moved closer, tree to tree, until he was no more than ten feet from the spot he had mentally marked. Nothing was there. Taking a few steps to the side to get a different perspective, he lost sight of the flickering light.

Whatever had caused it was gone. Perhaps it was an insect like a dragonfly that caught the sunbeam and reflected it off its wings. Didn't sound right, but at this point, it was as good an explanation as any. He looked at his phone. It was getting late. He'd have to start back within a half hour to make it back to the car by dark. He decided to go another fifteen minutes and be done with this little adventure.

Jeremy stood, stretched, and moved forward. As he reached the spot of the strange light, he had a sudden heavy feeling like walking through water. His movements were slowed by some unseen force. He stopped, afraid it was the first sign of a heart attack. He grasped his arm, waiting for the sharp pain he'd always heard about. A minute passed, then another. Still he felt strange, but no other symptoms came.

What was it? The air felt denser, like it refused to be breathed. Curious, he pushed forward. Each step took more effort. This was crazy. He needed to get back to the car before something serious happened. How long would it take for a rescue team to get to him in this remote area? How would he even describe where he was? The only landmarks were trees. Thousands and thousands of them.

He staggered forward another ten feet, and to his relief, the pressure ceased. He could breathe again, and he did in huge gulps. After a short pause to refresh, he moved on, taking out his phone. It no longer lit when he pushed the button to open the screen. Had the battery died or had he lost the signal?

A gasp startled him. He fumbled the phone and it fell. As he bent to retrieve it, he glanced up to see who he'd come upon. A young woman older than Daria stood in front of him. She was wearing a brown peasant dress and held one hand to her mouth and the other clutched her chest over her heart. Before he could speak, she whirled and ran.

She wasn't expecting anyone to step out of the woods. He squatted over his phone, hand inches from contact, and stared in amazement. A village of twenty assorted size huts made of hand-cut logs was in front of him. Thatched roofs made Jeremy think he'd stepped into a medieval Renaissance festival. The dwellings were all roughly the same size. A few had cooking fires blazing in front of them.

He heard voices. Lots of excited and perhaps hostile voices. He grabbed the phone and stood, thinking it was time to go. A score or more men and women all brandishing weapons, ranging from knives and clubs to bow and arrows came from around the huts. They spread out and advanced on him in a semi-circle.

Jeremy threw up his hands. "Whoa! Whoa! I'm not a threat to anyone. I stumbled upon you by accident. I'll just turn around and leave. I won't bother you again."

He backed toward the trees as the mob edged forward. Their faces held a mix of anger, hatred, and fear.

"I'm leaving. Don't shoot me. I'm not an enemy."

Jeremy was about to turn and run when a strong deep voice shouted.

"Halt!"

Jeremy didn't know if the speaker meant him or the mob, but he wasn't sticking around the find out. He spun and ran. Before he made it to the trees, the female voice shouted, "*Frozenco!*" and Jeremy could no longer move.

CHAPTER THIRTEEN

Heart pounding, Jeremy struggled against the invisible force holding him in place. He couldn't move. Not his feet, his hands, his arms, or his head. Had he been tazed? No. That didn't make sense. He'd be on the ground, rolling in agony if someone had sent an electric charge through him. This was something different; something unknown.

A man older than Jeremy stepped in front of him and looked him up and down. *Oh please, God, don't let him be a cannibal.* The man gazed at Jeremy's face, his dark gray eyes boring into him as if doing a full computer background check.

"Who are you? How did you get in here?" His weathered face was angry. His long white beard stuck out in all directions.

Jeremy wanted to speak but the strange force that controlled him also prevented him from talking. He moved his lips, but a garbled sound was all that came out.

"Who sent you? Are there others in the forest?" The man's face contorted with rage.

"Jno," a voice called. "How can he answer if you don't release him from the spell?"

The man looked past Jeremy.

A woman stepped into view. Her dark features were seductive; almost sizzling, yet her eyes looked more threatening than the man's. Her soft voice belied the danger she held inside. Her smile made him think of slithering poisonous snakes. She surveyed Jeremy from head to toe. With a whispered word, she snapped her fingers and Jeremy was free from his invisible restraints.

"Jerricka," the angry man said. "We don't know a thing about him or who might have sent him. He might be a danger to us all."

"Nonsense, Jno. He isn't dangerous." To Jeremy, she asked, "Are you?"

Her eyes narrowed, and for a moment he felt as if he'd been hypnotized. Jeremy gave his head a quick shake.

"There, now. See? He isn't a threat at all."

The man eyed her and seemed to be reassured by her words. "Still, we need to know how he was able to get through the barrier and how he can see us."

"Agreed."

Though they spoke to each other, neither took their eyes off Jeremy.

"What is your name, sir?" Jerricka asked, her honeyed tone making it impossible for him not to answer.

"Jeremy Kline."

"And why are you here, Jeremy Kline?"

He thought about lying. He didn't want to cause trouble for Daria, but even as he thought it, he said, "I was checking to make sure Daria made it home safely."

Whatever they'd expected to hear, based on their expressions, that wasn't even close.

"Daria?" Jno asked. "How do you know Daria?"

"I helped her escape some wild creatures."

They exchanged glances. "There's more to the story, though. Isn't there?" Jerricka said. The softness in her voice was gone.

He nodded.

"Let's get him inside where we can question him in private," she said to Jno. "And where is Daria?"

"Currently in Biatta's care."

Jerricka scowled. "Have her wake the girl and bring her as well. We need to get to the bottom of this, and fast. I sense there is something else going on here that isn't good."

Before she could move, a young couple walked through the camp. Jno and Jerricka froze and watched. Evidently on a hike through the forest, they kept a steady, fast pace.

"I was thinking about trying the full Appalachian Trail next year," the woman said. "What do you say?"

They passed between Jeremy and Jno, inches from them without acknowledgment of their presence. It was as if they hadn't seen them.

The man answered, "You're talking about months on the trail?"

Their words faded as they crossed to the opposite side of the small village and disappeared down a narrow path.

"Obviously, the spell still works," Jno said.

"Yes, but our magic doesn't have the same strength as it does in our world. Have some of the others add more layers to the shield." Jerricka swung her dark gaze toward Jeremy. "All the more reason to discover who he is and why it didn't work on him. Bring him."

She walked away, her long dark gown flowing behind her as if it were alive.

Jno motioned to two men who each took one of Jeremy's arms and led him away.

"No! Wait," Jeremy said. "I must get back before it gets late. I'll never find my way in the dark."

His words did not affect the men. Their stone faces looked straight ahead and their grips held fast. He was taken to a large log structure in the center of the huts. Inside, the floor was polished. It reminded him of a log cabin he'd stayed at in the Smoky Mountains. It was a large open room with wood furniture. Four doors lined the walls on the left and right. A kitchen was in front of him.

One of the men dragged a chair from the kitchen table into the center of the room forced him to sit on it. Though he wasn't bound to the chair, the men left no doubt he wasn't to move.

Jerricka and Jno stood to the side holding counsel. Jeremy heard the man say, "I've sent for Aric, Chase, and Favyan. Let's wait for them to proceed so we can all hear what he has to say."

Jerricka responded, "Have Biatta bring Daria."

"She may not be in any condition to—"

"She'll have to get in condition," Jerricka said with force. "This is too important."

Jno nodded. "I'll see to it." He walked off and spoke to another man, who left the cabin.

Jerricka focused her cold eyes on Jeremy, then advanced. The air seemed to chill in her path. He found his voice and forced enough courage to use it.

"I insist that you release me. I must get home. Others will be looking for me if I'm late." That much was true. If Chandra called to check up on him, she'd have a fit and he'd pay the price by having to listen to an angry lecture.

"Not until I have answers." She stopped in front of him and crossed her arms as she set her penetrating gaze on his.

Jeremy'd had enough. He was not going to sit in an inferior position, forced to look up at the tall woman. He stood abruptly, startling her. She took a step back and her hands unfolded in a flash and moved in some sort of dance or martial arts move. The two men assigned to guard him stepped in front of her, one with a knife in hand and the other moving to shove him back down.

The move shocked him. He backed away, bumping into the chair and almost falling into it. He placed his good hand on the table for balance, then stood erect.

"You will not hold me against my will. I'm leaving." He made a move to walk around the trio. In an instant, he was pushed back. The chair slid along the floor, clipping him behind the knees and he was seated. He wasn't as surprised to find himself back in the chair as he was that none of them moved to put him there, except for a flick of a wrist.

"You will be staying until I decide what to do with you," Jerricka said. To a guard, she said, "Take him into one of the rooms until I send for him."

At that moment, Jeremy was afraid. But even more, he doubted he would leave this place alive.

The outer door opened and a crowd of people entered. They all swept gazes over Jeremy, then huddled in the far corner of the room with Jno and Jerricka. Though their voices were hushed, their tones and mannerisms came through loud and clear. His presence had caused grave concern. They were angry, concerned, and unless he was mistaken, afraid. Somehow he had to convince them he did not pose a threat to them or their community.

The door opened again and another tall woman entered, this one dressed in white. She studied Jeremy with a look of curiosity rather than worry. As she stepped aside, Daria was ushered in by another woman. She was between the ages of Daria and the white-clad woman.

Jeremy thought, *Good.* Daria would vouch for him and the matter would be cleared up in minutes. But when her already dazed eyes lit on him, all color drained from her face and her knees buckled, and any hope he had of a quick release vanished.

CHAPTER FOURTEEN

The woman behind Daria managed to catch her before she hit the floor. The woman in white moved to assist the other woman and Daria was carried to a chair. The woman in white placed a hand on Daria's cheek and whispered something. Daria's eyes opened and her head jerked up. A look of confusion crossed her features. Her eyes swept the room and stopped on Jeremy. The color that had returned fled in an instant, but this time she did not faint.

The woman in white turned and advanced on the group. "I must protest this treatment. The girl is too weak to be put through your interrogation."

Jerricka held up a hand. "There are far greater concerns here than the well-being of one girl, Biatta. She made contact with an outsider and led him to us. We must find out what she knows, and now, before others come. We must be prepared to defend or flee as the circumstances warrant."

Biatta glanced over her shoulder at Jeremy. She nodded and looked back at Jerricka.
"Very well. But I will attend her. If she begins to falter, she must be given a break to recover."

"That will depend on what she has to say and the urgency of the situation she has placed us in."

They formed their circle again and the discussion became heated. After several minutes, Jerricka, who appeared to be in charge, raised a hand and said, "Enough. Let us begin." She moved from the circle. "Biatta, give her a boost to keep her stable. I don't want her slipping away before we get answers."

Biatta crouched in front of Daria and whispered. She placed both hands on Daria's temples, still whispering, and a strange white glow emanated from her palms. Daria stiffened for a moment. Then, as the woman released her, she slumped in the chair. Moments later, she shook herself and sat upright, somehow revitalized. Her eyes looked clearer but still held fear when she looked his way.

"Now then, Daria, why don't you tell us the story of how you arrived here?"

In a meek voice, she said, "Yes, Mistress." She swallowed and kept her eyes focused on the floor.

Jerricka moved to her. For a moment Jeremy thought she would strike the girl, but to his surprise, the woman squatted in front of her, placed a gentle hand under her chin, and lifted. In a soft and warm voice, she said, "Now, now, Daria. You have nothing to fear here. This is very important, though. We need you to tell us what happened so we can be prepared for what is to come. You understand?"

Daria nodded. Her throat moved as she swallowed.

"Okay. Tell us everything, child. And I do mean everything."

Daria spoke, the words rushing from her mouth.
"Bradenbaugh knows where we are. He's sending his minions through to find and destroy us."

A hush descended over the room, followed by gasps and excited chatter. Jerricka lifted a hand and the room fell silent.

"That explains the Harpy," Jno said.

"Who sent you with this message?"

"Master Rowan. He said to warn you and for you to take all necessary precautions."

Jerricka turned from Daria, crossing her arms and pacing. She moved to the far side of the wall, then turned. As she walked back, she said, "Jno, see to the defenses. Put everyone on alert."

Jno nodded and left the cabin.

"Okay. Now tell me about your journey and how you met this man."

Daria did not look at Jeremy, but he saw her swallow hard again. She twisted and untwisted her fingers, intertwining them in constant motion. "I was transported here by Master Rowan and made my way along the path he had me memorize. I was the only one who'd been here before, so I was the best person to send. Along the way, I was attacked by a Harpy."

More gasps and chatter. As before, the raised hand brought instant silence.

Jerricka turned and said, "Chase, find Nika, Neveah, and Allyra and have them bolster the dome. They need to keep it invisible and undetectable but reinforced against an aerial attack or scan."

"Yes, Mistress," the man said, and hurried from the room.

Dome? Aerial attack? Invisible? What was going on here? Not for the first time, Jeremy wondered what he'd stumbled onto.

"Continue, child."

Though she faced straight ahead, her eyes glanced at Jeremy. "I-I was forced to use magic to get free."

Another gasp, this one cut off by a stern look.

"I know I'm not supposed to use magic, Mistress, but it was the only way to get free so I could deliver the warning."

"There, child," Jerricka soothed. "We won't worry about that for the moment. Though magic is not permitted, it was a difficult situation and necessary. We'll discuss that further at another time. Please continue."

Daria cleared her throat. "I fell a long way, crashing through trees. I hit the ground hard. I'm sorry, but I don't know how long I was there."

"Understandable. You're lucky you survived to tell the tale."

Bolstered by the kind words, Daria grew more confident, her voice stronger. "When I woke, I was lost. I got turned around once the Harpy had me. I didn't want to continue on the same path in case it was scanning for me, so I took an alternate route. I stumbled through the woods, eventually finding a small shed to hide in."

"Why did you hide instead of coming straight here?"

I was too weak and it was almost morning by the time I hid myself, and I felt the Harpy above trying to locate me. I thought it best to hide until daylight."

"Okay. Then what?'

"I, ah, I fell asleep. I'm not sure how long I was out."

"It's important to know the elapsed time. Take an educated guess."

Daria sobbed. "I think it was an entire day."

At that, Jerricka lifted her head toward the ceiling and muttered something. She whirled and paced away, moving much faster now. She stopped at the wall and stood staring at it. The room remained silent until she turned, revealing the hardened expression on her dark face.

"You mean to tell me this warning is coming two days late?"

Daria couldn't speak. She merely nodded as another sob erupted from her frail frame.

Jerricka blew out a sigh, then said, "Go on. There is no time for your tears, girl. Get on with the story." Any pretense of being comforting was gone.

"If you would stop badgering her like a criminal," Jeremy started, as surprised by his interruption as everyone else in the room, "she might be able to give you the answers you want. Can't you see she's frightened of you?"

Jerricka's glare halted further words.

Daria wiped at her tears. "I left in the morning."

"But you're not sure which morning, right?"

"Yes, Mistress." Another wipe of her eyes. "I tried to find my way back to the path, but as I grew closer, two tusked hunting boars found me. That's how I met—him." She pointed. "They were after me. I tried to get away, but they were too fast. Jeremy was driving past and saw me. He stopped and helped me up the side of the road just as the boars got there. He led me to his car and drove me to safety.

"I swear I didn't tell him anything. He drove me around until I discovered the path. Then I got out of the car and took the path alone. I did not tell him anything about the village."

"That's true," Jeremy said. "She didn't tell me anything."

Jerricka swung her gaze at Jeremy. He felt the chill attack him like an arctic blast. "I'll get to you in a minute. Don't interrupt again." She returned to Daria. "And?"

"I found the path and came here as fast as I could. But just before reaching here, the Harpy came after me again. That's when you found me, and...well, you know the rest."

CHAPTER FIFTEEN

Jerricka kept a steady gaze on Daria. "What are you not saying, child? I can see into your heart."

Daria almost fainted again. Biatta raced to her side. "She needs a break. You got what you needed. Let me take her back to the clinic."

"No. I'll give her a break, but she stays here." She strode to Jeremy. "Now let's hear your version.

"It's as she said. I found her and tried to get her to go to a hospital. She was in desperate need of medical attention."

"And did you take her to the hospital?"

"No. She insisted she was all right, although clearly not. We drove around for several hours until she found a familiar spot. She got out and entered the woods."

Jerricka waited for more. Jeremy wasn't going to make it easy for her. "Explain how and why you are here."

"Daria—"

"Did she tell you her name?"

This seemed important. He wanted to protect her from any more trouble. "No. I heard that lady say it." He pointed at the woman in white.

Jerricka looked at Biatta, perhaps trying to remember if indeed she had mentioned Daria's name. A minute later, she shifted her attention back to Jeremy.

"Go on."

"I was concerned about her being out in the woods alone. She was in no condition for a long hike. She was injured and bleeding, and her...I was sure her arm was broken. I was afraid something bad might happen to her, so after a few minutes of debating with myself, I decided to follow her. Just to make sure she got here safely."

"How did you know there was a here?"

"I didn't. She said she needed to get home. I assumed home was through the woods."

"I see you have similar injuries. How did you come about yours?"

"I was in a car accident." He willed himself not to look at Daria.

She faced a dark-skinned woman. "Retta?"

"He's telling the truth. For the most part."

"What were the discrepancies?"

"When he was talking about what Daria said."

Jerricka looked from Daria to Jeremy. Daria's face scrunched up as she fought back tears.

"What are you leaving out?"

Jeremy didn't know who she was asking, but he answered to save Daria. "I can't remember everything that was said. I asked her multiple times who she was, where she lived, and what she was doing out on her own, but every time she either put me off or ignored the question. She didn't give anything away. When I followed her, she was nowhere in sight. I just kept moving until I got here. The fact I discovered this place at all is a miracle. I was about to give up searching for her when you found me."

Jerricka walked away and motioned for the others to join her. The discussion lasted fifteen minutes. Jno rejoined the group. His voice was louder and Jeremy heard him say, "The defenses are bolstered. No sign of any intrusion. I sent scouts out in four directions to give advanced warning."

Jerricka nodded her approval. The meeting broke up a minute later.

To Daria, she said, "You have been found guilty of multiple violations of our laws. Though an extreme situation, you have caused a breach in our security, thus threatening all who dwell here. I will decide your punishment later."

"You can't be serious," Biatta said. She moved inches from Jerricka's face. "It is not this child's fault your defenses have been breached. You still haven't asked the most important question of all."

"And that is?"

"How he managed to breach the barrier. Wasn't it created to confuse and shift intruders to another place? That didn't happen. And in case of a breach, this entire village should have been invisible to him. How is it he can see and hear us? And if I'm not mistaken, the wards and defensive dome were created by you and your team. If there's a failure here, perhaps it's best to turn your inquisition inward to discover who has failed this community." Her words were crisp. Anger reddened her face.

Jerricka's, however, showed no sign of ire or even mild irritation. She accepted the rebuke, gave it thought, then said,

"Perhaps you are right. My team and I will analyze the spell and work to improve it."

Biatta softened and looked at Jeremy. "I'm sorry for the harshness of my tone. The fault is neither yours nor your team's. There is something different about this man. I can sense it. The fault isn't yours. It is because of whoever he is."

Huh? That took a turn he hadn't anticipated.

He glanced around the room to discover every eye upon him, including Daria's. Since he had no idea what was going on in this village, he could offer no explanation or defense.

"A very astute and valid point, dear Biatta. Only someone of aligned magical ability would be able to penetrate the field." Her scrutiny of Jeremy increased. "Who are you, Jeremy Kline? Do you have magical properties? If so, how did you come about them?"

"Lady, I have no idea what you're talking about." Yet, somewhere deep in the hidden recesses of his mind, a thread of memory surfaced. Just a tiny morsel. Not enough to feed upon and grow stronger memories, but something stirred within him.

"He's lying," Retta said. "He does know something. He's just not sure what it is."

"Interesting. You have become quite a curiosity, Jeremy Kline. The question is, what to do with you?"

"Ah, I have no idea what's going on here, but I am certainly no magician. As for what to do with me...that's easy. Let me go. Now." He stood, but not so fast as to draw reprisals. He faced the strange woman dressed in black. Her long dark hair swirled around her face as she turned to the side. Eyes still on him, she asked, "Anything?"

Retta responded. "He speaks the truth as far as he knows. If he does have any abilities, they are latent. Perhaps even concealed. Whether or not that was self-imposed or done to him, I cannot determine."

"But he's male," another woman said. "How is it possible he has abilities?"

A man responded, "Some males have minor potential but either lack the connection to reach it or can only use those abilities for small tasks or unless they're set in an object."

"That's obvious, Chase," the woman said. "The question is why this man was not affected by a very powerful spell."

"Then he must stay here until we know more," Chase said.

"Is that wise?" Jno asked. "We know nothing about him. For all we know, he is a beacon leading Bradenbaugh and his legions right to us."

"It may not be wise, but it is necessary."

"What if we discover he is an agent for the evil one?" Retta inquired.

"Then he shall be dealt with," Jerricka said.

Jeremy did not like the sound of that. Being dealt with had a sense of finality about it.

"We could just erase his memory," Biatta offered.

"Yes, that is an option."

A better option than being dealt with, thought Jeremy.

"Let's question him further later. Have some of the guards keep watch over him while we see what needs to be done for our protection. Biatta, perhaps you can come up with something to ensure he is not transmitting a signal to the dark one. Retta, do some research into the name Jeremy Kline." She paused in front of Jeremy. A myriad of thoughts swirled behind those dark, cold eyes. "Everyone has their assignments. Let's get to them."

The interrogation over for the time being, Jeremy was taken away by two men with firm grips and hostile eyes. To his consternation, night had fallen. How long had he been there? He thought about the car—Miranda's car—and wondered if it would still be there when he got back. If he got back. Then he thought about Chandra. Oh dear Lord, what would he tell Chandra? She was going to be furious. Worried too, but it was her fury that concerned him at the moment. She was the only woman he knew who could match evil glares with Jerricka.

He was placed in a small hut and warned not to try to escape. The door closed. He was alone in a dark room, in a strange place with crazy people.

Now what do you do, old man?

CHAPTER SIXTEEN

Chandra set the phone down with a soft touch that belied the roiling sea of emotions coursing through her. She didn't know whether to be concerned or angry that her father hadn't picked up the phone the last five times she called. Why couldn't she be both? She wanted to believe he was asleep and didn't hear the phone. A very real possibility. But her gut told her otherwise.

Had he gone out? Did he take Mom's car? Doubtful. He never liked that car. 'Too small,' he'd always said. But if he really wanted to go someplace, would that stop him? Maybe the better question was, what would be so important that he'd need to go out? And where would he go?

The answer came immediately. She should have realized it before allowing him to stay at his house. He went looking for the girl he said he saw on the road; the one who had caused him to swerve off the road. Had she been real? Chandra wanted to give her father the benefit of doubt, but she was afraid it was just his night vision and his overactive imagination.

She had to know for sure. She picked up her phone, her keys, and her purse and walked into the bedroom. Cliff was coming out of the master bathroom, dressed to go out.

"Where are you going?"

"Oh. I'm meeting some of the guys down at the club for a few drinks and to watch the game."

"No."

His face retracted like he'd been slapped. "No, what do you mean, no?"

"You want me to wake one of the kids to explain the word to you? I said no. I need to go check on my father. He's not answering the phone."

"You know how he is. He's probably asleep. You worry too much about him. He's gotten along fine since your mother passed. I'm sure he's okay now."

"Are you? How precognitive of you. I'm going to check on him and you need to stay here with the children."

"The children?"

"Yeah. You remember them? The two tax deductions that run around here all the time."

"Honey. Chandra." The smooth, sugar-coated tone that had once so enthralled her now sickened her to her core. How long ago had that happened? Didn't matter.

"I'm going. You're staying. End of discussion. Do not leave this house. If you do, I'll know. Believe me. And you'll wish...well, you'll wish you never did." She whirled around and stormed out of the bedroom.

Seconds later, she was driving toward her father's house with a mix of emotions racing through her. Though worried for her father, she was ecstatic at finally standing up to Cliff. She was tired of him being a part-time husband and less of a father. Connor and Harper deserved better. She deserved better. Now she was angry. Her father's dislike for Cliff had finally rubbed off on her. Wait until she got to his house. Now that she was on a roll, he was gonna get it too. If he was home, that is. Now she was worried again.

* * *

Daria could not sleep. She had let everyone down and was going to pay the price. Would they dispose of her or just banish her? She was too terrified to think. Maybe the best thing for her to do was leave before they got around to deciding what to do.

Her thoughts fell on Jeremy. Why had the old man interfered? If he'd just driven away, no one would know about her failures. Now he would most likely get the same fate as her. What was she going to do?

She fought to calm herself to be better able to think, but that was like trying to ride a dragon. There was just too much motion to calm her racing mind. It was hot in the clinic. She pulled the sheet back to cool off and realized it wasn't hot. She just wanted to be ready to run. Why wait?

Daria sat on the edge of the bed and looked for her clothes. They had probably been burned since they were in such ruin. All she had on was the long nightgown. That would have to do. She placed her feet on the floor and crouched, feeling around for her shoes. They were dirty but still good. She brushed against them under the bed and pulled them out. She had them laced and was ready to sneak out when she heard a floorboard creak. Someone was in the outer room. Biatta, she surmised. As long as she had a patient, she wouldn't leave the clinic.

A long thin line of light filtered beneath the door. To her dismay, it was broken by shadows. Someone was at the door. As quickly and quietly as possible, she slid back under the sheet, keeping her shoes on. If someone came into the room, it would be apparent she was wearing them and would know why. She sat up to yank the shoes off, but the soft click of the latch announced it was already too late. She flung herself back and turned her ankles to the sides, hoping to conceal them better from that position.

The door swung open and light filled the room, causing her to squeeze her eyes tighter. That would let whoever entered know that she was awake, so she tried to relax her facial muscles. The door closed, blocking out the light. Soft footfalls sounded. The bed shifted under the weight of someone sitting. A soft hand touched her knee and gently ran down her leg. Once it reached her ankle, the hand ripped the sheet off and snatched her foot. The shoes were yanked off, the sheet replaced, and the weight lifted.

"You do not need to run, little one. You have made mistakes, but not so bad as to fear your fate. You will always have me to protect and watch over you. Your job now is to rest and get well so to better face the challenges ahead of us all."

She moved toward the door.

"Biatta?"

"Yes, child?"

"How did you know?"

Daria heard a chuckle. "Sleep well, Daria. I will see you in the morning."

She exited and Daria sighed.

* * *

In a darkened room in another world, the evil one stirred. He dwelled in a pit below the surface of the land where it had been kept prisoner for nearly a century. Over the past decade he had found a way to communicate which eventually connected him to his trusted collaborator to find him. The time was drawing near for his release. This time there would be no stopping him. He had been inactive for far too long. The one benefit of being idle was the amount of time he'd had to scheme and plot the destruction of those responsible for his current predicament. It was coming soon. In fact, it had already begun.

Bradenbaugh had proved a masterful partner. With his cunning and Bradenbaugh's unquenchable thirst for power, the mages had already fled this world, leaving but a token force to protect it. Even though his long-time foe and tormentor Rowan Vandalue was among them, they lacked the power to prevent what was to come. It was his time to rule, and once he was free from this prison, everyone who stood before him would perish in the most brutal and agonizing way possible. He already had plans for Rowan. The mere thought of his destruction brought renewed energy. He could taste the man's fear even from this great distance. And soon...yes, very soon, he'd taste his blood.

The ground shook with his sinister laugh.

* * *

Jeremy paced the small hut. It only took four strides to cross, so he pivoted as much as paced. His mind flooded with ideas how to make his escape. None sounded promising, especially if things got physical, but that didn't stop him from trying to figure something out.

He thought about Daria. How much trouble was she in? He hoped he hadn't made things worse for her. *Well, that was a stupid thought. Of course, you made things worse. You followed her and got caught. Just an old bungling fool.* No matter what, he had to find a way to make it better for her.

Suddenly the ground began to shake. His balance was thrown off and he reached for the wall to keep from falling. What was happening? Was it an earthquake? It ceased almost as fast as it had begun. As he regained his equilibrium, a foul sensation came over him.

He was transported to another place, somewhere in the deep recesses of this world. The dank odor of musty earth mingled with something foul and he gagged. It felt like someone else was inside his head; another entity possessing him. A thought entered his mind. It wasn't an earthquake. It was something far worse and pure evil.

Then he was back in the small room and his body began to shake like the ground had moments before, only his trembling continued much longer.

CHAPTER SEVENTEEN

Methen Bradenbaugh sat back from the ebony table and steepled his fingers. His thoughts were dark; angry. It took all his will to keep from smiting the messenger where he stood. From the way the man shook, he knew he was near death. If the Harpy had been dispatched somehow, the boars would be running free, since they were under her control. With no one to guide them, they would revert to their feral ways.

The woman to his right, Madelyn "Mad" McGrew, cleared her throat, distracting him from his contemplation.

"Do you wish me to search for them, my lord?"

"No. I need you here. I doubt that runt of a girl could have handled Jaselda by herself. She had to have help. That means we're on the right track. Jerricka and her young whelps are in that alternate dimension. We're close to eliminating them all. Once I've defeated Rowan, this dimension will fall fast. With this world secure, we can bring the Dark Lord back and allow him the pleasure of destroying those who incarcerated him."

Madelyn croaked in what passed for a laugh and rubbed her hands together in a vigorous and excited manner.

"Oh, this is going to be such fun."

The other two men at the table, General Perva and Toradon, shot nervous glances at each other.

Bradenbaugh said, "Still, it would be best to keep track of the exiles. Send Jaselda's sister Angwella. If her sister has been killed, she will want revenge. Tell her to reconnect with the boars. She is to find and eliminate the staff, but not kill any of the leaders. She can do what she wishes with the young brats."

"Yes, my lord," Madelyn said.

"General Perva, have you devised a plan to root out the last remnants of Rowan's resistance?"

"Yes, Lord Bradenbaugh. My forces are moving into position as we speak. As soon as this meeting is over, I will be joining them. I'll keep you informed as the battle is engaged."

"You're sure you have them bottled up?"

"Yes, Lord Bradenbaugh. We have them trapped. There will be no escape."

"There had better not be. Go. Get this done."

General Perva stood and left the room.

"Are you assisting him, Toradon?"

"Yes. He will need my expertise and power to subdue what Rowan will throw at him. They will be desperate, and I anticipate stiff resistance. Much more than our overconfident general gives credence to."

"Very well. If the battle looks like it is going other than as you expect, take control and see to it they are defeated. I need their combined power drained to weaken their hold on the Dark One."

"As you wish." He stood and left.

"Madelyn, you have your assignment. See to it and report back. We will have preparations to make once the rebels are destroyed. I will need your added power to assist with opening the prison cell."

She cackled and leaped to her feet. "Oh, with pleasure, my lord."

Bradenbaugh's forehead crinkled into deep furrows. "Send a small team through to the other world separate from Angwella. They are not to interfere with her mission. I'm not sure Angwella will be able to contain her rage if she finds her sister is indeed dead. The team is tasked with capturing any member of Jerricka's clan and bringing them unharmed to me."

"How many?"

"More will better the leverage, but one will suffice to begin."

She skipped from the hall, leaving him to his thoughts. He could taste the victory. Once the Dark One was freed, he would rule this world. Bradenbaugh would then ask to enter the new dimension and conquer that as well. Well, maybe not ask. With the Dark One in control of this world, he'll have little need for his services and in fact, may decide to rid himself of Bradenbaugh's desire for power. Perhaps the best path was to enter the other world, destroy the portal, and take that world for himself. Yes, things were looking up. He fought to control his excitement. Alone in the room, he allowed a smile.

* * *

Jerricka sat at the table with the other members of the council. To her left, the magical sector was represented by Gianna, Nika, Neveah, and Allyra. On the military side were Jno, Chase, and Aric. From logistics sat Favyan and Retta. The only section not represented was medical. Biatta was either busy with her patient or refused to attend. It didn't matter one way or the other, as her role would be limited; at least at the beginning. Jerricka made a mental note to have a talk with her regarding appearances. She could not have dissension in their ranks, especially with what was at stake.

She looked around the table. Tired, concerned, and nervous faces looked back. She couldn't blame them. Not more than two months ago, they'd been the teaching staff at the Academy for the Arts, a private educational facility for the young gifted of their world. It had existed for centuries, training and educating virtually every noted wizard, mage, and magician over that time. Some of the most famous names in magic had been trained at the Academy.

Now many of them were dead or on the run as Bradenbaugh struck without warning, assassinating many of the most powerful practitioners of the arts in his first wave of terror. Rowan had managed to round up some of them, but unless he could find many more, he was vastly outnumbered.

The last hope might very well be those sitting at this table, but none had any real wartime experience.

"I know this won't be a popular statement, but we need to start thinking of ways to get the children to safety." She held up a hand to prevent protests already on many of their lips. "It's best to be prepared, should the unthinkable happen. If the Dark One returns, it may already be too late for us. In the final battle, many of us will not survive. It is a hard thing to realize, but it is nonetheless the truth. If that should happen, we need to ensure the children will be taken care of. I need your ideas."

"Mistress," Jno said. "Shouldn't we be discussing the best course of defense instead?"

"Our best defenses may not be enough, considering the amount of power leveled against us. These children have been entrusted to us, not just for their education, but their safety as well. We have to have a plan in place before the final battle commences."

No one spoke. The door opened and Biatta entered.

"Forgive my tardiness, Jerricka. I was tending to our patient." She found an empty chair and sat.

"How is she?" Jerricka asked.

The question caught Biatta off guard. Jerricka usually showed no concern for the students. "She is healing and afraid."

"As are we all. Biatta, I have asked for suggestions how to safeguard the students, should we fail in our defense."

"A good point. I have an idea."

The corner of Jerricka's mouth twitched in the beginning of a smile. She knew Biatta would have an idea. She halted the smile before it showed.

"Please enlighten us."

"This won't be popular, but to ensure their continued safety, we need to find them homes with different families in this world."

The explosion of protests was predictable. Both Biatta and Jerricka waited the dissenters out.

Jerricka held up a hand for quiet. Usually it worked instantly but not this time. "We will hear Biatta out, then discuss it in a calm and professional manner. I am open to all suggestions. You should be too." She motioned to Biatta, who had been waiting in remarkable calmness. "Continue, please."

"Keeping them together will only make them targets. If our defenses fail, we will not be able to protect them if they are discovered. If we hide them individually, they will not draw any attention. Safety in numbers does not apply here. They look like all the other children in this world. As long as they act like it and do not use their magic, they will be safe. If any of us survive, we can continue to monitor them and bring them together when the time is right to take back our world."

"What if that never happens?" asked Gianna.

Biatta turned in her chair to face the other woman. "Then isn't better they can live out their time rather than die at the hands of the Dark One?" Her words hung over the table.

Jerricka asked, "Are there any other suggestions?"

"Yes," said Jno. "We uproot the entire camp and relocate."

That brought looks but no comments.

Jno continued. "I can send one of the men out to find another secluded area. I'd like to relocate at least five hundred miles from here. We're too close to the transfer point. If Bradenbaugh has indeed sent minions through to this world, he knows where it is. I had some of our people drag the Harpy's carcass deeper into the woods to our east, but if discovered, they'll search the entire area. I know you have great confidence in your ability to conceal us, but if you fail, we'll be in for the fight of our lives."

"Do you doubt the Mistress?" asked a defiant Nika.

Jno's face reddened. He was about to answer when Jerricka interrupted.

"I did not take the comment as a negative, Nika. Jno is only worried about protecting the children. Isn't that right, Jno?"

If any at the table thought she had been easy on Jno at first, they did not doubt her warning in the second.

Jno bowed his head and said, "Yes, Mistress."

Neveah broke the tense silence. "Let's be honest, here, because as you say, this is about the children. We cannot hope to survive a long battle head to head with Bradenbaugh's forces. Once he finds us, he will send everything he has against us. We do not have enough people, strength, or time to defend properly. So if we are truly thinking about the kids, perhaps whatever we do should have several levels to it."

"Such as?" Jerricka prodded.

"I agree with Jno about finding somewhere safer. But I also agree with Biatta about developing long-term survival placements for the children. I also think we will need local support to survive whatever is to come."

Encouraged by her support, Jno said, "Whatever we do, it has to be now. If a Harpy was sent, it won't be long before he sends larger search parties."

Jerricka swept the table with her gaze lighting on Biatta.

"I agree. Jno, send out a scouting team to search for potential locations. Give us three choices to select from, as we may see something your men don't. Neveah, explore partnerships. Go into town and observe and question. Find groups that we might join that may have secondary benefits. Perhaps some of us can take up employment. That will benefit us not only by the connections, but to have local currency to purchase food and supplies."

Then her eyes settled on Biatta. "I am intrigued by your suggestion. Though a last resort, it is a good one. Whether here or wherever else we may land, having reliable people we can settle the children with will be lifesaving. That is your task. Find those people. Vet them. Explain what is expected of the children, should we have to resort to your plan. My only concern is the lack of time necessary to develop those kinds of relationships."

She sat back and scanned the intense faces. "There is no doubt we are in for harder times than we have ever faced. I am encouraged by your willingness to do whatever is necessary for our continued survival. Let's pray it never comes to that, but let's also be prepared for when it does. Thank you. There is much to do. Go. Get it done."

Chairs scraped back across the hardwood floor. The council departed except for Biatta. Jerricka stood and moved next to her, sitting on the table.

"I'm glad you decided to attend."

Biatta sat back and crossed her legs. "Why wouldn't I?"

Jerricka shrugged. "It seems as if we've been in opposition since the crossing."

"We disagree on some things. That doesn't make us enemies."

Jerricka nodded. "Still, having you here adds a voice of reason to the council. We can disagree, but once a decision has been made, I expect you to support it—if only for the good of—"

"The children?"

Jerricka smiled at Biatta's interruption, though it didn't reach her eyes. "I was going to say the entire community, but you understand my meaning."

Biatta stood. "I do understand your meaning. But understand mine. I respect you and your authority more than you realize, but if any decision puts the children at risk, I will do what I deem necessary to ensure their safety, thus our people's survival."

"I wouldn't expect anything less."

"Then I have work to do, including a new assignment given to me by my Mistress."

Jerricka watched her old friend go. So much had changed since they'd been forced on the run. They had once been close; the best of friends, but since attaining a higher rank and taking charge of the school, Biatta and some of the others were unhappy with some of the administrative changes she'd implemented. It had caused a rift that had not yet healed. Her one solace was knowing that each staff member would put the children's needs and safety ahead of their own. That was all she could ask.

CHAPTER EIGHTEEN

Rowan Vandalue looked both ways for oncoming traffic, then scanned the sky before darting across the cobbled street. He ducked into an alley and sprinted the length. Nearing the end, he stooped behind a row of garbage bins and watched for pursuit.

He made a series of motions with his fingers, hands, and wrists, each with a definite purpose. Years of practice and experience had honed the muscle memory to perfection. He recited the words and extended his hands with his right forefinger pointing down the alley and across the next street.

He ran from behind the bins and down the alley, looking around. He buried himself deeper undercover as he stopped at the end of the alley and looked both ways before crossing the street. His body became smaller the greater the distance. Once he was out of sight from himself, Rowan waited patiently and quietly. He didn't have to wait long.

A large black bird flew down the alley and across the street, perching on a powerline it watched the retreating astral projection of Rowan. Rowan had his creation turn the next corner to be out of sight, then vanished it. The bird sped down the alley. As soon as it lifted off, Rowan stood and hurried back the way he came.

He pressed against the red brick wall, placed his fingers against the slight indentions in the brick, and pushed. The wall faded. Rowan stepped through, the wall reforming behind him.

A short dark hall led deeper inside the building. This secret section did not exist on any plans and was known to only a handful of trusted individuals. The hall turned right and ended twenty feet farther at a false door. Rowan stopped short of the door, turned to the right, and pressed his right eye to a small circular screw head. He held it there for several seconds. The screw moved to the left a quarter turn, telling him he was recognized as well as what to do next. He switched eyes, blinked once, paused, blinked twice, paused, and blinked once. The door slid up and Rowan stepped inside. He took a long winding metal staircase down to a circular room with no exit. He stooped under the staircase, uttered a magical phrase, fanned his fingers, and stepped through the final door to the inner sanctum of the resistance.

To each side stood wizards ready to attack, had someone other than he entered. Those in the room seemed to relax at the sight of him.

"Oh, thank God," Professor Wilden said. He collapsed into a chair. "You're late. We were worried."

"Sorry," Rowan said. "It's getting harder to move through the city unseen."

"What did they use this time?" Mr. Tarney said.

"A black crow."

"What gave it away?" asked Rhylie, the youngest member of the Arts Academy staff.

"The size, for one. Entirely too big. And the way it stopped every ten to fifteen feet. Whoever it was did not know how to control the body. It flew into a wall twice. Still, it's getting harder to get away from the watchers. Eventually, they'll be satisfied with just capturing me and hope everyone else will flee."

"You can't let that happen, Rowan," Tarney said. "You're too important to the cause. Everyone very well may flee without you holding them together."

"That can't happen," Rowan said, his voice hard. "No matter what happens to me or any of us, we cannot allow the Dark One to return to this world. You and Wilden were there the first time we had to battle him. It was hard enough then to imprison him and we had twice the numbers and much more talent."

"You're right, of course," Wilden said, "but I'm sick of all this sneaking around and hiding. We need to act. To go on the offensive. If we sit back and do nothing, eventually we'll be discovered and they'll attack us. I'd rather be on offense than defense."

"I'm not saying I disagree with you, but we have to be smart about what we do. It has to be fast and decisive. If it fails it may be the only chance we get."

Rhylie said, "And if you think we're hunted now, think about how it will be if the attack falls short of whatever goal we set."

That left the group silent, each lost in their thoughts.

Wilden said, "How many can we count on when the time comes?"

Rowan knew this question would be asked. He was ready for it but didn't want to give the response. Instead, he said, "We've got enough if used properly."

Tarney snorted. "In other words, not nearly enough."

Rowan sighed. That was all the confirmation the others needed. The silence lingered before Rhylie said, "Do you think she made it?"

No one had to ask who he was talking about.

"I hope so," Rowan answered, his voice just above a whisper. He stared into the fire.

"It was a mistake to send such a young and inexperienced person," Tarney said.

Rowan sighed. They'd been over this before. He gave the same answer he'd given then.

"Our options were limited."

"You should have let me escort her."

"Perhaps," he conceded.

"It'd be nice to know for sure," Rhylie said. "And we could sure use the staff's abilities when the time comes."

Wilden said, "What if they find a safe place to hide the students? Will you recall the staff?"

"It's possible."

Annoyed with the response, Tarney stood abruptly and paced.

Minutes passed.

"All right. Enough commiserating. Let's start making plans," Wilden said.

CHAPTER NINETEEN

They moved around a table and Wilden passed out blank paper to everyone. "Write down your ideas and what's needed to accomplish them. We'll compare notes and come up with one solid plan."

The four men did a lot of staring and not much writing. Finally, Tarney threw his pen down and rubbed his face. "This is a waste of time. None of us has a clue what needs to be done. None of us has done anything remotely martial in decades. We're out of practice and old."

"Hey! Speak for yourself," Rhylie said.

"Yeah, whatever," said Tarney. "If we screw this up, you'll never reach old age."

"All right. Listen," Rowan said. "We need to pinpoint where Bradenbaugh is. We need intel on his routine. The best way to win this war is to take him out. Without leadership, the Dark One's forces will collapse. We don't need to beat the entire army. We just need to kill Bradenbaugh."

"Huh," Tarney said. "You make it sound simple."

"Well, it's as simple as killing him, however simple that might be. Again, we need to know where he will be to devise a plan with a reasonable chance to succeed. We need to identify one of his followers and do some tailing of our own. Tarney, who do you have skilled in surveillance?"

Tarney gave a wry smile and nodded. "Suddenly, this seems possible. I know just the man."

Rowan smiled inwardly. He knew who Tarney had in mind.

"Leave the logistics to me," Wilden said. "I'll have my boys locate several targets and have a detailed report for you in two days."

An older man entered through a sliding panel near the back of the room. He carried a tray with tea service upon it.

"Ah, Kanter. Good to see you," Rowan said. "How are you?"

"I'm fine, sir," he said in a deep voice. His pure white hair lay in tight curls against his smooth black skin. For a man reputed to be in his early hundreds, he was in remarkable condition. His youthful features led many to believe he'd found the magical equivalent of the Fountain of Youth. He was legendary for his knowledge, his wisdom, and the training he imparted to the young students at the Academy. "And you?"

"I'm still alive." He knocked on the heavy wooden table. "At least for the present."

"And may that continue, sir."

"Thank you. And how are the twins?"

Kanter's twin daughters were equally legendary. In their early eighties, Olivianna and Delphina were just as notable as their illustrious father, but for different reasons. The two firebrands also taught at the school, and though well respected, they were known for their devious and detailed pranks on both students and staff alike.

"They are quite well and anxious to begin the defense of our world."

"As are we all," Tarney added, a touch of impatience in his voice.

"Please join us, Kanter," Rowan said.

"As you wish, sir."

He set the service tray down on the table and poured tea for everyone with hands as steady as a surgeon's.

Not much was known about Kanter or his family, though old tales surfaced of a family who traveled the countryside exorcizing demons from the young decades before Kanter applied for and was accepted as a teacher at the Academy. The stories were never confirmed and Kanter and his daughters never acknowledged it was them. However, whenever the question arose, Olivianna and Delphina glanced at each other with a dark intensity.

Even more ancient stories spoke of a thin-framed black man who had fought in the first war of magic when the Dark One's forces made their first attempt to free their master. The battle waged on almost equal footing until this mysterious man appeared. His magic was neither dark nor white, but some hybrid in between. It was his skill at out-weaving the then-leader of the Dark One's minions, ripping the man's atoms apart and scattering them across the universe. The raw power and horrible destruction the man had caused made many on the white side fear and shun him. Before any could question the man or discover his name, he vanished, never to be heard from or seen again.

Kanter served the others, then poured a cup for himself and sat in a cushioned chair to the right of Rowan.

"We're forming initial plans for our counterstrike. We'd love to hear your ideas or recommendations."

He blew across the ornate teacup, then took a tentative sip. Satisfied with the result of his brewing, he turned his almost purple eyes toward Rowan. "Very well, sir."

Rowan had tried for years to get the man to stop calling him sir, but the older man said it was a sign of respect for Rowan's position. Rowan knew it was more. For one moment similar to this, though in more relaxed circumstances, Rowan had brought up how Kanter always served others. Rowan said, "You are not a servant. Others should be serving you."

After a thoughtful pause, Kanter said, "I do what I do because that was how I was trained. I come from humble beginnings, where serving was expected and punished if not performed to expectations. I freed myself and for a while raged against the machine of the times, but those were dark and unpleasant memories. I serve now not just out of respect, but because it reminds me to never be forced to serve anyone. I serve others because I enjoy doing so. It is when I cease to serve that you should worry."

Rowan did not know how to respond to that, so he didn't. But the words had stuck with him ever since. He could feel the man's energy and power and knew instinctively that Kanter was not a man to anger.

"I heard your plans, or lack of, to be more exact." He spoke in a slow, deliberate manner with clear speech, as if each word was searched for and tried out in his head before passing over his lips. "I agree that taking out Bradenbaugh would hinder the Dark One's rise, but it will only delay the inevitable. The time to put the rebellion down was years ago at the first hint of the rising. I sensed it; others should have too. The situation could have been ended then, the danger defused, and deathless broad. Now, it is too late to prevent the rise of the Dark One. He will come. We need to be unified and strong. Much stronger than now to put him back in his prison. But his rise or attempted rise will reoccur unless he is banished in such a way that he can never be a threat again."

Tarney leaned forward in his chair. "You're serious? You don't think we can win?"

Kanter took another sip, staring into his cup as if divining the answer from the tea. He swung his eyes toward Tarney.

"Those were not my words."

Rowan noted the eyes had grayed and the word sir did not accompany his response. Was there a problem between the two men? If so, he needed to know what it was to keep it from affecting the defense of their world.

"I said we could not prevent him from rising. We can still stop him from his goal. It will just be more deadly than it might have been. We will lose many good people in the upcoming confrontation. We cannot prevent that. We can only hope to have the skill and the determination to see the task through, or our world will be altered forever."

"What do you suggest?"

"Is that my place?"

Wilden said, "Why wouldn't it be? You are a part of this world. You will have to share what is to come should we fail. Every man, woman, and child has a place in the defense."

His eyes were now dark brown with a spark of red in the center of the pupil. "I meant, sir, is my place to preach to the leadership of the rebellion?"

Rowan cleared his throat. He had to gain control of the discussion before it got out of hand. He very much wanted to hear what Kanter said.

"Kanter, I speak for all here that you are a respected member of this staff. Your advice is not only sought, but is needed, and perhaps more than any other here. As far as I'm concerned, you are a part of the leadership and always have been, just like every other member of the staff is considered to be. Please don't ever think otherwise."

Another sip. Another pause. Then Kanter leaned forward, set the cup and saucer down on the table, and moved his gaze around the table, catching and holding every man's eyes. When he reached Rowan, he held there.

"Very well. For us to win, we need a lot more power than we have currently."

"Where do we get more?" Rhylie asked. "Everyone still alive is scattered throughout the land or in the alternate world."

"There are options. Other races. Some more ancient than the ground we walk on. Many will not respond, but some may. Also, we need to find the lost tribe of Salemnon."

"Salemnon?" Tarney said, his mind seeking a thread of memory. "Where have I heard that name before?"

"Who is that?" asked Rhylie.

"A small band of people who chose not to fight during the last attempted rise because of a feud between Salemnon and your great grandfather." He pointed at Rowan.

Rowan felt the shock of the man's words deep in his chest. "My great grandfather?"

"What does his great grandfather have to do with this?" To Rowan, he said. "Rowan, you know what he's talking about?"

He shook his head. "No. I don't understand. He died during the first defense. I never knew him, though the stories that have been passed down tell he was the administrator of the Academy when it first opened and he sacrificed himself to save the students."

"All that is true," Kanter said. "But it was his ego and his refusal to accept help from those who lived on the fringes of accepted magical norms."

"The fringes!" Tarney said. "So they were into the black arts?"

"Black. White. Terms for the same thing. Just like with people. The good and the bad are not in the color but in the person wielding the magic. Just as not all black, white, brown, or yellow peoples are good or bad."

"We've always been taught black magic was a demon's tool and never to be practiced," Rowan said. "Both my grandfather and father were very strict about following that rule. Are you saying we've been wrong all this time?"

Kanter nodded. "You see, in the more rural areas where proper education and form are not known, the people use whatever tools are necessary or available for their survival. The magic is neither good nor bad. It is just a necessity to the task at hand. The evil only comes when the wielder is either too weak, too untrained, or not well versed in the arts to keep the demons at bay. If they open their hearts to the seductive lure or are tricked, the evil will wear them down and make them slaves to the power rather than the magic becoming a slave to them. For the most part, few of those who use dark arts know their evil nature or heed the call."

"Where did this lost tribe go?" Wilden asked.

The flicker of a smile passed Kanter's lips. He bent to retrieve the cup and saucer, took another sip, then said, "To the very world you sent the students."

The accompanying jaw drops around the table were satisfying to Kanter as his eyes glowed a dazzling blue.

CHAPTER TWENTY

General Perva's bulky form was difficult to conceal in the open alley. His thick frame was more hide than skin. His large head had little curved arch and bumps, ridges, and square cuts made up his facial features. He focused his eyes on the back alley building that his captain was pointing out to him. The man had a face like a ferret on steroids.

"The bird saw our prey go into that building before it was terminated. Other members of the resistance council have been seen in the vicinity. They are in there, sir."

"You'd better be right, for your sake." The voice rasped. The word's effects were obvious by the captain's rigid stance.

Toradon glided up behind him as if coasting on a stream of air. Though necessary to the upcoming fight, the general was not a fan of the arrogant man. His mere presence gave him a creepy sensation like an invading insect army running just under his hide.

"Is your man sure this time?"

To take the attention off himself, Perva asked, "Well, Captain?"

"Ah-ah, yes, sir. We have multiple verifications."

"Are your forces ready, General?"

"They are."

"Very well, then. Allow me." He stepped away from the wall. His body seemed to elongate and grow taller. With an overdone sweep of his hands, fingers splayed in the proper position, he spoke words in an ancient tongue. None but he could see the yellowish lines snaking from his fingers and floating on the air. They reached the target building and slithered along its surface. Seconds later they ceased moving, clinging to the dark red brick wall.

"Hmm. Curious!"

"What?" inquired Perva.

"Once again, I ask if you are sure this is where the council is hiding?"

The captain no longer sounded confident. "Ah, yes." He swallowed. "Sir."

"What is it, Toradon?"

"I would have thought the place would have some form of magical protection around it."

"And there's not?"

"Not a smidge."

"Well, maybe they didn't want it to be obvious and left the outer portion unprotected," the general said.

"Perhaps. Proceed."

Perva nodded to the captain, who signaled his forces. From the shadows, a dozen black-clad men moved toward the building's entrance.

"Do not let them get too far in. I will want to sweep the interior as well," Toradon said.

Once the twelve men were inside, the three leaders entered. Toradon placed his palm flat on the outer wall and the snakes slid back into his fingers. Inside, he set them loose again. They stopped at a rectangle of wall down the hall to the right. Their color changed from yellow to red and blinked like Christmas lights.

"Ah. It appears you may be right, after all. There is a hidden and protected door."

"Can you open it?" asked Perva.

Toradon rolled his eyes and scuffed at the notion. He flicked a wrist to have them move aside. He traced the outline of his snakes, mumbling, then placed both palms flat on the wall and pushed. The door opened inward. With a flourish of hands and a slight bow, he motioned for them to enter.

The twelve men entered and found stairs leading down. The captain nodded and the men descended.

***

In the lower level room, Tarney sat erect, hearing a strange buzzing. The others became aware, and attuned to his various forms of strange communications, watched him in silence. He did not blink, appearing to be a long way off. Then he blinked, shook his head, and looked around the group, taking in the concern on their faces.

"Gentleman," he said in a much too casual tone. "It appears we are about to be invaded."

***

At the bottom of the hidden stairs, the men halted. The space was too narrow for more than one at a time. From below, the word was passed up that they had reached a dead end.

Toradon said, "Everyone, duck." He didn't wait to see if they complied. He sent the snakes out again. Within seconds, they outlined another secret door. Though unnecessary, the men squeezed against the left side to make room for Toradon to descend. The wizard altered his shape and his elongated form slithered along the wall, taking human form once at the bottom. There he repeated the spell and slinked back up.

The lead man pushed on the door. It flew open, revealing a large ornate room with old-fashioned furniture, a blazing fire, and the shocked expressions of several men.

The force burst in, shooting everything in sight. In seconds, the acrid smell of gunfire wafted upward to Perva and Toradon. They waited for word.

"Ah, General Perva," the captain said. "You need to see this."

***

The door burst open. Rhylie jumped to his feet in shock and panic. Rowan grabbed his arm to steady him. Twelve men exploded into the room, sending bullets flying in every direction. "Not yet, my good man," the professor said.

***

The two men walked down the stairs, Perva leading. They stopped at the threshold and took in the carnage. Perva did not expect to see five men staring at him. With all the rounds poured into the room, he fully envisioned seeing red Rorschach patterns on the walls. He moved to enter, but strong hands grabbed his shoulders and held him back. He swept his hands from top to bottom of the doorframe and a translucent shape shimmered in front of them.

***

"There they are." Wilden pointed. "Now, Tarney."

***

In a blinding flash, the room was filled with an ozone-smelling flash. A horrid odor arose amongst the shrill cries of the twelve men. Thirteen shocks fell upon each other, sounding like a large insect being fried on a bug zapper. Smoke filled the space making it difficult to determine what was happening.

In a whoosh, the foul stench was sucked from the room by unseen ventilation. The room now showed thirteen dark, ashen smudges and the forms of five men still calm and still looking at the doorway.

"What the bloody hell just happened?" Perva demanded.

In typical annoying fashion, Toradon said, "Well, for one, your men are dead. Two, you'll need to appoint a new captain. And three, I just saved your life. You're welcome." He released the general, turned, and floated up the stairs.

"I don't understand. They're right there in front of us."

"Holograms, dear General. It was a trap. Pray our Lord Bradenbaugh doesn't think to replace his general too."

***

"Well," said Wilden. "We missed a big score."

"Sorry," Tarney said. "Just a fraction too soon."

Rhylie stood at the liquor cabinet and poured a stiff brandy into a glass with shaking hands. He set the decanter down and gulped the amber liquid straight down, gasping afterward.

"You all right, Rhylie?" Rowan asked. Low laughter filtered through the air. "We were never in any danger."

"Well, that would have been nice to know beforehand."

Another louder chuckle reddened his face. He filled the glass again.

"Yes. That was a golden opportunity to do major damage to Bradenbaugh's army.

"My God!" Wilden exclaimed. "He not only sent Perva, but Toradon as well. We could've crippled their efforts in one blow."

The group sat in silent contemplation.

Kanter said, "One thing is for sure. The kid gloves are off. There was no attempt to capture. Only to kill."

"But what's changed?" Wilden said.

Tarney answered, "He's getting desperate. Maybe the Dark Lord is putting pressure on from beyond this world."

Rowan clinked his fingernails on his glass. "Or it could mean he no longer needs us to find the students."

All eyes shot up and stared at him.

Tarney said, "We need to send a team to warn and support them."

"Yes," said Rowan. "See to it at once."

CHAPTER TWENTY-ONE

Jeremy had had enough. He pounded on the door and shouted. When no one responded, he kicked at the door. His body still ached from the accident, but he was too angry to notice. With each kick, his anger flamed higher, and he put more power behind each kick until the door bounced against the frame. He was rewarded for his efforts by the sound of cracking wood. The sound also drew attention from whoever was outside.

He lined up his next kick; heart pounding, breathing labored, sweat dripping. But as he delivered it, the door was flung open. Unable to completely stop the kick, he caught the equally surprised guard in the chest, propelling him out of the doorway. Even with the way now clear, Jeremy found himself off balance. He stumbled, fell against the door frame, and took a moment to regain body control.

He darted for the outside, but the guard was more agile and quicker. He lunged for Jeremy's legs, wrapping him up like a cornerback and tackling him before he reached the ground. He fell hard, his injured wrist banging off the wooden steps. His head hung over the first step and his forehead bounced against the second. He groaned, slightly dazed, yet still fought for his freedom.

The altercation drew attention. People came running from several directions to help corral Jeremy.

"No! Let me go! You have no right to hold me!"

He was quickly subdued and lifted to his feet. Blood dripped into his eye. Too exhausted to offer resistance, he was all but carried. Instead of taking him back to the hut, he was taken back to the main cabin in the middle of the compound. Jerricka and two others were waiting for him.

"You need to let me go, right now."

"Do I?" Jerricka asked, her smug expression making him angrier and more afraid. "Seems to me I don't have to do anything of the sort. If I wanted to, and believe me I am tempted, I could make you disappear without a trace."

Her announcement stopped any further comments. It also stopped his heartbeat and caught his lungs short of breath. The cold manner in which she delivered the statement only made Jeremy realize the truth of her words. No one would ever know where he was, at least until they found the car. Even then, searching the woods might take a long time and his body might not be discovered.

"Fortunately for you, others have spoken out against such an act." She sighed as if to emphasize her disappointment. "I have considered their requests and decided on an alternative solution. I don't know who you are or how you managed to pass through our veil, but I cannot take a chance on the safety of my charges. I pray I am not making a mistake, so listen carefully. I will not hesitate to end your life if I find you anywhere near this location again." She turned to the woman behind her and motioned with her head. "Allyra, if you would, please."

"Yes, Mistress."

She stepped forward and lifted both arms. Mumbled words came from her lips, but they were in an alien language that Jeremy did not recognize. Something stirred deep within him as if her words were awakening some life force living inside. Panic raced through him. The fear had him trembling.

Allyra closed on him. A dull blue-white current crackled in her palms as if she were connected to an electric power source. His eyes widened to the point of popping, yet he could not move. His body refused to respond to his brain's panicked cries to save himself. All he could do was watch in absolute terror as the blue-white charge grew in intensity and moved ever closer.

In the distance he heard a voice.

"This will not hurt you." It was Jerricka. Her words were not comforting. How could he believe her? "You will feel sleepy. You will dose. When you wake, you will have no memory of this village, of Daria, or any who dwell here. If you drive past the place where you entered the woods, you will not recall this foray. From the moment you sleep, this portion of your life will be scrubbed clean of any trace."

Allyra's voice grew louder. Her hands clamped down on his temples and the current shot through his head. For an instant he felt mind-numbing pain, then all went white. The pain subsided and he was out.

* * *

Jerricka thanked Allyra and dismissed her. She paced a few times in a slow circle around the room before sitting at her desk. Jno waited for direction. Jerricka dove deep within her mind searching for the answer to the question of who Jeremy Kline was. Her biggest concern was that the old man had somehow duped her into thinking he was harmless. Though her threat about making him disappear was mostly bluff, she would not hesitate to end him, should he become a threat to her students. Had she made a mistake? Only one way to know for sure.

"Jno, after you deposit Mr. Kline, have one of your men follow him. Let's make sure he is who he claims to be. If he appears to be a potential threat, I want to know. We may have to leave here sooner than expected."

"Yes, Mistress." He gave a slight bow and left Jerricka to her thoughts. There was something peculiar about Jeremy Kline that she could not decipher. She did not get the sense he was hostile, but given their current situation, she could not afford to take the chance.

Then a new thought came to her. She rose from her desk and went outside. She motioned for Chase. When the tall muscular man stood before her, she said, "Bring Daria to me and ask Allyra, Biatta, and Nika to join me."

"Yes, Mistress."

She closed the door and went back to her desk to wait. Her mind whirled with thoughts and questions. She needed answers and needed them now.

Ten minutes later, the three women and Daria were in the cabin. She motioned Daria to a chair she pulled in front of her desk, then met with the three staff members for a conference.

"I am going to question Daria about her involvement with this Jeremy Kline. I want Allyra to scan her memories and Biatta to read her emotions. I need to know what she knows and did and whether she's lying about any of it."

"You're going to interrogate one of your students?" Biatta asked, astonished. "Not to mention, the poor child is recovering both mentally and physically from her ordeal."

"When the safety of every other student may rest on what she says or is concealing, you bet I am. If this is too beyond your sensitivities, then you are excused. Send in Neveah. She is equally as gifted in empathy. She will not have the same qualms as you. I invited you because of your connection with the girl. I thought you could read her easier and with less discomfort to her, but if you'd rather leave the task to Neveah, I'm fine with that."

"Don't play me, Jerricka. I've known you far too long. I will do what you ask, but I do disagree with it."

"Very well. Let's get started."

She took a seat at the desk. Allyra stood behind Daria. Biatta and Nika stood on either side. The terrified girl looked from one to the other. She was so pale she looked on the verge of fainting.

"Wh-what's going on? Are you going to hurt me? Or-or—"
She couldn't continue.

"Now, now, Daria," Jerricka said in a soothing tone. "We're
not monsters."

Biatta grunted.

Jerricka shot her a warning glance. "We are not going to hurt
you. But we do need to know exactly what occurred when you
were with that man."

"But I already told you."

Jerricka offered a smile that wouldn't have comforted
anyone. "Of course you did, dear. But often times small details
are overlooked. You may have forgotten or repressed them,
but we do need to know. I'm going to ask you some questions.
Answer to the best of your ability. Okay?"

The nervous girl nodded but bounced in her seat like
someone had set her controls on high.

Allyra mumbled her words and wove her fingers in a pattern.
Daria glanced over her shoulders.

"What is she doing?"

"Do not worry about her. She's helping to form the images you remember into a more complete picture. Now, take me back to when you first crossed into this world."

"Okay." Her voice was meek. "Rowan brought me to the transfer point."

"Rowan himself?" Jerricka asked, surprised.

"Yes. Is that wrong?"

"No, child. Just surprised he would take you himself. Was there a reason?"

"Yes. He said he needed to give me a lot of information but time was short, so he told me everything on the way to the site."

"What sort of information?"

"About what to say and precautions I should take."

"And what did he tell you to say?"

"That the situation was getting worse. Bradenbaugh was increasing the pressure. He had captured a few of our people and tortured them for information. One of the people tortured knew the transfer point. He feared it would soon be breached."

Jerricka hesitated to ask the next question but couldn't help herself. "Did he give you the name of the captured person?"

"Yes. It was Doniel."

Jerricka hadn't realized she was holding her breath until she blew out a sigh of relief. A gasp from Nika drew her attention. Too late she realized it hadn't been who she feared. It was Nika's man. Nika clutched at her throat with one hand while the other covered her face.

Jerricka made to rise and comfort her, but Biatta was faster. She embraced the other woman and whispered something in her ear. Nika nodded and bolted from the room. As Biatta returned to her position, she shot a withering glare at Jerricka that held enough venom to make her cringe. She hadn't meant to be that obvious or audible with her sigh, but she couldn't help the relief that swept through her hearing a name other than Jeter, her husband. She regrouped and put her focus back on Daria. The girl was crying.

"I'm sorry. Did I say something wrong?"

"No, child," Biatta said, kneeling at her side. She stroked the girl's hair. "The truth is the truth. We can do nothing about what has happened, but we need to hear the rest of what you know to help prevent more pain for all of us in the future.

Please continue. And don't leave anything out." She stood and stepped back.

Daria wiped at one eye and continued her story. It took almost two hours before Jerricka was satisfied they had pried the entire saga from Daria.

"Okay, Daria. You did well. Go back to your hut and rest. If we need anything else, we'll call for you."

Drained, Daria didn't speak nor make eye contact. She slinked from the room as quiet as possible.

CHAPTER TWENTY-TWO

Jeremy woke with a start as a large truck drove by, shaking the little car. Confused, he scanned the area. *How did I get here?* Had he fallen asleep and pulled over? That was the only explanation he could determine. He started the engine. Where was he? He got his bearings and pulled from the side of the road.

The sun was getting low. How long had he been asleep? As he drove, he searched his memory why he'd left the house. He couldn't remember anything. Maybe he was getting senile. Or perhaps he'd sustained a more severe head injury that he thought in the accident.

Accident.

He remembered that. How many days ago had the crash happened? He wasn't sure. He had lost track of time as well as his memory.

It took half an hour to get home. It was dusk as he turned down his street. Chandra was waiting in front of his house. If the sight of her standing there fuming wasn't bad enough, she was speaking with two police officers. His first thought was to turn around and flee, but that would only delay the inevitable.

Jeremy pulled up the driveway, afraid to get out of the car. For the first time, he noticed the items on the passenger seat. What was all this stuff? He had more important things to be concerned about. He exited the car. He barely had both feet on solid ground before Chandra stormed at him.

"Dad, where the—heck have you been? I've been worried to death about you. I called the police, thinking you'd been in another wreck. I thought we agreed you would stay home for a few days. What was so important that you had to leave? I don't understand you at all. Well? What have you got to say?"

One of the officers, a Hispanic woman with Perez on her name badge, stepped forward. "Ah, miss? Maybe if you gave him a chance to speak." She turned toward Jeremy. "Sir, are you all right?"

"Yes, I'm fine."

"You're not injured? Haven't been in a crash?"

"No."

"Did anyone force you from your house?"

"No."

"Did you experience a blackout?"

Jeremy hesitated a moment; just long enough to be suspicious. "No."

"Sir, I need to ask this, and please...be honest. Have you taken any drugs, prescribed or otherwise, that may have caused a blackout or loss of memory?"

"No."

"What about alcohol? Have you been drinking?"

"No."

She turned to Chandra as if to say, *See? He's fine,* then said to Jeremy, "Is there anything you need to tell us?"

"No. I'm fine. Everything's fine."

A crooked smile creased the officer's face. "Well, perhaps not everything." Her eyes rolled toward Chandra. "We'll be going now. Take care." She turned to Chandra. "Things will cool down if you let them. I can see that you're still upset, and perhaps with good reason. I hope we don't have to come back here for a domestic dispute."

Chandra's jaw dropped. The officers left her stammering for a response. As they drove away, Chandra rounded on Jeremy.

"Explain yourself. Now!"

The story came to him in a flash. "I went to get the things from my car. They're on the front seat. Then I went for a drive."

"Did you forget your phone? I've been calling you for hours. Really, Dad. Have you no common decency? A simple phone call would have saved me a lot of stress and worry. It's bad enough I have to worry about my kids, let alone my father, not to mention the added stress you've put on my already strained relationship with Cliff. Oh, sweet Jesus! Cliff. I left him hours ago with the kids. He'll be fuming." Her voice softened. "Are you sure you're all right? No hangover from the concussion?"

"I'm fine. Really. I'm sorry I put you through this. I guess I was deep in thought and lost track of time."

"You worry me. Anyway, I have to go." She gave him a hug and a frustrated groan. "I'd tell you I love you, but I'm still too angry. Stay home."

She hurried to her van, waved as she drove off, and sped from view.

***

Jerricka sent out for food before resuming the conference. As it was brought in, they moved to the round table and sat. She was tired. The day had taken a toll that only sleep could remedy, but it would have to wait. She took a bite of a vegetable omelet and washed it down with a sip of tea.

"What did you see, Allyra?"

"She was deliberately concealing the use of her magic. Her use of it to get away from the Harpy was understandable, but she was responsible for the man's accident, though she didn't do it on purpose. The sudden appearance of the car caught her by surprise. She reacted without thought, creating a force field that, though weak, was enough to deflect the car off the road. She was not responsible for him rolling down the hill. She also used her magic to create a light to see if the man was alive. If the Harpy was close by, it would have detected the magic and come hunting her. She was fortunate."

"Anything else?"

"She spent hours in the man's company. Though she doesn't remember it, she gave him the information he needed to track her."

"Yes, that was apparent."

"Biatta."

"She's been traumatized by the situation. I think she handled herself with remarkable skill for one so young and untrained. Yes, she did lie about using the magic, but she did not lie about how long she was with him or what was said. She had no idea she gave away vital information. There was no intent."

"She is not on trial, Biatta."

"Isn't she? Could have fooled me. I doubt she feels she isn't. What are you going to do with her?"

"Do?" She snorted. "Tell me, Biatta, what would you have me do? Pat her on the back and say, 'Nice job?' You want me to give her a slap on the wrist? Her actions put us all in jeopardy."

"You can't be thinking of—"

"Of what? Executing her to make an example? You have such a low opinion of me. No. She'll be restricted to the grounds and placed on kitchen and bathroom duty. Hopefully, she won't get the two confused. Regardless of what you might think of me, I am no monster."

Biatta lowered her head. "I apologize for saying that. Forgive me."

"I'll think about it." She pushed from the table. She was so tired, yet still had so much still to do. "Thank you both for your time and assistance. It's late, and we all have duties to attend to. Goodnight."

With that, she whirled around and headed for her bedroom, leaving the meal clean up to them.

CHAPTER TWENTY-THREE

It was late, yet Jeremy was not tired. *It must be the long nap I took in the car*, he mused. There was more to his insomnia, though. Something tickled the back of his mind; something important. Whatever it was refused to budge from the shadows there. Feeling a sudden urge to eat, he made a peanut butter sandwich and sat at the kitchen table.

His mind worked as he chewed, never tasting the food. The phone rang, jostling him from his trance. He glanced around the room and stared at the sandwich in his hand. When had he made that? He set it down and picked up the phone. It was Chandra checking up on him.

"Yes, beloved daughter?"

"I'm just checking to make sure you're all right."

"I am and I'm home."

"That's good. I'm too exhausted to come back over there."

"How are things with Cliff?"

"A little chilly, but I don't want to talk about that. Get a good night's sleep and I'll talk to you tomorrow."

"Okay. I love you, Chandra."

"Love you too, Dad."

He set the phone down and realized he was still holding the sandwich. It was half-eaten, but he had no recollection of taking a bite. Jeremy got up, placed the remains of the sandwich in a plastic bag, and put it in the refrigerator. Then he went to bed.

Still unsettled by the day's events, sleep was an adversary he battled. Finally, it landed a knockout punch and he tumbled into darkness. If he sought rest and recuperation, his mind had other notions.

He was chasing a young girl through an endless forest. No, that wasn't right. He was chasing the thing that was pursuing her. It was a large and faceless creature with malevolent intent. He followed mere seconds behind, yet never once caught or got a good look at the beast. Several times he lost its trail, only to be reconnected upon hearing a distant scream. Just as he caught up and moved to save the girl, he woke.

***

Daria slipped unseen from the village. She had messed up and put the entire camp in danger. She had no way to make it right. Her best option was to leave and never return. It was better if she faced the danger alone rather than risk her fellow students.

With extreme care and stealth, she passed the first line of guards, creeping slowly until she was sure of the placement of the second line. Once past, she hastened her pace to put as much distance as possible between herself and the village. She planned on staying in the forest and traveling until dawn. Then she would find a place to rest and not start again until the night. Daria had no idea how she'd survive, but the memory of her failure motivated her beyond rational thought.

With no idea how long she had been traveling and only a vague notion of her direction based on the moonlight that filtered through the dense overhanging canopy of trees, Daria began to feel the solitude of her journey. She was cold, tired, hungry, and yes, afraid, but she would not, could not stop.

Something large flew overhead, momentarily blocking out the moon. She paused and crouched. Fear doubled as the memory of the Harpy resurfaced. Was it another one? She did not know, but knew if it was, she was sorely outmatched. Regret over her rash decision to flee added to her stress. Frozen to her spot and too terrified to move, Daria began to tremble. Her entire body felt ice cold. A sound from somewhere behind her caused a whimper to escape her throat. She clapped her hands over her mouth. Her eyes widened, taking in the dark shadows that surrounded her.

Another crack of a twig came closer now. Afraid to move for fear of giving away her location, Daria shrunk lower to the ground. Her mind fought against the panic and searched for a spell, but she knew so few and had mastered even less.

Then something snaked around her head, yanked her back, and clamped over her mouth. The hold was so tight she struggled to breathe and move. She kicked and squirmed until she felt warm breath at her ear.

"Stop moving or you'll give us away," a voice whispered.

Though panic still consumed her, she forced her body to go limp. She attempted to turn her head to see who held her, but the strong grip did not allow her to move. Once again, the moon was blotted out. Daria glanced upward. If the Harpy was still in the sky, then who was holding her?

She waited an eternity for the grip to relax. When it did, she snapped her head back, making solid contact. A bolt of white shot through her head. Though dazed, she gripped the fingers and bent them back until she broke free. Daria ran with all her strength. She made it five steps before arms wrapped around her and bore her to the ground. Her face smacked into a root and she cried out in pain. The body clawed its way on top of her, pinning her arms to the ground. A face appeared inches from hers.

"Stop, you little pain in the butt, or I'll leave you for the Harpy."

She recognized the voice now. Shadows hid his features. It was Jno. But was that good or bad She stopped fighting. The pain in her face pushed everything else from her mind. A minute later, Jno stood and yanked her to her feet.

"You have two choices: either walk back on your own or be carried over my shoulder."

With tears streaming down her face, she said, "I'll walk."

"Good choice." He took her hand and led her back through the forest. It didn't take as long to return as to leave, leading her to believe she'd been going in circles.

Back inside the village, she was taken to Biatta's cabin. Biatta stood in the doorway waiting for her.

"Thank you, Jno."

He grunted and handed her over. Though Biatta's hand was softer than Jno's, her grip was just as firm.

"Oh, child. What were you thinking? Running away is never the answer. You made mistakes; we all do. Learn to live with them and learn from them. Come. You'll stay with me tonight. We'll decide what to do with you in the morning." Biatta led her into the room and closed the door behind them. Once out of sight, she jerked Daria to her. "This must stop. Do you understand? Your actions endanger us all. It's time for you to grow up and act like the trusted student I thought you to be. Can you do that?"

Daria nodded and burst into tears. Biatta held her close and stroked her head.

"It'll be all right. Now, let us both get some much-needed sleep."

CHAPTER TWENTY-FOUR

The village was a hub of harried activity the next morning when Biatta and Daria exited the cabin.

"I have matters to attend to and can't be following you around today. Do I have your word that you're done running?"

Daria hung her head. "Yes, Biatta. I promise."

Biatta slipped a finger under Daria's chin and lifted it until their eyes met. "We all have more important things to do than worry about you. Do you understand?"

"Yes. I'm sorry."

"Don't be sorry. Be better. Now go. I'm sure tasks are awaiting your attention."

Daria jogged away, heading for the girls' dorm. She had been stupid. She understood that now and vowed to make it up to Biatta and the entire village.

She reached the long rectangular log cabin that housed the female students. Most of her classmates were busy outside doing chores. Only three girls remained inside, all picking up bedding for laundry. Two of the girls were in the senior class.

She moved toward the third girl, ignoring the piercing glares of the older girls.

"Daria!" her friend shouted. "There you are. We were so worried about you. Are you all right?" The exuberance of the greeting surprised and warmed her.

Gwynedd was smaller framed than Daria but taller. Her dirty blonde hair seemed darker than she remembered. She dropped the load of sheets in her arms and embraced Daria.

"You're really all right?"

"Yes. I'm fine."

"We heard crazy stories about you being attacked by a Harpy and leading a strange man here. An outsider, no less."

"I'm afraid it's all true."

One of the older girls huffed and said to the other, "See? I told you she was a traitor."

Gwynedd whirled on the girl. "She is not, you—"

Daria snared her friend and stopped her from saying more. "It's okay, Gwynedd. Let them think what they will." She bent and picked up the sheets. "Here. Let me help with the laundry."

"We don't need *your* help," the older girl said.

"Oh, you need help all right," Gwynedd said. "Just more mental."

The other older student said, "Come on, Lisa. They're not worth our time." They carried their loads outside, leaving the younger girls alone.

"So, you fought a Harpy?" Gwynedd's tone was incredulous.

"I wouldn't call it a fight. It pretty well had me. I got lucky and burned its underbelly with a fireball and it dropped me."

"A fireball!" Gwynedd cried with a mix of shock and awe. She leaned closer and whispered. "But we're not supposed to learn offensive spells until next year. How did you learn it?"

Daria glanced around to make sure no one was listening. "I snuck into a private lesson with Master Rowan and a senior boy."

"Weren't you scared?"

"Petrified, but once I was there, I couldn't leave without giving myself away. So I kinda listened."

"And you were able to do it? How did you develop enough capacity to perform the spell?"

"I practiced a few times to make sure I had the words and hand motions right. I can't do a very big one, but it was enough to get me free."

"Wow! That's amazing. Can you show me?"

"I don't think it's safe to do magic at the moment. Besides, I'm already in enough trouble."

Gwynedd looked disappointed.

"Hey. I'll show when it's safer to use magic, okay?"

She brightened. "Yeah, that'd be great."

They gathered the sheets from every bed and hauled them outside. They followed the path down to the brook where the other two girls were washing the blankets.

***

Biatta watched the two girls leave the cabin and walk toward the stream. She held a mug of tea and blew over the rim before sampling the brew. Her face scrunched up. Bitter. One of the many things she missed from home was her special blend of tea. An aroma memory filled her thoughts, bringing forth fresh images of her room at the academy.

She stood in the bowed window of the third-floor tower in the teacher's wing. The tower had six stories, but she was happy with her level. It allowed for a picturesque view of the open grounds of the campus, past the stone walls and down the sloping forest-covered hillside. The river at the foot of the hill flowed in a long S-curve until it was out of sight.

In the distance the mountains surrounded the property, serving as protection against all who might pry or wish harm upon the school's unique students. It was lovely. Breathtaking. With the warmth of the fire that flamed behind her, the comfort of the memory of her special tea, and the vista, she had never felt calmer or more at peace.

It had been a good decision to seek a position at the school. For the first time in her life, she had stopped running and looking over her shoulder for those still searching for her. The school had been good for her and those in charge, Master Rowan, Professor Wilden, and Jerricka, had been welcoming and supportive. The staff too had taken her in as one of their own, though she had few she called friends, feeling the long-learned need to keep a distance. She liked them well enough, but it had been her experience that as soon as she got close to anyone, something always went awry. Either they learned too much about her, word leaked out where she was, or her hunters found her and she was forced to leave in haste.

By far, this had been the best decision she'd made and the longest she'd been in any one place since she was a child. Before she knew who, or perhaps better stated, what she was. At least here she was surrounded by others, though perhaps not the same as her, were at least as different.

Another sip of tea and the bitter taste snapped her from her fugue. Ah, reality. Now look at them. Not only was the warmth and protection of the school gone, but the world they now existed in had new dangers of its own.

She sighed and set the undrinkable brew down. At least the danger hadn't come from those hunting her. But from what she'd learned, this new danger might be even worse.

* * *

Rowan Vandalue watched as Bradenbaugh's minion tasked with tailing him walked by. The confused expression on the young man's face morphed into one of fear with each passing step. He imagined the thoughts racing through his mind. Where did he go? How can I find him? What will the boss do to me if I report I lost him? That last would be foremost on his mind.

Rowan did not sympathize. He would get what he deserved for siding with the dark one. He should have stayed true to his nature, though in retrospect, perhaps he had.

The boy, Javier, had been a third-year student at the academy. He'd never really excelled at any one magical trait but had progressed. Somewhat. He was too lazy to ever develop any great skill. As he thought about the boy now, it came to mind that Javier was the perfect candidate to be lured by Bradenbaugh's promise of easy power. The evil master must be desperate to send someone known to Rowan.

Then a chilling thought struck. Perhaps that was the point. He'd be so obsessed with watching and following Javier, he'd be unaware of a second, more dangerous spy lurking in the background.

In a fraction, he had his power ready to defend just as an icy blast lifted the hairs at the base of his neck. He whirled, ducked, and dodged left.

"Deflectis!"

Whatever had been cast from the shadows bounced off the invisible field in a shower of sparks and scattered along the high stone walls of the narrow alley where he hid.

Rowan hit the ground hard, rolled, and banged into the wall. By the time he reached a somewhat upright position, he had the next spell on the way.

"Luminous extremeus!"

A blinding bolt of light flew from his fingers, piercing through whatever counter spell had been raised. A scream followed. Something hit a hard surface.

He got to his feet and ran to the side while directing his hands toward the sound. The light faded but remained as an aura around the assassin. Rowan did not recognize the unconscious mage. That was bad. That meant Bradenbaugh had found a new source to build his army. He swung toward the alley entrance and scanned for Javier. The boy was nowhere in sight. Had he even been aware of the plan? Rowan doubted he'd been informed. The better to make an unassuming patsy.

With the idea of following Javier back to Bradenbaugh's lair now a fantasy, Rowan lifted his collar and stepped onto the walkway. Two steps later, he stopped and reentered the alley. The man stirred. Rowan was not a cruel man, nor did he enjoy killing, especially if it was someone unable to defend himself. But this was war, and the attempt had been too close. He searched his mind for the proper spell, cringed at the thought of using it, then sighed with resignation.

He bent, brought forth the words, and aimed his fingers at the enemy's digits. The skin smoked. The man's eyes flew open and he screamed. With a quick swipe of his hand, Rowan cut the sound off. The man stared at his now burning and withering fingers, his face contorted in a rictus of extreme pain.

Rowan stood and turned allowing the spell to run its course. It was a horrible thing to do to another person; especially another mage. He took no pleasure from the act, but the man had tried to kill him. He would be fortunate to regain any use of those fingers, let alone ever use magic again. If his lost ability brought disfavor from Bradenbaugh, so be it. Let him deal with his minion. Rowan's conscience would be clear.

Rowan scanned the street. Not seeing a threat, he stepped out and turned left, away from Javier's path. He would take the long way to his new residence, taking time to check for pursuit. It was obvious now that Kanter was right. Bradenbaugh had changed the follow and capture command to a kill order. Something had changed. Whatever it was did not bode well for him or the future of his team.

CHAPTER TWENTY-FIVE

Jeremy was lethargic; his troubled sleep had given little restorative benefits. His dreams were some of the strangest he'd ever remembered having. Not that he recalled many, but this one gave flashes of a girl, a woman, and a beast. Several types of beasts, at that.

Robotically he went about his morning routine, eventually settling at the kitchen table with a mug of steaming coffee. By the time the fugue lifted and he took a sip, it was barely warm. He shook himself. Where had he gone just then? He searched his recent memory but had no recollection. Whatever it was had jarred him. He had to wake up and get something accomplished today.

He stood and gave his body a good shake, then stretched. Placing the mug in the microwave, he caught sight of his reflection in the darkened glass. Something fought to come forth; some distant tidbit that felt important, but the beeping of the completed cycle snapped the thread he'd latched onto.

With the rewarmed mug in hand, he went out back to the patio for fresh air. The briskness surprised him. A shiver raced through him, but he let it run its course and sat at the patio table. He sipped the coffee and started a mental list of things to accomplish. It was important and helped him get through each day with a feeling of worth. It was something he'd struggled with since his wife's death.

He no longer handled chilly weather well without a jacket. He finished his coffee and stood. A sudden flash struck, dropping him back to his seat. The memory of another chilly day came to him out of nowhere. He was running. A man. His father? No, not his father. His grandfather held his hand and ran in front of him. They were surrounded by trees. The branches whipped at his face; scratched his arms and body. He cried out often, wanting to stop, but the look on his grandfather's face prevented him from doing so. The expression was sheer terror and it passed from his grandfather and through his arm to Jeremy as if by osmosis.

"Hurry, boy. Your life depends on speed."

What? Where was this memory coming from? This was not something he'd lived through. Was it a daydream?

His grandfather looked back over Jeremy's head at something behind them giving chase. Something evil.

His chest heaved to the point of bursting, yet still he trudged on. How old was he? Five? Six? What was happening? What had happened to cause this desperate dash through woods? What happened to kindle this long lost memory? Was it a memory? He didn't think so. And what triggered this terrifying scene?

He wanted to look behind him to see what it was chasing them, but his grandfather's constant pull on his arm did not allow for slowing. A branch cut deeply into his cheek just below his temple. He winced. Something leaked down his face. His fingers rose to touch the spot. Wet. Red. Blood. His blood. His panic increased.

"Hurry, boy! They're gaining. We're almost there."

They? They who?

He felt something on his back, a touch or a breath. Whatever it was spurred his little legs to pump harder. A floating oval of light that didn't make sense shimmered in front of them. In a fraction, he was lifted and hurtled toward the light. His body rotated. He caught sight of his grandfather's face. A mix of relief, sorrow, and something else. Regret? No. More like resignation.

He turned away as a pack of shadows descended upon him. The light narrowed and vanished, leaving him confused, terrified, and alone.

The shattering of glass broke the vision. He looked for the source and found the mug in shards on the patio block. His eyes blurred. A sharp, throbbing pain ignited at his temples, causing a groan. He rested his head on his arms now laid across the table and waited for the pain to ebb.

Minutes stretched on, and still the pain remained. What had happened? What was that vision? He searched in vain for the spark that had set the images into motion, but nothing came. It became more difficult to capture the scene and keep it clear in his mind. Frustrated, he forced his breathing to slow and his muscles to relax. After another five minutes, the headache had faded to a dull throb. He stood. His foot kicked something. He glanced down to see the broken mug.

"Now how the heck did I do that?"

He stood and went inside to retrieve the broom and dustpan. He needed to clean it up before Miranda saw it. She'd be angry and accuse him of daydreaming again. He cleaned the mess, deposited it in a plastic bag, tied it up, and placed it inside the kitchen garbage container. He looked around, trying to decide if he was about to do something, but couldn't remember. Instead he went to his room, crawled back into bed, and pulled the covers up high as if to protect against something more than just the chilled air.

***

Angwella squeezed her massive bulk through the tight passage that led to the so-called new world and sniffed at the air. There was something foul about the scent of pine and crisp air. Deep-socketed evil eyes darted from place to place, taking in every bit of the landscape. She was in a wide open field surrounded on three sides by a large forest. To the left was a long narrow path covered with a hard surface. Beyond that, more trees. There were no mountains. She had no high perch from which to watch and scan.

Taking two long running strides, she leaped and unfolded her short but powerful wings. The strong downward thrusts lifted her slightly forward-leaning torso into the air. She coasted above the trees, keeping to their tops for cover from below.

Her sister was here somewhere. And if she was dead, as was rumored, Angwella would unleash her fury on this world until all was destroyed.

***

An hour later, a head poked out from the passage. From a distance, it must have looked as though a headless body floated several feet off the ground. Seeing no one near, the tall, slender, dark-haired woman stepped out, touching down for the first time in another world.

She stepped to the side to keep watch as two shorter men with rat-like features followed. The three beings loped for the safety of the trees. She set the two minions to work finding a scent that might lead them to her mission. While they were occupied, she took on a form of her own. Montack was a shape-shifting wizard. Not as powerful as some of the other wizards, Montack had been trained for stealth. Where other shifters had more impressive forms, hers were meant for surveillance and eavesdropping. She could become a toad for land and water pursuits or a dragonfly for aerial tailing. It was the dragonfly shape she assumed now.

Her body convulsed as it shrunk to size. Bones creaked. Muscles folded in on themselves. Head squeezed to the size of a large grape. She hovered above the two rat-men, then followed as they attempted to pick up a scent. Twenty minutes later, one of their heads popped up, its long snout sniffing the air. It chittered something to its partner and the two creatures scampered toward the road.

Once there, they sniffed the ground and the air, then licked the ground. Though they started off, Montack wasn't confident they knew where they were going. Still, something was better than nothing, so she flew above them.

To her surprise, only a few minutes later, they both stood upright and turned to her. They nodded in unison and started following the road. More than an hour later, they entered the grounds of a house that sat up on a hill. Montack gave instructions for the two to hide while she flew up and checked it out.

She buzzed along the large window at the back wall of the house, then flew around the house and peered into every window that wasn't covered by a curtain. It appeared to be deserted.

Now it was a waiting game. The house wasn't big enough to hide the entire group. Either only some of them lived here, or they knew where the group was hiding. Her partners had picked up their scent. There was a connection somehow. She flew back to her partners, filled them in, and they all hid in the valley below the house to rest.

This world looked nice, but she dared not think about staying here or wandering off. Bradenbaugh and the Dark Lord were not the forgiving kind. She would capture whoever lived there and torture them for details about the rebel hiding place.

Montack envisioned returning to Bradenbaugh with the location and reaping his praise.

CHAPTER TWENTY-SIX

Jerricka was nervous. She couldn't push away the feeling something bad was about to happen. No. She had to stop thinking like that before her thoughts made it come true.

They had lots to do. Too many of their group members were away from the village on errands for her. If any of them got captured, the entire village was in danger. She'd like to start moving some of the students away today, but as yet, they had nowhere to send them. It was best to remain in the village to be protected rather than get caught out in the open.

This was not what she thought she'd be doing when she first signed on more than ten years ago as an instructor in defensive arts and potions. Of course, she never envisioned becoming the headmistress of the school, either.

It felt like another age when Rowan had first discovered her roaming the streets of London, using her untrained natural ability to pickpocket. She was but eight at the time. One of her victims was a young but wise man with intelligent deep purplish eyes and a disarming smile. He'd tracked her to her favorite hiding place and caught her as she was rifling through his billfold. Startled, Jerricka tried to run, but an unseen force held her firm. She squirmed, and when that didn't work, she shrieked like a banshee and accused Rowan of molesting her. However, before she could get more than a few syllables out, her mouth was clamped shut by an invisible hand.

He smiled. "You are a feisty one, aren't you? Well, little miss feisty, I'll take back my billfold, thank you very much." He did so and secreted it inside his overcoat. "Now then, urchin, if I remove the gag, you must not scream or I will be forced to replace it. You have nothing to fear from me. I probably have more to fear from you. Can we agree?"

With wide eyes, she gave a curt nod. He gave her a crooked smile, the one she now knew he put on when he doubted a person's sincerity. No sooner had the gag come off than Jerricka was screaming. The unseen gag was slapped back in place. It took several more attempts, and each time the gag was replaced, it took on either a foul smell or a horrid taste. By the fifth time, she was retching.

"Okay. Okay. No more. I quit."

"Good. Perhaps you'd be so kind as to tell me your name."

She shook her head.

"Well, that's rather rude. My name's Rowan. See how easy that is? What's yours?"

Again, she gave a hard shake of her head.

"I tried to be nice. Guess I'll have to turn you over to the authorities."

With eyes wide, she blurted, "Jerricka."

"Nice to meet you Jerricka. Are you hungry? Would you like to get some lunch? I think we have a lot to talk about."

With suspicion, she eyed him and backed away. "What is it you want?"

"Nothing bad. I promise. We'll be in public where people can see us. You'll be safe. You have my word."

"Yeah, like that means anything."

"It does to me. It's mine. It's important to me. If I give my word, I mean it. Shall we?"

"If I try to run, you're just gonna catch me again, aren't you?"

"Yes, I think I might. You're a curious little girl and I'd like to know more about you."

"What is this, an interview?" she scoffed. "More like an interrogation."

"In a way, both. I'd like to learn more about your, ah, shall we say, interesting skill."

She froze in place. "I-I don't know what you're talking about, mister."

He gave her that smile again and she felt relaxed. "Sure you do. You know. The one that does this." He levitated her off the ground a few inches before setting her gently down."

Her jaw dropped.

"Careful now, Jerricka. We're in an alley. Unless you like to eat flies."

He fed her and questioned her, gave her some money in exchange for a promise not to steal again. She gave the promise readily enough, though he never believed she'd abstain. Before they parted, she became pensive.

"Can you show me how to do...you know, what you do?"

"Jerricka, that's what this is all about. I wanted to see if you were qualified for a special training program."

She grew excited. "And am I?"

"We shall see. I'll be watching you. Remember, no more stealing. No doing anything illegal. If you get caught and draw attention to yourself, you will no longer be considered for the program. It requires absolute secrecy. Consider this your entrance exam."

Over the next few weeks, Jerricka was on her best behavior. She lived on the streets and had no one to support or look after her. On the verge of starving several times, she almost broke down and stole a bit of food, but Rowan's words and the promise of learning something more prevented her from breaking her word.

One cold morning, she was ready to give up. Her stomach growled in a continuous rumble, announcing her approach to all she passed. She stood a few feet from a produce stand and stared at the large, delicious apples. Her mouth watered. Just one would make a meal. Just one. She gathered her will and extended her fingers. The apple rose, but her resolve stiffened. She set it down and walked away.

As she shivered in her small cubbyhole, footsteps approached. Rowan pulled back the tattered rag covering the opening and smiled down.

"Congratulations. You've been accepted."

She was taken to the Arts Academy. She studied, grew, learned things beyond her wildest imaginations, and rose to the top of the rolls. Upon graduation, she was offered full-time employment as a teacher.

Now she was in charge of the education, training, and safety of more than sixty students during the darkest period in the Academy's long history. She thought of her old mentor.

"Oh Rowan, I wish you were here now."

A knock sounded at her door. "Come."

Jno hurried in. "Mistress, we have a problem."

She frowned. Great. Another crisis. "Yes?"

"I've been keeping someone near the portal watching for crossings."

"And they spotted someone?"

"Two different crossings. The first was a Harpy; this one, much larger than the first. The second was a wizard and two followers. I think they were tracking someone. They spent a long time sniffing the area before setting off down the road."

"So, they picked up a scent and are heading here?" She held the rising panic in check.

"That's what's strange. The scent they picked up led them in the opposite direction down the road."

Jerricka let that play around her mind for a moment. "That's a good thing, isn't it? I understand how the Harpy is a problem, but as long as our shields hold and no one leaves the village, we should be safe. But if the other team is searching in the wrong direction, it gives us time to prepare."

"I agree to a point. The question is, whose scent did they pick up?"

Jerricka had to think. "We have teams out searching for a new place to set up."

"Yes, but they are all north and east of us. They went south."

"South. Who could be—wait. Oh no. You don't mean that outsider, do you?"

Jno nodded. "He was here. He spent time with Daria. He carries Allyra's touch in his mind. What if they're sensing him?"

Jerricka's brain worked fast. "But I had you send someone to follow him."

"He returned late yesterday, unable to follow the fast-moving vehicle. Concerned with who might be watching, he took a circuitous route back here moving west then north before turning east. The pursuers went nowhere near his route."

"So it has to be the stranger. Okay. It shouldn't matter. He has no memory of ever being here. There's no way he could lead anyone here."

"Still, I'd feel better if I sent a team to watch him."

"No. Absolutely not. That just gives them more scents to acquire and places us all in jeopardy."

"Not necessarily. One of those who crossed is a wizard. A shape-shifter. We can have spells cast upon us to cover our scent. I'm told it is a simple spell."

Jerricka turned away and paced. So much depended on their secrecy that taking this gamble could put them all in danger. Yet, it was better to know where the enemy was, if only to have an advantage. She whirled around.

"Jno, only your best people can go, and you can't be one of them. No more than two, and they are forbidden to engage. You understand our safety relies on them not being seen. Can you track them without the use of magic?"

"It's harder, especially since they will not be leaving much of a footprint, but they were rat-men, so if we tune only to them, we should be able to find them."

"Very well. Consistent reports, and they must be able to come back as soon as the word is given."

"Yes, Mistress."

"Jno, things are moving too fast. We must have options and now."

"Understood." He left the cabin, leaving Jerricka's already frazzled nerves about to snap.

CHAPTER TWENTY-SEVEN

Jeremy fell into a troubled sleep. Sharp images popped up in staccato fashion, flashing before him and blinking out. A floating light, a flying shadow, a floating girl. Then a beautiful woman dressed in white, followed by Miranda wagging a shameful finger. Next, he was in the forest surrounded by strange beings. A village popped up. The lady in white and the floating girl were there. They vanished, replaced by two large charging beasts with sharp tusks.

He woke; sweaty, confused, and worn out, as if the sleep was more tiring than replenishing. He swung his legs out of bed and sat for a time rubbing his face. It was then he realized the sun was up and not just rising. He glanced at the clock. It was after one. Why had he slept so long? Hadn't he got up once? He couldn't remember. What was going on with him? Maybe he'd developed Alzheimer's overnight. That wasn't funny. Besides, you didn't just catch it. There were signs, though he couldn't recall those at the moment either, reinforcing his belief he was losing his mind.

He walked into the kitchen. He should be hungry, shouldn't he? He couldn't think. He needed coffee. He opened the cupboard and looked for his favorite mug. It wasn't there. It wasn't in the sink either, and he never used the dishwasher; not for the few dishes he had at each meal. A thought struck him that maybe he hadn't finished yesterday's coffee and had placed the mug in the refrigerator, but it wasn't there. Another unsolved mystery. He reached for a different mug, his second favorite. The one Connor had given him that read *World's Best Grandpa.* He set it on the counter next to the coffee pot and reached for the coffee and filters only to discover there was coffee in the pot. He touched it. Cold. Was that from yesterday? This had better be a bad dream because the alternative meant he was losing his mind.

He replaced the mug, deciding he no longer wanted coffee. He emptied the pot, washed it, and returned to his room to dress, even though he felt like he'd already missed half the day. As he pulled off his sleepwear, he felt a strange desire to get back into bed. The pull was strong; an urge that could not be denied. He sat and was about to swing his legs up when the house phone on the nightstand rang. He reached for it.

"Hello?"

"Dad?" It was Chandra. "You okay? You sound groggy."

"Yeah. I'm fine. I didn't sleep well, I guess. What's up?"

"Nothing. Just being a good daughter and checking up on you. I tried your cell phone, but you never answered."

A dark thought ran through his mind. *More like the warden checking on his prisoner.* He shook his head. Where did that come from?

"Well, thank you for that. It's good to know someone's watching out for me."

She had been trying to sound upbeat, but that faded. "Seriously, Dad. I'm worried about you. Are you really all right?"

He placed his fingers to his temple and massaged. "Of course, dear. I'm doing fine. Really. I appreciate the concern, but you have plenty to worry about with your own family. You don't need to add me to the mix."

"That's going to happen regardless. Got anything exciting planned for the day?"

Now she's trying to wheedle information out of you so she can control what you do. What was going on? Again he shook his head to clear the alien thoughts.

"No. Nothing's on the agenda. I plan on staying home today. Perhaps dive into a new book."

"That's good. You always liked to read. Oh. I've got another call coming in. Can I call you back?"

"Chandra, you don't have to. Call me later tonight if you want to. Go do your thing with your family."

"Okay. Love you, Dad."

"Love you too."

He hung up the phone, got up, and finished dressing. After splashing cold water on his face, Jeremy went back to the kitchen to make a sandwich. He pulled out some packaged ham, bread, cheese, and mustard and readied to create when the phone rang again. The sound annoyed him. It was Chandra calling back anyway.

He picked it up. "Chandra, I thought you—"

"Dad?" The voice was faint, concerned, and male.

"Nick? Oh, dear God. Is it really you?" The excitement swelled inside him, instantly lifting his spirits. He hadn't spoken to his son since after Miranda's funeral. Nick had been shaken by the loss. Never a strong boy in body or mind, he was easily prone to long bouts of depression, and Miranda was concerned he'd gotten hooked on drugs.

"Dad, are you all right?"

"All right? Of course, I'm all right. Why do you ask?"

The answer came to him in a flash. Chandra must have called Nick to fill him in on all their father's recent escapades. That's all he needed. Two meddling kids.

"I've been having these strange dreams lately about you and-and bad things chasing you. Dad, they seem so real. I've never had dreams like this before. It's as if something has woken up inside me. You promise you're okay?"

The excitement drained from Jeremy, leaving his body weak. Miranda had been right. He was on drugs. Nick sounded crazed and on the verge of a breakdown. "Where are you, Nick? Are you someplace safe?"

"Safe? Why do I need to be safe?" Then his pitch escalated. "Are they coming after me too?"

"No. No, Nick. No one's coming after me or you. It was all just a dream, remember? I'm just concerned for you. You want me to come and get you?"

"I'm...no. I'm...Something's wrong. I can't make sense of any of it. So many images. So many bad people. Dad. I'm scared."

Something buzzed at the window. He glanced up and caught sight of a dragonfly hovering along the glass.

"Tell me where you are and I'll come get you." No answer. "Nick?"

The buzzing continued. The dragonfly bounced into the glass several times as if trying to get inside.

"Nick, answer me."

His voice was louder, more forceful then he could ever remember. But this was his son and now he was getting scared for him.

"Dad, be careful. Something's out there and it's coming for you. The lady in white can help." The line went dead.

"Nick!" he shouted. The dragonfly buzzed louder as if it had somehow worked its way through the glass. As Jeremy pushed the buttons to dial Nick's number, he looked up, did a double-take, and froze. He moved closer to the pane of glass and studied the strange insect. It took a moment for his eyes to adjust to the closeness, but when they did, he jumped back with a cry of shock.

Did the dragonfly have a human face?

CHAPTER TWENTY-EIGHT

Montack flew around the house and back to the rat-men. "He's in there. We have to get inside and capture him. We'll tie him up, then figure out how to get him back to the portal."

The two nodded eagerly, their beady eyes sparkling with excitement. They ran for the rear of the house, their forms growing to their natural size by the time they had reached the corner of the house. Above them was a window. One climbed up the other and stood on his shoulders. He pried at the window as Montack hovered nearby.

The window didn't budge and the top rat-man turned and shrugged to Montack. She buzzed at the man. He ducked.

"Get me inside. Now!" she commanded.

The top man reached into a rear pocket and pulled out a ball bearing-filled sap. With a deft move, he snapped the leather pouch against the bottom corner of the glass hard enough to crack it. He tapped the glass, loosening a shard, and wiggled it free. With room to insert his long finger, the second fragment came out fast.

Without waiting for the gap to widen, Montack flew to the opening, settled to draw back her wings, and stepped through. Once inside she took on her human form. Motioning for her partners to move to the patio door, she crept to the door of the bedroom she now occupied. She pressed her ear against it and listened.

Beyond, she heard her quarry talking. Was he with someone else? She listened more intently but no one answered. He was talking to himself in a voice too low to make out, but from the tone, it sounded like the rantings of a crazy person.

She cracked the door to get a view. The strange man walked toward a side door with something in his hand. Now was her chance. She tiptoed fast from the room and into the open space of the main room. Keeping an eye on the door he passed through, Montack veered to the patio door. She unlocked it and slid the door slowly along its track. It glided without a sound. The two men entered and she pulled them in close.

"He went into that room." She pointed. "Stand on either side of the door. I'll open it and draw him in. Then you pounce."

Their eager faces lit with the excitement of the moment. They hurried to the doorway, but before Montack could open the door, a strange rumbling sound came from the opposite side. A look of confusion crossed her face as she pressed an ear to the white wooden door. With a start, she realized the cause and whipped the door open hard and it smashed into the rat-man behind it. She stuck her head out as the garage door lowered, cutting off the sight of the retreating car.

"Hurry! We must follow him. He cannot get away." She whirled and ran for the front door. One rat-man followed and the other staggered. She reached the door but could not open it. She fumbled through the series of three locks before finally getting the door open. The car was already making its way down the street.

Montack took two running steps, leaped, and assumed the dragonfly form. The rat-men scampered behind. She pushed to the limits of her speed but quickly fell behind. She hovered, watching as the car turned a corner and was gone. She'd missed her chance.

"Let's go hide inside the house this time. We'll be ready when he returns."

***

Jeremy was agitated but didn't know why. Something was bothering him that he couldn't quite get a handle on. It was unlike him to be so angry at nothing. He was usually the calm, laid-back parent. Miranda was the one who went on rants. Was this the result of delayed mourning? Couldn't be. He'd mourned intensely and deeply enough to be well past any overdue reactions. No, something else was at the core.

Was it triggered by the strange dreams, or had his sudden fit of ire been caused by the notion he was losing his memory? That might make sense. Who wouldn't be afraid of losing a lifetime of memories? He tested himself, recalling details about Miranda and special dates of family importance. Birthdays, holidays, and vacations.

He moved on to the kids, Nick and Chandra. He could see their faces as clear as if they were there with him. A sudden jolt struck then. What had Nick said? *Something's out there and it's coming for you?* That was certainly a thought-provoking statement, but how much credence did he give to a son who had clearly slipped over a drug-induced edge. No, it wasn't the statement. It was knowing his son needed help, and Jeremy had no way of finding him.

That was surely the reason for his angst. Every parent's concern—the safety of their children. His son needed help and there was only one person who might be able to give it. Jeremy pulled into a fast-food parking lot, stopped, and searched for his cell phone.

"Ahh!" he screamed, realizing he had left the house in such a state of disconnect that he forgot the cell phone.

A car passed, the woman driver giving him a worried look. He tried to smile at her to let her know he wasn't crazy, but he was beginning to have doubts himself. He sat for a few minutes until he'd calmed down enough to drive without flying into another frenzy. He'd go for a drive to think and sort things out, then head home and call Chandra. Maybe she knew how to reach Nick.

The drive took him through the valley and along the tree-lined road that led through the forest. He had no destination in mind, but fifteen minutes later, he found himself slowing and staring out the passenger side window at an open field surrounded by trees. He'd been past this spot hundreds of times before. What held so much interest for him now?

A car horn blared behind him. He started, unaware the vehicle had closed. He pressed the gas pedal down harder than intended and the car lurched forward. He pulled off the road at a small clearing to allow the car to pass him, but before he moved on, the image of a young girl running through the field and disappearing into the trees came to him.

He had the feeling he knew that girl, but not being able to place where he knew her from set him off again. Too riled up to sit and not trusting himself to drive, Jeremy got out of the car and walked. His path took him back the way he'd just come. Head down, thoughts whirling, he was like a storm ready to erupt.

He lost track of time and how far he'd walked. Eventually he calmed and slowed, and rational thought returned. For the moment, the turmoil had passed. He turned his head to the sky.

"Miranda, help me make sense of this."

He continued watching as if expecting a sign. Then it came. Not in the shape of a dove or a warm breeze that carried his wife's scent, but as a dark shadow.

Jeremy followed the path, catching sight of something just before it disappeared over the trees. It looked like a strange bird, and the largest he'd ever seen. Was it real or one of those whirly things? A drone? He'd never seen a dragon, but if one did exist, he imagined it'd be a little larger than whatever that thing was.

Bursting from the trees came two large, tusked forms as big as bulls. They exited one side and followed the path of the flying creature. A sharp pain sliced into his temple. He crumbled to the ground where the stones and other debris dug into his legs. Jeremy clutched at his head, massaging vigorously with his fingers. He moaned, then stiffened as a memory surfaced with a force that drove the air from his lungs.

A girl. The same girl he'd seen in a dream before was running across a field directly toward him. The beasts were in pursuit. The same brutes he'd just seen...or had that been a dream too? The fear on her face was beyond anything he could imagine.

No, that wasn't right. He'd felt fear like that, only it wasn't for his life, but Miranda's. He identified with it. Understood it. Lived it. That's why he had to help this girl. He couldn't save Miranda, but he still had a chance to save the girl.

He reached for her. A car horn blasted the memory to pieces. He yanked his hand back as the car whizzed past. Jeremy glanced around. Where was he? What had just happened? Was he hallucinating?

He stood with a grimace. The stones had cut through his pants and into his skin. He brushed them away and turned to face the woods. He felt the answers to his questions were somewhere out there.

He glanced down the road for the car. It was not in sight. He'd walked farther than he thought. Jeremy looked from the road to the woods, then up at the sky. It was still midday. He had enough sunlight to explore for a while. Feeling a pull he did not understand, he stepped over the guard rail, down the slope, and into the field. He angled left and soon was at the tree line. He stopped and turned an ear to the forest sounds. Nothing was out of the ordinary. No heavy pounding hooves, no rumbling roars, no fire-breathing monsters.

At least not yet, a small voice inside said.

That gave him pause. He was going insane. He was hearing voices now. Suddenly, he lost interest in going farther. This was more foolishness that confirmed he was heading toward dementia. He strode away. What would Chandra say if she knew what he was doing? She'd lock him away in some nursing home and visit him once a month when she could get away. He was a foolish old man who desperately needed something to do with his life.

And a nap. A nap sounded great.

He stopped, stood still, and closed his eyes. His body swayed with the breeze as another vision entered his mind. The woman in white. Where had he heard that? Nick. Nick had said, 'The lady in white can help.' Lady in white. Biatta.

His eyes opened. Where did that name come from? Why did it sound so familiar? Daria. That name caused him to take an awkward step backward, almost falling. He caught his balance and whirled toward the woods. The girl who was running from the beasts was named Daria. He knew that beyond a doubt. For the first time, he believed she was something more than a dream. He had met her. Had helped her. Brought her home to Biatta. And that home was somewhere in those woods.

With a sense of purpose, Jeremy Kline walked toward the woods, determined to know the truth. The question was whether finding the truth vindicated his sanity or proved the lack of it.

CHAPTER TWENTY-NINE

Connor sat at the kitchen table next to his sister. The two of them colored while their mother made them a late lunch. Without looking up from his creation, he said, "Mommy, Pe-Pop's in trouble." His voice was casual, as if asking for a cookie.

Chandra's mind was occupied and only heard the word trouble. "Hmm? What are you having trouble with?"

"No, Mommy. Not me. Pe-Pop."

Chandra gazed curiously at her son. "Pe-Pop's fine. He's just a little...tired."

He went on coloring for a few more seconds.

"Bad people are coming for Pe-Pop."

Chandra dropped the knife she was using to spread peanut butter on a slice of wheat bread. She turned to face him.

Harper said, "Yep. Bad people." She too kept her head down on her picture as she spoke.

"Whatever gave you that idea?"

"Saw them," Connor said.

"Saw them? Where?" A tight knot began to form in her stomach.

He looked up, his face calm yet distant. He pointed to his head. "In here."

Harper nodded. "Yep."

"You dreamed Pe-Pop was in trouble?"

He thought about that for a second, then shrugged. "I guess."

Chandra relaxed. "Honey, it was just a dream. Pe-Pop is fine."

His gaze never wandered from hers as he shook his head. This time when he spoke, his voice was a whisper and did not sound like his own.

"Pe-Pop's in trouble, Mommy. We have to help."

Her blood iced.

Harper said, "Big trouble."

Heart racing, she reached for her phone. She'd heard about these types of things among family members. Premonitions of things to come or things that had happened. The call went through, but she got no answer. With each ring, the tightness in her stomach grew until she felt like she'd just done a hundred sit-ups.

"Answer the phone, Dad," she willed. It went to voicemail. Working to keep her voice calm, she said, "Hi Dad, just calling to see how you're doing. Call back when you get this. Bye."

She tried the house phone, then called the cell twice more without leaving messages. Her children had their heads down as they worked away at their drawings. She cleared her throat to make sure it didn't crack when she spoke.

"Connor, honey, when did you see this picture in your head?"

"Before."

"Before? You mean earlier this morning?"

"Yes."

"And you saw something bad chasing Pe-Pop?"

He nodded.

"Something bad," Harper said.

"Harper, did you see it too?"

"Yep."

"How is that possible?" she asked, more to herself.

Her daughter shrugged and pointed to her brother. "Got it from him."

"He told you about the bad people?" That explained Harper's knowledge of the dream. She was reacting to what Connor had told her.

"No, Mommy. I saw the picture in Connor's head."

That stymied her.

"And what did these bad people look like?"

Connor and Harper put down their crayons, glanced at each other, then lifted their drawings. Chandra moved closer to get a better look. She gasped and put a hand to her mouth.

Connor's image was clear and detailed. It was the best artwork he'd ever done by far. It depicted a large, winged creature flying over trees. There was also a figure in the trees.

With a start, she realized Harper's picture, though cruder, was of the same scene. She squatted next to her son, stroked his hair, and searched deep in his eyes.

"Connor, who is that?"

"The bad flying lady. She's looking for Pe-Pop." He pointed to the figure in the trees.

Harper nodded. "Yep. Flying bad lady."

Chandra felt the color drain from her face. For a moment she thought she might faint. Holding onto the table for balance, she waited the spell out before attempting to stand. Once she felt she could move without falling, she grabbed the phone. This was crazy. Why was she giving credence to the drawings and the story told by two children? It was something they must have picked up on TV. Nothing she'd let them watch, of course, so obviously Cliff had. She was going to have strong words for that man when he got home.

It dawned on her then that she'd been having strong words for him a lot lately. She pushed that aside. One problem at a time. Once more, the call went to voicemail. She set the phone down harder than she wanted and checked the screen to ensure she hadn't cracked it. She was allowing a story told to her by her children to drive her into a frenzy. This was nuts. But then, everything with her father had been lately.

"Where are you, Dad?" she muttered.

"Trouble," Connor said, back to work on the drawing.

"Big trouble," Harper said.

* * *

Jno rushed into Jerricka's cabin without knocking, something he'd never do unless it was urgent.

"Mistress, Angwella has been spotted to the east. She is circling the area where we killed her sister."

Jerricka pushed up from her desk chair and placed her palms on the desk. "But you removed the body, right?"

"Yes. It was too large to move, so we were forced to make smaller packages. Her remains are in four different graves in four opposite directions."

"Yet she has scented out the kill zone."

"Yes, Mistress. It would appear so."

The question was whether she could locate the remains or if she would be satisfied with the knowledge her sister was dead and come looking straightaway. Regardless, they were out of time. Their combined power should be enough to take her down, but she was twice as powerful as her sister and had magical abilities. She could cause severe damage to the students before she was ended.

"Very well. Keep me updated. Send in the council, please. We must be ready to move, and sooner than expected."

Jno gave a slight bow, which was an ingrained reaction to his time serving the royals of their world, then spun and hastened out. While waiting for the council to arrive, Jerricka paced. She had to have her mind relaxed and ready to give commands by the time they arrived. This was happening too soon. She had to find a way to keep the children safe. That was her task, her mission. Their lives were entrusted to her and she was determined not to fail.

She sat at her desk, picked up a pen, and began making a list. By the time the first of the council stepped through her door, she was ready. Once everyone was seated, she said, "We are out of time."

Already on edge, the entire council sat up straighter and mirrored the concern of their Headmistress.

CHAPTER THIRTY

Jeremy plodded along with no idea where he was headed. The pull to this path grew stronger by the step. He became consumed by the notion his sanity was waiting for him at the end of his trek.

The cold began to settle in as the canopy overhead blocked much of the sun. There was a crunch of dried leaves to his left. He stopped to listen, but whatever it was had gone silent. Probably a squirrel, he thought, and continued his journey.

Somewhere far to his right, a bone-chilling screech erupted. In an instant, the forest was alive with movement and sounds. He didn't want to discover the source of the horrifying sound. Animals and birds cut through the woods heading west across his path and over his head without concern for his presence. He assumed a predator of some kind scared the denizens into a frenzied evacuation. They were more afraid of it than him.

His step faltered as the sudden realization struck that if it was indeed a predator, would it also stalk him? What could be so terrifying to these creatures that they chose to flee rather than hide? Steeling his resolve, he continued on his path still feeling the strange pull.

Seconds later, the screech ripped through the trees again. Creatures who didn't heed the warning the first time bolted now. Frightened deer, squirrels, and rabbits darted in terror. An eerie silence descended over the forest, so deep that Jeremy became attuned to the emptiness. He slowed his pace. Again, the screech came; this one deeper, more like a roar, and closer.

He stopped and crouched behind a large tree. He scanned behind him and either side of the trunk in front of him. He saw and heard nothing. It was like a scene in a horror story. The intensity of the presence hovering over the woods was a sensation he could feel on his skin, penetrating his bones and sinking deep into his core. Afraid to move for fear of drawing attention to himself as the only meal around, he hunkered down and waited.

Though the screeching roar did not come again, the thundering sound of running steps pounded through the trees to the east. Hair rose all over his body. Though no ice formed, the cold deepened, causing a constant shiver. Had the creature found him? Was it moving in for the kill?

Eyes wide and desperate to know what was coming, Jeremy lowered still closer to the damp earth and scanned the area to the east. Something crashed through the trees. He caught sight of dark brown, almost black fur sixty yards away. He saw two forms flash between the brush and the trees. Did bears move that fast?

The creatures barreled through spaces that offered only fractions of exposure and Jeremy couldn't determine what they were, but he envisioned the two monstrous boars he'd seen in his dreams.

They came closer. He tensed, pressing both palms over his mouth to keep the building scream from escaping. Closer. He caught a better glimpse of the first one and recognized the beast as the boar he'd seen. Considering the danger he was now in, knowing he wasn't crazy did little to comfort him.

They drew even with his hiding spot. This was it. He was about to die a hideous and painful death. He would probably be gored with those two-foot-long tusks, then eaten. He prayed his death would be quick. He didn't want to be alive when they began feasting on him. He closed his eyes, not wanting to see the end coming. Despite the cold air rushing through the trees, sweat rolled down his face.

Seconds passed like hours. He fought the urge to look. The screech took him by surprise. He jumped and his scream escaped. His eyes flew open wide with fright and anticipation, but nothing was coming his way. If anything, the pounding of their legs was retreating. They had passed him by. Did that mean he was not the target or just that they had missed him?

He didn't care. He stood on rubber legs and ran in a north-westerly direction, still trying to reach his goal but not on a close path with the boars. He fell once, grasping in desperation for branches to keep him upright. He missed and crashed down, banging his knee on a hidden root. He scrambled to his feet, running on all fours before being able to sustain his balance to run. He pushed harder than he'd ever run before. His heart thumped like the bass drum in a marching band. The pressure built in his head and chest and he thought his body might explode and save the boars from having to gore him.

He fell against a large tree. His breaths were so raspy and loud and he knew the boars would surely hear him. He listened intently for their approach, but his breathing blocked out all other sounds. He bent and placed hands on knees. It took a long time to recover before setting out again.

As he walked, he tried to feel the strange pull that had drawn him this far, but it was gone like the forest denizens. Great. Now what should he do? He slowed his pace as he tried to get his bearings.

Light filtered through the trees in front of him. The sight reinvigorated him. He wanted nothing more than to get out of these woods.

At the tree line, he stopped. Another field spread out ahead of him. A hundred yards beyond the field was another forest. His heart sank. He had no desire to traipse through more woods, not to mention crossing an open field where the predator might be able to see him better. If those boars discovered him in the open, he'd stand no chance. With a full-body shudder, he recalled how fast the creatures had torn through the forest. No, it was time to end this foolishness and head home. Surely by now, Chandra had called looking for him. She would be angry with him again. Facing her wrath frightened him almost as much as the boars had.

He turned to leave when a loud whoosh drew his attention. He turned in time to see something rise from the ground and take flight over the trees. It let out a screech before disappearing from view.

So that's what was making that sound. But what was it? He was too far away to catch any details, but it looked like a large bird of prey with legs like an animal. The hair on its head was wild and mangy and didn't look like fur. He stepped from cover and shielded his eyes to catch another glimpse of the creature, but it was gone. Then he heard the snorting and without looking, knew he was in trouble.

At the far end of the field stood the two boars. One faced away from him and the other appeared to be looking straight at him. It lifted its huge head and sniffed the air. Jeremy ducked back into the trees. Afraid to move, he slowly lifted his head to look. He had to know if they were coming.

They were no longer in sight, and that scared him to a new level.

In the distance, he heard the crashing again and knew they were in the trees. If they were hunting him, he had no hope of survival. He couldn't outrun them and staying in the trees was no longer safe. He glanced across the field. The grass and plants there were tall and would offer some cover. But what good was cover if they caught his scent? He could make his way across and lose himself in the other section of woods.

A snort caught his attention. It sounded too close to delay any action. He ran crouched across the field, wanting to look back but not daring to. He didn't want to slow down to look, and truth be told, he didn't want to know if death was closing in behind him.

He stumbled and fell, rolling over his shoulder. When he sat up again, woozy from the contact with the ground, he was facing back the way he came. He cleared his head and stretched his neck, feeling the strain. He heard the beasts snorting and sniffing somewhere behind him but couldn't see them.

He turned and began to run on all fours. Sticks, roots, and stones bit into his palms but he kept moving. Something wet coated his hands. He didn't want to know what was on them and didn't want to look. He kept going. No sounds followed him. He prayed that was a good thing. Maybe they'd lost his scent.

He stopped to rest and get his bearings. He was halfway across the field now. He could do this. He risked a second look behind him and caught sight of a massive head scanning the field. They knew he was out here; just not where.

The knowledge increased his panic and blocked all rational thought. He couldn't take the cat and mouse chase anymore. He pushed from the ground and sprinted for the trees. His lone idea was to find a tree to climb.

One grunt was followed by a second, and then came a full-blown snortfest. He took a quick peek. They were coming. The fear was too much and he began blubbering like a baby. Tears flew off his cheeks. He gave no thought to stopping despite the protests from his heart, chest, and muscles. The woods loomed ever larger, but he could now hear the heavy thudding of the hooves getting louder.

He drove his legs and arms hard, pushing every ounce of energy from his body. He exploded into the woods unsure how much of a lead he had on the beasts, but knew it was disappearing fast. Frantically he searched for a tree, afraid to slow down. A branch cut his forehead. Blood trickled down his face mixing with the sweat. It rolled into his eyes, stinging and blurring his vision. He dodged right, scanning fast.

Ahead to the left, he spotted a tree with a low branch. He could scale it, but he didn't have time to check for the next foot and handholds. He just knew time was running out and he had to get up fast.

The snorts and hooved steps were closer. He envisioned them being right at his back. At any second he expected the pain of being lanced with a tusk. His brain could barely function beyond the terror. The tree loomed ever closer. He just might make it.

Then he tripped. He rolled several times, stopping with a solid thud at the base of the tree. He sat up shaking, shook his head. Pain spread everywhere. One eye was swelling and closing fast. The other wished it was as the two monsters rushed toward him. The first one lowered its head, intent on impaling him. The speed of the approach would skewer and pass through him, pinning his torso to the tree.

From somewhere deep inside, all thought faded away. He hoped his life would flash before his eyes. He'd have images of Chandra and the kids. Instead, a long-buried memory rose to the surface. The figure of an old man cloaked in dark robes flickered to life like an old-time movie reel. As if led by the image of the man, Jeremy's arms extended in a futile attempt to block the oncoming impalement. From his depths, a word rose, forcing its way past the terror and exploded from his mouth.

"Deflectus!"

Before he passed out, he heard a squeal of pain and a loud crack, then impact as something crashed into him.

CHAPTER THIRTY-ONE

Jerricka was considering several proposals from the council. One such held that they stay and wait out whatever was to come. Surely if they prepared, they could overcome a Harpy, regardless of her anger and power.

Though she didn't like the idea of staying put and letting Angwella come to them, it had the advantage of less movement and preparation to flee would entail. However, the one sticking point was the safety of the students. If they failed, the children died. Even if they won, there was no guarantee that some wouldn't perish in the fight. There could be a stray blast of a spell or a slice with the razor-sharp talons. Any number of accidental attacks could prove fatal to the students, not to mention the loss of members of the staff. It had merit, but to her mind also had too many downsides.

"I just don't like the idea. I don't mind facing Angwella, but not with the students here. They have to be moved regardless."

Nika countered, "Some of the senior class are quite capable to aid in their defense."

That idea sent a soured expression across Jerricka's face.

Nika was angry. Her mate, Doniel, was captured by Bradenbaugh. There was no question of his chance to survive. She wanted to lash out; to get some revenge for the loss. Jerricka understood the welling emotion but doubted Nika was thinking clearly.

"No. I will not put them in a position to make those types of life and death decisions."

"Mistress," Neveah said. "We might not have a choice. They need to be prepared for the worst."

Jerricka sucked in a deep breath to begin a tirade.

Biatta saw it coming and intervened. "Mistress, what of the other proposals? They both have merits that need to be explored."

All eyes swung her way. Tension eased from the table.

"We have a new location to move to. The problem is that it is not yet developed. It will be more rustic than even this place, but it took time to make this village into a home. All homes are merely temporary anyway. The end goal is to survive and eventually return home. What's a little inconvenience if it means avoiding conflict?"

"But that isn't the question, Biatta," Nika said. "It's how long the next location will be safe. And the next. We have to make a stand and end the current threat now."

"Using that logic, how long before the next threat appears?" Biatta countered. "One way or the other, unless we can put a stop to Bradenbaugh's attempt to raise the Dark One, it's all temporary. The primary effort must be for the students' safety. Once we know they are safe, we will be free to engage in conflict."

Allyra said, "The truth is now that they know where we are, nowhere will be completely safe. We have to ensure that no matter what happens, there will be survivors. I favor the plan that sends students to separate locations to be fostered by people of this world."

"But we don't know enough people willing to foster this many students," Nika said.

"So we foster the students we can and relocate the rest. At least we'll know some of them will be safe," Allyra said.

"Enough!" Jerricka said. "We're just rehashing the same arguments. We must decide. It is up to you to vote. I will abstain until the end and make the final decision."

The nine members of the council fidgeted. None wanted to make the wrong decision, but they knew a choice had to be made.

"In favor of staying?"

Three hands went up. Jno, Chase, and Nika.

"Moving to the new location?"

Biatta, Aric, and Gianna voted.

"And to seek fostering?"

Allyra and Neveah raised their hands.

"It's between staying and relocating," said Jerricka.

All eyes focused on her. She eyed each of them, holding their gaze for a moment before moving on. She used the time for a final sweep of the proposals given. As she readied her response, a loud rap on the door interrupted her decision. One of the men rushed in and whispered to Jno. He stood abruptly, knocking over his chair.

"Mistress, I have urgent business to attend. Make your decision fast. Angwella is getting closer to discovering us. She has the boars with her."

"Go. See to our defenses."

Aric and Chase followed.

"No one plan is ideal. My decision is to do all three." She turned to Allyra. "How many students can be fostered right now?"

"Eight for sure. Two more possibly."

"Take the eight, one of the men, and a sister. Pack what you need and go now. Bring me a list of the students and where you'll take them before you go."

"Yes, Mistress." She left.

"Biatta, split the remaining students into two groups. Have them pack everything they can carry. Take food and water. Gianna will go with you. Assign a female and male staff member to each group. Set up routes with the destination being the new location. Make sure all groups know how to get there. Send them out in different directions. You will be short-staffed, but it's all we can do. The rest of us will stay. We will give the groups a chance to get as far away as possible. If we can stop them, we'll join you later. If not, use whatever means necessary to cover your trail. Understood?"

A chorus of, "Yes, Mistress," came, and she stood.

"I don't need to remind you what is at stake here. Be brave for your students. Now go."

Chairs scraped back and all left except for Biatta.

"You are leaving your defenses short of firepower," Biatta said.

"What else can we do?"

"It's been ages since any of us had to use our abilities in a real fight."

"That's true. But this war will be won or lost depending on how quickly we shake off the rust and how determined we are to survive."

"I should stay."

"No, you should go. You will look after the students and make sure they are safe."

"You should be the one leading them to safety."

Jerricka smiled. "I don't want to be insulting, but truthfully, who will be stronger in the fight to come, you or me?"

Biatta blanched at the directness of the statement. It was true. Jerricka's abilities were better suited for combat. Hers were more for healing. Still, the words slapped her.

"Do not do that to me, Jerricka. I do not want you to sacrifice yourself because you think I am too inept in a fight. That is not fair, and not a burden I want to carry with me."

"Dear Biatta, it's what being in charge is about. Making hard decisions. I appreciate the concern, but this is the best course of action and what I have chosen. Don't think me so ready to sacrifice myself, as you put it. I plan to be around to see the students back home again. I am not throwing my life away. I am doing what I deem to be right for the defense of our wards. I am counting on you to do the same. You have much to do. Go see to it."

Biatta held her friend's eyes for a moment. They steeled before her. "As you wish." She turned and exited the cabin.

"And be safe, old friend," Jerricka said to the closed door.

She looked around the empty cabin. It had served its purpose well, and it was time to move on. With luck, the next location would remain a secret much longer. No, strike that, she thought. She didn't want to get used to settling down away from their home any longer than necessary. If this was to be the first battle of the war to come, she was determined to make it a victory.

She strode with confidence toward her room to prepare for the coming fight.

CHAPTER THIRTY-TWO

Chandra could take no more. She'd called her father twenty times at least and still no answer. She was worried; not just about him, but also about her children. She had no explanation for what had occurred before lunch. What explanation could there be? It was creepy how they both had told the same story, drawn the same picture, and insisted Pe-Pop was in big trouble. As soon as the kids were finished with their lunch, she packed them up, put them in their car seats, and drove toward her childhood home.

The drive went fast. She pushed the speed limit the entire trip. To her surprise, the kids stayed quiet. The usual talking and arguing never came. It was as if they understood the seriousness of the situation. Maybe so, since they had given the warning.

She wanted to believe it was some strange reaction to a TV show Cliff had let them watch, but it just felt off. She convinced herself that her father would be home, maybe sleeping or outside doing yardwork and had left his phone inside. It wouldn't be the first time, and the way things were going, it wouldn't be the last.

That brought up a new worry. Was her father losing it? He had seemed off these past few days. She prayed she'd never have to talk him into moving to a senior complex. He'd hate being away from his home, and eventually, he'd hate her. She didn't want to think about that now. But if she had to keep driving across town to check on him, something would have to change.

Perhaps she could convince him to move in with her. She cringed, thinking of Cliff's reaction to the request and her father's refusal. Her dad didn't much care for her husband. She wished they got along better but doubted that would ever happen. Her dad, for all his idiosyncrasies, had always been a good father. They might not have had the money or done things other families did, but he was always there for her and her brother. He made family time important, something Cliff lacked the understanding and the desire to do.

The street came up and she made the turn, climbing up the winding road to her father's subdivision. It was a nice area with lots of trees and scenery. It had always been a pretty place, though as a child she never appreciated the serene location.

She pulled up the driveway. The house looked like it was empty. A chill swept through her like a premonition of doom.

Despite her anger at not being able to reach her father, she feared what she might find inside. She hesitated, studying the house and sucking on her lower lip. She turned to the kids. Connor was excited and was already unbuckled from his seat.

"You two stay in the car."

"What? Why?" Connor said. "We want to see Pe-Pop."

Chandra whirled on him, her intensity level at its highest point. "You do what I say," and pointed a finger at him.

His lip quivered. Instantly she regretted her tone, but if something had happened to her father, she didn't want the kids to see.

With a softer tone, she added. "I just want to see if Pe-Pop is here. There's no reason to get out if he's not. Okay?"

Connor nodded as a fat tear rolled down his face. Guilt hit hard. She placed a hand on his cheek and gently wiped the tear away.

"I'll be right back."

She got out and locked the doors. She scanned the windows for movement, hoping to see any sign of life. Nothing. She dug the house key from her purse, angry for not having it out already. She unlocked the door and instantly noted the lack of beeping from the alarm. That didn't necessarily mean anything. Her father was always forgetting to set it when leaving the house. Still, it was another sign something was wrong. She pushed open the door but didn't step inside.

"Dad? Dad, are you here?" Did she hear something coming from the hallway leading to the bedrooms? "Dad, it's Chandra. I brought the kids to visit."

She took out her cell phone in case she needed to call 911. She entered and a thought struck. She called his number and heard the phone ringing. She found it on the kitchen counter. He either wasn't here and forgot his phone, or—

She refused to think about the possibilities. With dread, she moved down the hall.

She checked the bathroom first. The door was shut. She rapped lightly.

"Dad?"

No answer. She tried the knob. The door opened. She swallowed hard and stepped inside. It was empty. She realized she'd been holding her breath and let it out in a huff. This was silly. She was letting her imagination off its leash.

Exiting, she stepped across the hall to Nick's old room. It was empty as well. She wondered when the last time anyone had even entered this room. She backed out. Two rooms left. She reached for the door on the left, her old room, but stopped. He wouldn't be in there. Grabbing her parents' room doorknob, she twisted, exhaled, and shoved the door. She pushed harder than intended. It bounced against the door stop and swung back. She stopped it with her foot as her eyes swept the room.

The bed was disheveled. He had at least slept there. What was unusual was that it wasn't made. He always made the bed. Mom insisted she and Nick made their beds before doing anything else, and her father always did too. It was ingrained in them from an early age. Was this yet another sign her father was slipping?

Her steps faltered as she moved toward the master bathroom. The door was closed. She said a silent prayer and rapped. No response. She tried the knob. The door opened. Another hard swallow before the door swung wide. To her relief, her father was not there. The feeling did not last long. Now she had a new worry. Where had the old man gone?

The garage. She should have checked that first to see if the car was there. She exited quickly and halted halfway down the hall. She turned back.

Might as well check my room while I'm here.

Without hesitation, she opened her door and scanned the room. As expected, the room was empty, but the bedspread was rumpled as if someone had been lying on the bed. Strange. Had her father been lying there reminiscing? She'd add it to her list of questions for him when she found him.

She backed out the doorway, but movement near the window drew her attention. The curtain billowed out. It was nothing. Was the window open? Curious now, she walked to the small window at the back of her room. Her foot scraped on something. She glanced down. Glass. Instant panic flashed through her. She ripped the curtain back, exposing the small break in the pane. Since the glass was on the inside, it had been broken from outside.

What could have caused it? An errant baseball? No kids lived on either side of them and behind the house was the valley. Then the darker thoughts came. Had someone broken in? She turned and ran from the room, examining everything she thought might be of value. The large screen TV she'd bought him last Christmas. The laptop computer. The old stereo system her mother and father used to listen to and dance to. No, everything was still right where it had been. Had her father been kidnapped?

She ran to the garage door. It raised, displaying the open space where the car had been parked. He wasn't there. Again she felt relief, but then fear just as quickly. Where was he? It was hard enough worrying about him being alone at home, but how would she find him?

She turned to go back inside the house when she heard a noise behind her. Before she could turn to see what it was, hands wrapped around her and pinned her arms. A rough, smelly bag was placed over her head and she was lifted from the ground.

CHAPTER THIRTY-THREE

Jeremy opened his eyes. He had shut them immediately upon seeing the massive animal standing only a few feet away. He cringed, whimpering and mumbling.

"Oh, no. No. No."

He quickly recited every prayer he knew. Jeremy had known fear before, especially over the past few days, but this was a new level. His brain was so locked up he could barely think. A minute later when no pain had come, he risked barely opening his eye. The boar sat on its haunches eyeing him with malice-filled black eyes.

Why hadn't the beast skewered him? What was it waiting for? Was this some sick game it played with its food? Where was the other one? Maybe that was the cause of the delay. It was waiting for its partner to join in the feast.

Jeremy glanced around, trying not to make any sudden moves that might incite the boar. It snorted as he turned his head. He froze. When nothing else happened, he let his eyes move but kept his head still. In his periphery, he caught sight of the other boar lying on its side. Was it sleeping? Did they need to take a nap before devouring him?

He moved his head to get a better look. The boar in front of him roared and rose to all fours. Jeremy screamed and drew his body in tight. The scream backed the beast off a step. It snorted, roared, and paced, but did not approach. He risked angering the boar further by turning to get a better look at the sleeping one. It looked to be sleeping or at least at peace.

A memory flashed. *She looks so peaceful.* One of their friends had said it to him at Miranda's funeral. The memory made him look closer at the bulky form. He saw no rise and fall of the massive chest. He noticed its head was at a peculiar angle. Surely that wasn't right. Was it dead?

As if in answer, the living boar roared again. It pounded a hoof on the ground like a bull ready to charge, but when it approached, it did so with tentative strides. The head lowered and raised as if probing the safety of approaching. Despite his body shaking fear, Jeremy could not look away.

It came closer, now within three feet. He could feel its breath on his face and smell the rancid odor of it. A steady flow of sound flowed from his mouth. It lifted the tusks toward him. This was it.

He braced for the pain. Instead, the tusks sparked against something. The air appeared to shimmer around him and fade. What just happened? Had it struck a rock and sparked like steel to flint?

The beast moved to the side and continued to probe. The same strange shimmering occurred. It raised its horrid head and roared. Strangely, Jeremy thought it sounded like frustration. It huffed and snorted and patted the ground preparing to charge, then thrust its huge head with two-foot-long tusks straight at his chest. Jeremy screamed again, turned to the side, and closed his eyes. A bright flash penetrated his closed lids. It sounded like an electric current.

The beast howled in pain. Jeremy opened its eyes to see the beast backing away. This was too much to bear. His body began to shut down as fear intensified.

From a distance, a loud screech added to his overloaded mind. He felt his sanity slipping away. Before him, the beast roared as if in answer to the screech. The closeness of the noise startled him alert. The beast eyed him, then walked to its partner. It prodded with its tusks but got no movement from the monster on the ground. It lifted its head and bellowed a mournful wail. With one last malicious look at Jeremy, it ran off.

Unable to comprehend what had just happened, Jeremy slumped to the ground and passed out.

* * *

Daria and Gwynedd were ushered into the large room used for community meals and meetings with students. Biatta was at the front motioning for quiet. She glanced around. It looked like there were fewer students than usual.

She turned to Gwynedd and whispered, "Where is everyone?"

Her friend shrugged.

"I need everyone's attention now," Biatta said, her voice authoritative.

Daria and Gwynedd exchanged glances. When Biatta raised her voice, they knew it was important.

"We are about to evacuate the village."

A murmur rose. Biatta quieted them again.

"It is important that you listen and do exactly as directed without delay. There is a good chance of imminent attack. We can no longer safely stay here. We have devised a plan to move to a new location. It will be quite a hike from here, so we must get started as soon as possible. That means fifteen minutes from dismissal. You will return to your quarters, pack your backpacks, and report to the designated areas. You will be assigned to a group, given important items to carry, and set off. We do not have time for questions. Trust that this is in your best interest and do not delay or cause a problem."

She paused to scan the room. Her voice softened.

"You all know the situation and what's at stake. Our survival depends on how well you function under duress. At no time should any of you use magic unless instructed or under direct threat. The creatures hunting us are attuned to the flow and will be able to use the residual threads to track us. You will have fifteen minutes to report back here, where you will be divided into your groups. Go. Now."

The din rose to eardrum-shattering in a second. Biatta's voice rose above them.

"And do it quietly."

Daria and Gwynedd exited fast and made for their cabin. Four cabins had been constructed to house the students. Two for the boys, two for the girls. Each cabin was assigned a senior leader. As they arrived at the cabin, their senior leader Aby was hustling students along.

"Hurry! Hurry! Load whatever will fit in your backpacks. Anything else will have to be left behind. Only take essentials. Leave anything not vital to your survival. If things settle down,

we may be able to return to retrieve those items at a later
date." She spied Daria and shot her a scowl.

Daria cringed away. What had she done to deserve that
look?

As Daria packed, she wondered if the girl thought her
responsible for their current situation. She looked around the
cabin. No one else paid her any attention, yet she felt she was
the magnet for their resentment. If she hadn't been caught by
the...Her body shuddered from the memory. She couldn't
bring herself to say the word; even think it. And if she hadn't
used magic to escape...But if she wouldn't have, she'd be
dead.

"Are you okay?" Gwynedd said. "You're pale as a spirit."

Daria could only nod as she continued packing. She scooped
a handful of clothes and shoved them into her pack. A small
cross fell on her bunk. She stared at it for a moment, not
recognizing it at first. Then it came back to her. It belonged to
Jeremy. It hung from the mirror in his car. She had been drawn
to it and snatched it. It was yet another in her long line of
momentary lapses in judgment. A brief dart of guilt lanced
her. She shoved the cross into her pocket and finished
packing.

* * *

Once again, Jerricka's door was opened sans knock. Jno hustled in with one of his men close behind. Her first thought was, *Now what?*

"Mistress, I apologize for the brash interruption. Martine just returned from following Bradenbaugh's henchmen."

"Yes, and?'

"They picked up his trail and followed it to his home. Though the man left before he could be captured, they waited for his return. Instead, a woman arrived and they grabbed her. Martine was dispatched to report and get instructions. Larrinan is there watching."

She looked at Martine. "Do you know who has her?"

"Yes, Mistress. It is a female wizard and two rat-men. I do not know their identities."

"But the man was not taken?"

"No. He drove away."

"Was he aware of the pursuit."

"Unknown."

"What are your orders?" Jno asked.

Jerricka thought about it and could spare no more time. "It is no longer our concern. Once we leave here, he will no longer know our whereabouts. It sounds cruel, but we can no longer afford to deal with the situation and further split our forces. Return and bring Larrinan back as fast as possible. Do not intercede."

He shot a nervous glance at Jno, then said, "Yes, Mistress," and left.

"You think my decision too callous?"

Jno frowned. "It is not for me to question your decisions."

"That's right. It's not. My sole concern is the people in this village."

"But we are sacrificing a life for our safety."

Jerricka slammed her hands on the table and glared at him. "This is not the time or place to challenge me, Jno."

Jno bowed. "My apology, Mistress."

He turned and exited.

CHAPTER THIRTY-FOUR

Jeremy got to his feet and walked on shaky legs. He was filthy. His dirty clothes were torn and bloody. His legs were bruised, his hands scraped and bloody. His shoulder thumped and the left side of his face burned. Despite all that, he was determined to get as far away from these woods as he could. He had no idea where he was or what direction he was heading. The forest had grown colder and the filtered sunlight appeared to be dwindling. How long had he been here?

He stumbled on, using trees for support. He wanted to sit and rest, but fear kept his legs churning. To stop now may be to invite the bloody and painful end he was miraculously avoiding. He had lost track of time but kept moving. He stopped and leaned against a tree, unable to take another step. He wondered if anyone would find his body or if it would be eaten by the forest creatures. If they devoured him, at least he'd be dead and wouldn't feel any pain.

Something to his right caught his attention. At first, he thought the boar had returned to finish the job, but then voices drifted through the trees. Voices. His hope renewed. Voices meant people. People meant help. He pushed off the tree and with an adrenaline bump, made his way toward the sounds.

It wasn't just a few voices. It was several and they sounded excited. The other commotion reminded Jeremy of a construction site. He kept moving. Tree by tree he grew closer to the voices.

* * *

Daria shouldered her pack. It was nowhere near as full as some of the other girls', but she didn't have much. She walked down the stairs behind Gwynedd. Her friend was handling the situation in a calm and poised fashion. Nothing seemed to rattle her. Daria envied her friend's demeanor and wished she could be more like her. Daria usually put on a good face but inside she roiled with fear and worry. Still, she had faced down a...that creature and survived.

Gwynedd spoke over her shoulder. "I wonder where the new camp will be. I hope we get put in the same group."

Daria hadn't thought about that. She hoped so too. She didn't have many friends. It would be a long, lonely hike without Gwynedd to talk to. As they walked from their cabin toward the meeting room, Daria caught movement near the tree line. She glanced up and saw the man, figuring he was getting ready to move out of the camp. However, five strides later, she stopped as a recognition flicked on in her mind. She whirled, bumping into a girl behind her.

"Hey!"

But Daria did not respond. Instead, she moved on stiff legs toward the apparition coming from the woods.

"Jeremy?"

The old man looked stunned. He was hurt. Had he been in a fight? She started to run toward him, but thought better, and sprinted toward the meeting room, dropping her pack along the way.

She bolted up the stairs bumping into students and forcing her way past them. They muttered comments about her aggressive behavior but she plowed through. Once inside, she stopped and craned her neck, searching for Biatta. She found her on the far side of the room speaking with staff members and looking over a piece of paper.

She ran, again knocking into her fellow students. The commotion she caused was loud enough to raise Biatta's head. Her brow furrowed as she spotted Daria.

"Child," she commanded. "Slow yourself down."

Before she got any farther, Daria burst into fast speech. "He's here. He's here. He's here."

Biatta grabbed her arms and shook her. "Slow down. What are you saying?"

Daria felt like she was going to vomit. She sucked in a breath and tried to slow her words. "He's. Here."

"Who's here?"

"Jeremy. He found his way back."

Biatta blanched, the color draining from her face. "That's not possible, child. Where did you see him?"

She pointed, though she couldn't see him from where she stood. "Coming out of the forest. It's him. I'm sure."

"Come with me."

Daria had little choice but to obey, since Biatta clamped down on her wrist and dragged her along.

"Clear a path," Biatta commanded.

The students fell away like water. They raced down the stairs and away from the building.

"Where?"

Daria pointed at a heap on the ground. No one had yet noticed him. Biatta whirled and crouched, grabbing both Daria's shoulders and squaring her up.

"Listen to me. Go get Jerricka."

"The Headmistress?"

"Yes, you silly child. Go and tell her."

She released her and gave her a shove. Then she straightened and focused on the crumpled body. As she moved, she motioned with her hands for quiet. Those around her paid heed and turned. Biatta was dumbfounded by Jeremy's sudden appearance. Perhaps he had stumbled back here by mistake. Perhaps a deep memory had not been erased. Was he the reason Angwella was zeroing in on the village? She didn't want to risk speaking to him if he couldn't see the village.

She stopped twenty feet away and watched. She first noted he was still breathing but had been through a conflict of some sort. He did not appear to have the strength to rise. He lay on the ground sucking in short, quick, raspy breaths, each sounding like it might be his last.

Less than a minute later, Jerricka and Jno arrived. Daria trailed behind and stopped a few feet to their sides. His whispered name escaped her lips.

"Jeremy."

Jerricka and Biatta both spun and gave her a harsh glare. Daria slapped her hands over her mouth.

The entire compound had gone still. No one dared move or make a sound that might draw his attention.

Jerricka leaned in close and whispered to Biatta. "How is this possible?"

"I do not know. You'll have to ask Allyra."

"Of all times, why now?" Jerricka said, but Biatta knew it was rhetorical. Jerricka turned to scan the village, then turned back. "We can't afford a delay. We'll have to continue packing. If he does notice, he will have to be dealt with."

"Dealt with? You mean kill him?" Biatta's tone and expression were incredulous.

"Do not give me that tone, Biatta. My sole concern is getting these children to safety. He poses a danger to the mission. If he sees us, he must go."

"Go, yes, but have Allyra do another wipe. By the time he returns, we'll be gone."

Jerricka was furious. Her eyes lit with a fire Biatta had never seen. "Do not challenge me on this, Biatta, or I will be forced to leave you behind as well."

Biatta felt the heat rise in her core. Before she could reply in her own harsh words, movement behind Jerricka stopped her short. She went from anger to worry in a blink.

"Daria, no."

Jerricka whirled and gasped. Jno moved to stop her, but it was already too late.

Daria crept closer and crouched. "Jeremy?"

He did not respond. She crawled closer. "Jeremy. It's me. Daria."

He didn't move, but a raspy dry voice said, "Daria?"

"Yes. Are you all right?"

"Daria."

"Yes. It's me. Are you hurt?"

"Daria. Lady in white."

Daria turned and looked at Biatta. She was dressed in white, as was her norm. Biatta's expression scrunched up in confusion. Daria looked back at Jeremy, then stood and moved away.

"He said my name. Then he said lady in white."

Jerricka looked at her. "We don't have time for this. Deal with it and let's get moving." She walked away.

Jno stayed and eyed her. "What do you want to do?"

"I'm not sure. He needs medical attention, but that's not something we have time for. If we leave him here, he may die."

"If we leave him here, Angwella may find him. He's not protected like we are."

The words made her cringe. "We can't leave him to that horrid fate."

"Do we know for sure that he sees us?"

They looked at Daria. She shook her head. "He never opened his eyes."

Just then, a massive wild boar burst from the trees and ran into the village. Jno placed an arm in front of Biatta and Daria and swept them behind him, drawing a long knife from his belt.

The beast roared and ran straight through the grounds, exiting on the opposite side.

"The beast has a small brain and is easily fooled by the magic barrier," Biatta said.

"Still, it's time to make a decision," Jno said. "You should know that one of Bradenbaugh's tracker teams picked up his scent and went to his house. They missed him, but they now have a woman."

Biatta's mouth dropped open. "Why weren't we told?"

"Not my call."

"How do you know this?"

"We have people watching the portal. They saw the team and followed them. They just reported less than half an hour ago."

"What was decided? Is your team going to rescue them?"

His silence told her all she needed to know. "This is our fault. These people are going to die because of us. We can't stand by and do nothing."

The boar came back, this time moving slower. It ignored them but moved straight toward Jeremy. It sniffed and probed the area between itself and Jeremy. It inched closer in a tentative fashion, poking with its tusks as if expecting something to happen.

Daria gasped. The beast stopped and sniffed the air. It looked around, then turned a complete circle. Even though they stood not twenty feet away, it did not indicate having seen them. It turned its attention back to Jeremy.

Daria wanted to say something, but Biatta covered her mouth and put a finger to her lips. The boar probed Jeremy. He didn't move or show signs of knowing the beast was there. It poked him again, growing more confident with each effort.

Overhead, a horribly loud screech forced everyone to cover their ears and collapse to the ground. The boar gave an answering roar. The Harpy came into view. The village went wild with activity. While staff worked to keep the students quiet and usher them to safety, others raced to take up defensive positions. The Harpy appeared as oblivious to their presence as the boar had.

It screeched again, and the boar replied. Then the Harpy soared away and out of sight. The boar slid its tusks beneath

Jeremy and lifted him. It turned and trotted toward the trees, bouncing Jeremy on its tusks.

Daria tried to break free and race after him, but Biatta held fast.

"We can't let that beast kill him! He saved my life!" She fought with anger, tears welling. "We can't let him die."

Biatta shook her. "Settle child. I have no intention of letting anything happen to him. But we can't start a fight here. We'll track him and take the boar down away from here."

Biatta turned to Jno. "Please inform the Headmistress that we are in pursuit and will join the others when we can."

Jno looked like he was ready to argue, but instead nodded and ran away.

CHAPTER THIRTY-FIVE

Chandra was placed on a kitchen chair. As soon as her feet touched down, she pushed back up. Blindly she kicked out and connected with something solid. She was rewarded with a squeal of pain and the grip around her lessened. She took advantage of the situation twisted, freeing herself. She reached up to remove the bag from her head when something slammed into her from behind, driving her to the floor.

She kicked and flailed but had trouble making contact since she couldn't see where to land her punches. Still, she would not go down without a fight. A second person joined the wrestling match. She might have been able to fight off one attacker, but two was more than she could handle. Soon they had her pinned again.

They taped her hands and legs together before they put her back on the chair. Then one attacker held her down while the second taped her to it. Finished, they released her. Chandra pushed off the floor and bounced the chair several times before a female voice shouted, "Enough!"

Chandra paused. How many attackers were there?

"You either stop squirming or I'm going to hurt you," the woman said.

Forcing the fear from her voice, Chandra said, "You release me right now."

"I don't think so."

Chandra began bouncing again. Slap. The bag deadened some of the blow, but she cried out.

"You chicken. Free me and I'll fight you. You're not woman enough to take me on without my hands bound."

"Oh, I'm more than woman enough. There is just no sense to it when I can get what I want without a fight."

The woman spoke with a slight accent that Chandra couldn't place. Was it Eastern European?

"What do you want?"

"Nothing much. Just some information."

"About what?"

"Where are you hiding the children?"

Chandra's blood iced. Children? Her children? Oh God, no. They didn't know the kids were in the van, but knowing

Connor, it wouldn't be long before he came to find her. Hands tied or not, she would not allow this madwoman to hurt her children.

"Children? What children?"

"Ah, yes. Play innocent with me. It will make extracting the information from you all the more fun."

"I don't know anything about any children."

"So you say. Maybe we'll wait for the man to come back and use you as leverage to make him talk."

That didn't make sense. What did her father have to do with these people?

"Let's start with who you are."

Chandra didn't speak.

"Well, who are you? Why are you here? Do you live here?"

Chandra remained silent. She expected a second slap, but she was still unprepared for it with the bag over her head. This one hurt and rocked her. She almost turned over the chair.

Just then, a car horn blared and Chandra's heart sank.

"Go see who that is," the woman said.

Light footsteps sounded against the kitchen linoleum.

A strange voice said, "Kidss. In the carr."

"Whose kids are those?"

Chandra remained silent.

"Hmm. I'm guessing they're yours. Talk, or I'll have the boys go out and get them."

"No." Chandra couldn't help herself. The word was out of her mouth before she realized. Her legs pushed up and she stood hunched over. The woman shoved her back down.

"Ah. So they are your children! That's perfect. Start talking."

Chandra was in full panic mode now. She had no idea what these people wanted, but she had to keep her children safe. Without her father here to answer questions, she would have to say something.

"Okay. Okay. Don't hurt them. Don't even go near them."

The horn blasted again. It wouldn't take long for Connor to get out of the van and come to the door. Had she locked it? She knew she hadn't. She had barely shut it. Connor would be able to push right inside the house.

She had to do something. To think of something. To get free. She had to stay calm for her children. Her babies. No harm could be allowed to come to them.

Through gritted teeth, she said, "What do you want to know?"

"That's better. It's easier when you're cooperative. Not as much fun for me, but easier."

Chandra lurched back as she heard the voice right next to her ear. "Tell me where the children are being hidden."

Huh? Children. She knew they were in the van. What was she talking about? It dawned on her then that this woman was looking for some other children. But what did that have to do with her dad?

"I'm sorry. I want to help, but I don't know anything about children."

"Go get the brats."

"No!" Chandra pleaded. "No. I don't know what you're talking about. I swear to you. I swear. I would never put my kids in jeopardy to hold out information. I honestly don't know what you're talking about. Please. Be more specific and maybe I can figure out what you want."

"The kids from the school."

"No help. What school?"

The woman's tone suggested her annoyance was growing. "The Academy of the Arts."

"Is that like the school for theater and acting and singing and art?"

"You're trying my patience."

"It can't be helped. There is a school for the arts here, but it's not called the Academy of the Arts."

"I don't want the school. I want the students attending it."

"I can look up the address and you can go there and see if any of the kids you're looking for are there."

The offer was met with silence. "Why would they hide brats from one school at another school? Hmm...perhaps that makes a strange sort of sense. Give me the address."

"I need my phone."

"Don't think so. Not letting you call for help."

"Well, get on your phone and Google it then."

"Google. What is a Google?"

"Seriously? The internet?"

"What is internet?"

Chandra was stunned. The woman had to be putting her on. It was a sick game designed for maximum terror. Well, she was succeeding.

"Get my phone and I'll speak into the phone. You can control it. If you don't like what I'm saying, just hang up."

"Where's the phone?"

"I had it in my hand when your thugs jumped me."

"Herrre it is." Whoever held it tapped it against her chin.

"Alexa, find the address for the School for the Arts."

The robotic voice answered. *"The School for the Arts is located at one...five...seven...four North Main Street. Twenty-two minutes from your current location."*

"There you go. It's only twenty minutes away."

"Come. You will take us."

"What? No. I told you where it is. Just drive there."

"You will drive us."

Just then, the front door opened and Connor walked in.

"Mom. Why are all these people in Pe-Pop's house? Are you playing a game?"

"Yes, Connor. We're playing a game."

"Can I play?"

"It's the sort of game that grownups play."

"You mean like the games you and Daddy play?"

"Ah...no...this is different."

CHAPTER THIRTY-SIX
_____

They sat in the library of the old English countryside manor. It stood miles from the nearest neighbor or village on lands that had been owned by the same family for too many generations to count. Though its exact age was unknown, it had been standing for two centuries. A fire blazed and the three men sipped brandy in front of it.

"Is all going according to plan?" Lord Drewmore asked.

"Yes. Moving quite well," Lord Fontworth replied. "I do believe we'll have an end to at least one group within the week."

"A week, you say?" Lord Barnabus said. "How is that possible? They've barely even started to fight. This Bradenbaugh character can't even find the little mischief-makers."

"He can now," said Fontworth. "The Headmaster of this so-called School for the Arts has a connection to the bank I own. I had my man follow him. He led to what they call a portal leading to another world. Perhaps dimension is a better term. I fed the information to this Bradenbaugh, who coincidentally banks at another of my holdings. From what I understand, he has sent some of his minions through to find the youngsters."

They sat in silence for a moment.

Barnabus said, "How much will we net after destroying them all?"

"Oh. Millions, old man," Fontworth said. "Millions."

"Not to mention we'll be rid of those sorts forever," said Drewmore. "Imagine. They believe themselves magicians, as if they could do more than pull a rabbit from a hat. No, the world will be a better place without their kind."

"And we'll be all the richer for it," added Fontworth.

"Do we have a preference about which side folds first?" asked Barnabus.

Fontworth breathed in the liquor, drawing in the aroma. "Not really. We have contingencies in place for either outcome."

"With that in mind," Drewmore said, "Do we want to send a team through this portal to ensure no one returns?"

The room was silent for several moments as the men pondered the question.

Fontworth spoke, steepling his fingers. "Rather than send them through, why not position snipers on this side to eliminate any who cross back? That way, we won't need an entire team to search for the others. They'll know exactly where they are. We can let everyone cross to the other side, and none will return. That will let us control this portal and thin the herd."

Drewmore nodded.

"Stellar idea," Barnabus said. "Portal to another dimension. Who would have thought? By the way, how did you come to discover this portal?"

"Once we discovered the existence of these so-called wizards, we formed our plan and set it in motion. The first stage was to set Bradenbaugh on the trail of resurrecting this dark lord they worship. Then we fed him information that his biggest opposition was the school. He took it from there."

Fontworth continued. "Yes, but we didn't want a full-scale war on our soil, so we tipped off the school of the upcoming assault. They fled by way of the portal, which was a most incredible thing. We thought about collapsing it once this mission is ended, but in truth, the possibilities of further financial gain seem boundless. We will simply control the portal."

"Outstanding," Barnabus said with awe.

They pondered, sifting and sorting their thoughts.

Fontworth asked, "Is there any chance they can actually wield or perform magic?"

"Are you serious?" Drewmore said. "Magic? As if they're straight from the stories of Arthur and Avalon? Good God, man. This is reality."

Undeterred, Fontworth pressed on. "Then how do you explain an entire school dedicated to learning magic?"

"A good con job. This Rowan Vandalue must be a magician when it comes to convincing people to pay handsome tuitions for an education in the arts, which he says includes learning magic." He chuckled. "I dare say he's a better con man than even you, my dear Barnabus."

"Anyone up for a wager?" Barnabus said.

"Willing to bet your share, old man?" asked Drewmore.

"Barnabus blanched at the thought. "Heavens, no. But something to make it interesting."

He got no takers.

"Imagine this Bradenbaugh character believes he's going to raise some evil dark lord to take over the world," said Drewmore.

"Whatever gave him that notion?" Barnabus queried.

"I did, of course," Drewmore said.

The three men burst into laughter.

* * *

Following in the wake of the boar was easy. It took the most direct path possible without running into a tree. The result was a trampled path wide enough to not be missed. Biatta hadn't moved so fast in years. It reminded her of running the city streets as a child, fleeing those who pursued her. She had released Daria's hand. The girl would have to keep up on her own, a task she easily appeared to be up to.

Ahead they heard a roar. Panic swept through her. Were they too late? She pushed harder. To her surprise, Daria surged past.

"No, child. Wait!"

But the girl kept moving, increasing her lead with long graceful strides.

Now Biatta was torn. She had already started drawing in energy for the offensive spell she was going to use, but with Daria putting herself in danger, again she had to switch to a defensive spell to protect the girl. If faced with a choice between saving Daria or Jeremy, she'd pick her student every time.

Her long slender fingers stretched toward the ground as she drew energy from the natural surroundings. The power flowed. She drew in deeply as if quenching an arid thirst. Ahead the roar ripped through the trees again, this time much closer.

"Get away from him, you hideous beast!" Daria shouted.

"No, child. No!" Biatta pushed harder, almost stumbling on a root.

Through the trees, she saw flames. "My God." She stared in disbelief. Had Daria just cast a fireball? *How did she even know an offensive spell? She shouldn't learn that particular spell until senior year.* The knowledge and use of such a spell was an expellable offense. However, using it now might prove deadly. *Surely, Angwella will sense its use.*

She rounded a large oak and stopped abruptly. The fiery hulk of the boar bore down on Daria at full speed. Though aware of the charge, instead of fleeing, Daria was weaving a spell. It looked like a defensive one by her finger positions. Biatta couldn't take the chance on her failing to cast it in time. She raised her arms and extended her fingers.

"Deflectus."

The air in front of Daria shimmered.

The boar screamed in rage and pain. It lowered its huge head, aimed its thick tusks at Daria's core, and exploded forward for the kill. Two feet before impaling the girl, the beast hit an invisible wall and crashed furiously, its hind legs lifting in the air. Its head snapped back. Flames rose from the seared fur. The ground trembled and Daria moved backward from the force of the impact, but the shield held.

The hind legs dropped. The boar shook its head, took a few steps, and collapsed. Stunned or dead didn't matter.

Biatta recited her next spell and an electric current flowed from her fingers. It singed the husk, then engulfed it in bright light. The body gyrated for seconds and lifted before the spell ran its course and the crisped carcass fell to the ground.

Weakened from the extreme effort, Biatta leaned against a tree, her chest heaving from the strain of the spell and the long run. Daria looked at her with concern that turned sheepish under the woman's withering glare.

"Child, you and I need to have a long talk when this is over."

Daria's lips thinned. She focused her attention on Jeremy, running to his motionless body. The boar had placed his body next to a dead boar. It was one of the pair that had attacked her previously.

Biatta came up next to her and studied the scene, then bent to check on Jeremy's condition. He was breathing. Though still recovering, she placed a hand on his head and his chest, closed her eyes, and called up a basic healing spell that was designed to stabilize rather than cure. It was the best she could do for the moment. Besides, stable was better than dead any day.

"Help me up, child."

Daria took her arm and lifted. Biatta held on for a second until her balance restored, then released the girl and pressed a hand to her belly. They stood silent for a while before Daria said, "Will he be all right?"

"He should be fine. He will need time to recover, but he will."

The scene before her was strange. Jeremy had been placed next to the dead boar as if being offered as a sacrifice. Did the boar, with its limited mental capabilities, believe its mate could be resurrected by such an offering? Or had Jeremy been responsible for the first beast's death and the boar was getting its revenge? Even stranger.

"What are we going to do?" Daria asked.

Biatta shifted her gaze from the scene. She looked at Daria.

"We can't just leave him here. What if more boars or other creatures find him before he can get up?"

That was a good question. Biatta was taken by Daria's compassion and concern over another's well-being. She might make a good healer. She had put herself in danger to save someone. Or was it just this man? What possible connection had they developed during their short time together?

"We may not have a choice. We can't take him with us and we don't have the time to see him to safety."

Then she remembered another crisis concerning this man. Bradenbaugh's minions were holding a woman hostage, waiting for Jeremy's return. She pondered telling Daria, knowing her response.

The girl was watching her and waiting for direction. Her brown eyes were wide and empathetic. Yes, she would be a healer if she survived long enough to learn the skills. Rushing to attack creatures bigger and more powerful than she was a sure way to die young. If Biatta hadn't been there, the girl would be dead meat on the boar's tusk. So young. So inexperienced. So brash.

The question remained. What did they do now? She frowned, knowing she was no different than Daria.

"Child, we have to get him home, and fast."

CHAPTER THIRTY-SEVEN

In the end, Chandra decided it was better to be in a moving van in the open where help might be found rather than locked in a house. She drove with the woman sitting in the passenger seat. Now that she could see, she took mental notes. If they got out of this, she wanted the police to have a good description of these crazies.

The woman was petite with short blue and black hair. Her facial features were small, giving her an almost elflike appearance. If not for the scar down her right cheek and the hard, evil eyes, she might have been considered pretty. Well, at least cute.

Her two partners were strange beings. They too were short and thin with long angular faces that gave them an eerie rodent-like appearance. They didn't speak much, but when they did, they rolled their Rs and hissed their Esses. Their beady eyes darted in quick, constant motion.

The kids were in their car seats in the middle row and for once, were quiet. Chandra thought they were perceptive enough to feel the tension in the van. They watched the three strangers with wide-eyed curiosity. The two rodents sat in the third row and leaned over the seats that held her children.

She set the GPS for the directions to the School of the Arts and headed toward it. As she drove, her eyes scanned the surroundings for a police car or avenue of escape.

According to the navigation, they had less than ten minutes before arriving at their destination, and nothing presented itself yet as a means to be rid of her passengers.

"How much farther?" the woman asked, her tone harsh.

Chandra glanced at the GPS. "It says nine more minutes."

"It does, does it? It had better be right."

"The only thing that might delay the arrival time is getting stuck in traffic."

"Then don't get stuck in traffic, or my friends may start nibbling on young ears."

Chandra's chest constricted. The thought of those two creeps being set loose on her children was beyond horrifying. Before she allowed herself to sink into a pit of endless fear, the protective anger of motherhood took hold and she vowed to ram the van into a brick wall before she would allow those two to touch her kids.

She made the turn onto the street where the school was and was forced to stop at the next light. A police cruiser pulled up next to them. The woman didn't seem to notice. Now was her chance.

How would she get his attention without causing alarm? If she rolled the window down to signal, it would be obvious. She thought about whipping open the door, taking the key with her, and banging on the car. But the thought of leaving the kids in the van with these insane people scared her too much.

She placed her hand by the window and waved back and forth, but the cop wasn't looking. She had to do something. The light would change in seconds and she might not get another chance. She twisted the wheel to the left a fraction. As the light turned green, she stepped on the gas and the van veered toward the cruiser.

The officer stomped on his brake and Chandra turned to the window and mouthed, "Help."

The officer either couldn't read lips or felt it was a simple mistake. He waved, misunderstanding her, and drove away.

Chandra felt the heat rise to her cheeks. She refused to look at the woman.

"You must be tired of having kids. Don't worry. They're about to vanish from your life."

Chandra didn't respond. It would give the woman more power over her. She turned into the driveway of the School of the Arts. The old building had outlived its usefulness and the board of education sold it to a charter school. The long one-story building sat between two shopping centers. The grounds stretched out behind it for a long distance and was filled with sports practice fields.

Chandra parked behind the building but did not shut off the engine. "Here it is."

The woman surveyed the building and the grounds.

"There are few vehicles here and the building appears deserted."

Chandra hadn't mentioned the school was closed for the day. She hoped the strange woman wouldn't notice. She turned her eyes on Chandra. Her irises seemed to change colors in kaleidoscopic fashion.

"If you have deceived me, it is your children who will pay the price."

That threat was too much for Chandra to handle.

"Honestly, I didn't know. I wouldn't risk their safety. Most schools are still open at this time. This one is special and must have different hours of operation."

"Hours of operation? You mean the students do not live onsite?"

That took Chandra by surprise. "No. This isn't a boarding school. The students come each day and go home for the night at dismissal."

The woman's gaze was penetrating, as if searching for the lie. "Then this is not the school I am looking for."

"I'm sorry, but it's the only School for the Arts in the city."

"That cannot be true."

"It is. I swear."

"Then we shall have to return to the house and await your father. He must know where it is. He has their smell about him. He has been in contact with at least one of the students. Residual magic lingers on him."

The smell about him? In contact? Magic? What was this crazy person talking about? Or more importantly, what had her father gotten involved in?

"Drive. We will have another discussion when we arrive. This time, it will not be as pleasant."

Despite her efforts to remain strong, a tear rolled down her cheek as she drove back to her father's house.

* * *

Once Jeremy stirred, Biatta woke him to ascertain his injuries. Other than bruises, scrapes, and cuts, he was in better shape than she'd estimated.

"Do you know who you are?"

"Yes, of course." But his response was slow and unsure.

"What is your name?"

"Jeremy. Jeremy Kline."

"Do you know where you are?"

He looked around. At first, he appeared confused. Then his eyes lit with recognition.

"The forest. I was following something." He scratched his head, as if the action would bring forth the something. "I was—" He met her gaze, then shifted to Daria. "You. You were in my dream. I think I was looking for you." Then he shifted to Biatta. "You're the woman in white. You were in my dream too."

The statement took Biatta aback. "What does that mean?"

"Mean? I dreamed about you. And something...I don't know what drew me to the forest." He cocked his head, trying to draw more information from that thread in his memory. "Then, a bad thing came. It chased me." He spun fast and stared down at the two dead boars. "Those." He pointed. "Those monsters chased me."

"Did you kill one of them?" Biatta asked.

"Me?" He recoiled at the suggestion. "How would I? Look at the size of those things. I don't even have a weapon. No. It wasn't me who—" A memory surfaced, giving him pause. A charging beast. What had happened? "No. Not me."

Biatta noted the hesitation and wondered if he remembered or blocked it away. "We have to get you home. Are you strong enough to travel?"

"Yes. I think so. Is it far?"

"I do not know. I have never been to your home. How did you get here?"

"Here?" He pointed at the ground. "I walked."

Daria said, "You have a car. Did you use it to get to the forest before you started walking?"

Jeremy tried to recall. "Yes, I must have."

"Do you remember where you parked?" Daria asked.

Biatta watched the girl, impressed by her questions.

Jeremy ran the question through his mind. "This way." He started walking. Biatta nodded to Daria and motioned with her chin for her to walk with him. She'd follow a few steps behind to serve as a guard in case anything else came through the woods searching for them.

She still had lots of questions to ask this man. Too many components didn't make sense. How had he found his way back to the village? It should have been invisible to all who passed by. How had the second boar died? It certainly hadn't keeled over on its own. By the acute angle of its head, the neck had been broken. She sensed a strangeness within this man; something she was unable to pick up on or decipher. Was he friend or foe? Who did he serve? She was risking so much to keep this man safe, yet Biatta felt the answers were important. She would see this journey through, but if she had an inkling of concern for Daria's safety, she would not hesitate to end this man.

CHAPTER THIRTY-EIGHT

___

The groups were ready to move out. Each leader knew their destination and the route they'd take to get there. All was as planned. Still, Jerricka did not give the word. Biatta and Daria were out there somewhere, aiding the strange man who had once again found the invisible village. How was that possible? She questioned Allyra, but the woman was just as puzzled as she.

"Unless he has some resistance to magic, he shouldn't have any clue where we were."

"Could it be the inhabitants of this world are less susceptible to magic than those from our world?" Jerricka asked.

"That's possible, I suppose. I don't have enough information about the people here to know for sure."

Jerricka nodded, but her mind was mulling over something Allyra had said. Was the man immune to magical suggestions? If so, was everyone? No. That couldn't be true. Others had hiked past the village without ever hesitating. They had no clue it was there. Two men had walked right through the grounds without pause just yesterday, engrossed in a discussion of some local sporting event. So if it wasn't all people, then what was it about this Jeremy that was different? She had no time to think it through now, but it would be a priority for later. Now, if only Biatta and Daria would return.

"Mistress," Jno said. "We cannot delay further. We risk discovery. Biatta knows where to find us."

Jerricka sighed. "Very well. Give the order."

He nodded and trotted off. In less than a minute, the first group was gone. The second and third groups moved into position. She'd ordered them not to leave at the same time.

A screech erupted from over the trees. The Harpy appeared suddenly, surprising her and sending the students into a panic. Though most remembered their training, some screamed and broke ranks, running into the woods.

"Keep them under control!" Jerricka shouted.

Though the staff ran to corral the students, the damage was done. The Harpy, sensing something amiss, hovered overhead, straining to pierce the magical veil over the village.

Jerricka motioned for groups two and three to move out. The staff got everyone moving. Jno, Chase, and Neka ran to Jerricka's side. She saw her start to prepare a spell in case they needed it. The men readied their weapons. It would take both physical and magical attacks to bring a being as powerful as Angwella down.

Above, the Harpy circled the area, screeching and flapping its powerful wings. The strokes were powerful and disturbed the ground around them, sending up a cloud of dust and leaves. As it lowered, the wind swept in cyclonic fashion, whipping around them and making it increasingly more difficult to see.

"Spread out!" Jno shouted over the din. "We must hit it from all sides."

Jerricka swept an arm wide across her body, indicating group four to move out. Once the Harpy broke through the magical barrier, it was important they kept her occupied to prevent her from targeting the students. She looked around at the concerned faces of those ready to give their lives for the defense. They were brave, but were there enough of them to make a successful stand?

The protective field over the village shimmered, showing signs of weakening. Angwella sent one magical bolt after another into the invisible shield, leaving no doubt she was aware something existed underneath. Long jagged cracks appeared. The Harpy increased her efforts, determined to break through and wreak havoc.

Two other male staff members, Devin and one whose name she could not recall joined the group. Good, she thought. The more the better, although she doubted only two wizards were enough to stop Angwella. She took one last look around the village to make sure all groups were away. With relief, she found they were.

How had it come to this? And so fast. She was missing something and had to believe Rowan was more on top of events then she was, hidden in this alternate world. If she survived, she would have to plot the facts and the timeline. For days she'd had the feeling that an unseen force was working against them; some yet undisclosed player whose motives were unknown. None of Bradenbaugh's people should have had a clue as to their whereabouts, yet here they were in the fight of their lives.

A fight *for* their lives.

The shimmering was constant now. In seconds, Angwella would be through and ready to kill all who stood in her path. Jerricka thought about reinforcing the dome, but it would only delay the inevitable and leave her drained. Well, if it was a fight she wanted, Jerricka was determined to give all she could and more.

She swept her arms down, fingers pointed to the ground to absorb every bit of power she could hold, which was a lot; more than any of her staff knew. She'd been preparing for a moment like this her entire life.

As the power engulfed her body, she was radiant. Her eyes blazed with raw power. Her hair lifted on end. A fiery aura surrounded her. As the last remnants of the shield dispersed, she lifted her face to the sky, called up her most powerful spell, and emitted a screech of her own.

As Angwella descended toward them screaming victory, Jerricka unleashed a deadly bolt of pure death. It struck Angwella full in the massive breast, driving it back skyward. The enormous bolt crackled with an electric current that lasted for a full minute before fading. Though the bolt had struck Angwella full-on, she had a natural resistance to magic and shook off much of the effects. With a furious screech of outrage, she zeroed in on her attacker and dove.

For an instant, fear gripped Jerricka. No. She would not die afraid. She fueled her fury, drew in another massive amount of energy, and targeting the blackened spot on the Harpy's chest, prepared to drive her back again. Angwella released a fiery breath at Jerricka, but her attack knocked the Harpy sideways and the fire struck the near dormitory, setting it ablaze.

To one side, Neka sent thin, piercing shards of pure energy into Angwella's face, attempting to blind and weaken her. The three men readied their physical penetrating weapons hoping to draw her black blood.

Jerricka ceased her assault and waited. She wanted Angwella close for this next attack. Closer she came, razor-sharp talons flexing and reaching for her. Jerricka sucked in a gulp of air and retreated deep within her soul to a place she shouldn't know, let alone resort to. She screamed the activating words and released the spell she thought would be her last. The dark magic flowed out in a black stream. It surrounded Angwella in a cloud of pestilence in the form of thousands of tiny spiderlike creations.

They swarmed over her, seeking places to penetrate or enter her body. They had little initial effect. Her speed carried her straight at the now spent and defenseless

Jerricka. At the last second before impact, she was thrown to the ground. As she rolled free, she caught sight of the man whose name she did not recall. He extended his blade upward. Angwella's momentum impaled her torso, but it continued to the ground, crushing the man beneath her.

Jerricka saw the body compress like a crushed aluminum can. He made no sound as he died. The sight mortified Jerricka, her sanity threatening to flee. Angwella's body slammed into the ground, sending shockwaves that lifted Jerricka.

Jno, Chase, and Devin closed in, hacking violently at the Harpy's extremities. Neka continued a steady barrage of various offensive spells, trying in desperation to find anything that would penetrate the tough skin.

With a vicious swipe of her talons, she cut Devin in half. The sight further enraged Jerricka. She pushed to her feet, determined no one else would die here today. She called upon another long-buried spell that she'd never used, but always retained; one she could be shunned for knowing, let alone using. The close distance she needed to be from the target made the spell impractical for battle like this but did not prevent her actions. As she moved toward Angwella, she could see the pestilence was beginning to eat away at her insides. It would eventually take her down, but how many more might die before that happened? And she had no idea how much her magical resistance would nullify the effects.

If the others could keep her attention, she might get close enough to end this fight. As she approached, she recited the words she'd learned decades before, in another time and another conflict. The energy flowed up her arms. They were engulfed in a glowing white light. Her hands shimmered with electric current and then disappeared.

A claw swept toward her. She ducked as the talon sliced through her hair. Severed strands fell in every direction. Jerricka rolled, coming up under the beast's heaving chest. She spoke the final words and ran the last few steps closer. With a hard straight punch at the chest, her hand phased through feathers, thick skin, and bone. The fingers stretched searching for their target. It touched the organ, causing Angwella to jerk back. The tone of her screech became one of fear, which encouraged Jerricka.

She shoved her arm in farther. Now aware of her mortality, Angwella beat her wings hard and fast. As she started to lift from the ground, she pressed a claw forcefully against Jerricka's back. Jerricka felt the pressure.

She couldn't take much more before her ribs cracked and her body was crushed like a tomato. But even if it cost her death, she would not stop.

Now thirty feet off the ground with her lungs on fire, she screamed for one more breath. She stretched to her farthest extension, her entire arm now inside the body. The pulsing organ was within her grasp. She encircled the heart. It was surprisingly cold. With the flick of her wrist, she snapped her fingers closed and squeezed hard.

With renewed effort, Angwella pressed Jerricka to her muscular chest. Jerricka had seconds before she would pass out and die. She yanked hard, feeling the organ stretch. As her vision began to close in around her, she dug violently into the throbbing muscle with her fingernails, hoping to at least puncture it.

Black circles surrounded her vision and narrowed to tiny circles of light. Blood vessels popped in her eyes. Something cracked in her chest. Her hand was cold and now sticky. With a final effort, she pulled back, her arm inching out of the body. Something snapped. Angwella's head jerked back and plummeted to the ground with a final death screech. Jerricka, her arm still deep within the Harpy's body, was unconscious. She never felt the impact.

CHAPTER THIRTY-NINE

Jeremy grew stronger as they walked. His color returned with some of his memory. He wanted to talk about what he remembered but didn't know how to broach the subject without sounding like he was insane.

He glanced at the cast on his wrist and flexed it. No pain. Was it healed already? It sure felt fine. Wasn't he hurt other places too? If so, why didn't he feel any pain?

They found his car and he was surprised they wanted to go with him.

"Uh, okay. I suppose that's all right."

Though he thought the request strange, in truth, he was glad. He wanted the chance to question them. They got in and he drove.

"Can I ask you something?" He caught the woman in white's eyes in the mirror. She smiled warmly.

"Why don't we wait until we get where we're going?"

Her smile and the warmth in her eyes put him at ease, yet he wanted to know. "Why are you coming with me?"

"We'll discuss that when we get there, as well." She changed the subject. "How are you feeling?"

He had to give that some thought. How was he feeling? Somewhat renewed, though he didn't know why. "I guess I feel okay. I mean, my body aches, but it's not awful."

"I'm glad."

He glanced at her. "You look tired. Are you all right?"

She smiled again. "Yes. I'm fine. I just need a little rest."

"How much farther is it?" Daria asked with youthful impatience.

"Not long. Maybe ten minutes."

"Can we make it sooner?"

"We can if you want me to speed."

"Yes. Please do."

"Daria," Biatta admonished.

"Is it a bathroom thing?" he asked.

"Yeah, sure."

He studied her. She seemed on edge. He kept getting flashes of memory about her.

"You were the one I dropped off in the woods, right?"

"Ah, yeah." She glanced at the mirror where the cross once hung. Her cheeks flushed with guilt.

"We went to the village?"

Daria looked behind her for a clue about how much she could say.

Biatta slid forward. "How is it you remember that?"

"Excuse me?"

"I just wondered how you found us."

"You mean this time or before?"

"This time."

"I'm not sure. I felt this strange pull and..." He shrugged. "I followed it."

"How interesting."

The remainder of the trip was made in silence. As Jeremy made the turn onto his street, he hit the brakes. Oh, this wasn't good.

"Problem?" Biatta asked.

"Ah...well, I hope not. My daughter's here."

"Isn't that a good thing?"

"Yes, but she's a little miffed at me at the moment."

"Oh, I have a feeling she's going to be very happy to see you."

"You think?"

"Of course. She's your daughter. She loves you no matter how miffed she is at you."

"I hope so."

"There's only one way to know for sure."

He pulled up the driveway and pushed the opener. While they waited for the garage door to open, Biatta said, "You go ahead and pull in. I'm going to get out here. Go inside. I'll be there in a minute."

Daria looked over her shoulder. Biatta nodded. "Stay with your friend. Keep him safe."

Daria nodded. Biatta got out and ducked around the side of the garage as the car pulled in. They exited and Jeremy stood at the doorway looking for Biatta. "Where'd she go?"

At a loss for words, Daria said, "It's a female thing."

"Oh, ah...well, let's go inside then. I'll leave the garage door open for her."

They walked toward the interior door. Jeremy pushed it open and Daria gave him a few steps' head start before following. She wanted room to act, should the need arise. He entered, took two steps, and stopped abruptly.

"What? What's the meaning of this?"

Hearing the words, Daria pushed past him. A woman was tied to a chair. Two sobbing children were seated on a couch, being watched by two strange-looking men. Behind the bound woman was a small-framed woman with a wicked smile.

"Ah, this little adventure just paid dividends."

"Not for you," Daria said. She flicked her fingers forward to free the spell she'd readied.

"Sleptidus."

In a blink, the woman disappeared. The woman bound to the chair slumped, head lolling to the side, but her captor was nowhere to be seen. Then she heard the high-speed vibrations and spotted the dragonfly racing down the hall.

The two men leaped the sofa and charged at her, twittering strangely.

From the left through the open patio door, Biatta said, *"Frezon."*

The two men froze in place. One was on his feet, but the other had leaped in the air and now crashed down face first, unable to move his hands to protect himself. Daria watched wide-eyed at the scene. The man only feet away could not move, but his eyes roamed wildly. It was like looking at a living mannequin. The man on the floor groaned.

Daria said, "The woman shifted into a dragonfly and flew down the hall."

"Stay with them."

As she walked past the now wailing children, Biatta swept her arm in a downward motion and the kids slumped forward, both asleep.

Four closed doors presented themselves down the hall. A noise came from one of the two back rooms. She moved between them and listened. Opening doors was something she learned to do as a child, even before she knew and understood who and what she was. If you couldn't do a few of the basics, you starved.

After some bad experiences and some training, she'd also learned a long time ago never to stand in the doorway when trouble might be on the other side. She backed away, readied the simple spell, and lifted both arms. The doors swung inward at the same time with speed. As soon as an opening appeared, slim blade-like darts shot from the room on the left and embedded in the wall to Biatta's right. No sooner had they touched than they disappeared, leaving only marks in the drywall.

Biatta ducked, pointed a hand inside the room, and released a spray of similar objects. A cry of pain told her she had struck at least once, but another lesson learned was never to assume anything. She shot a second wave of the small icy blades, then walked inside. This time, her attack was rewarded with a sharper cry. A small woman stood tugging at her arm, which was pinned to the wall. Blood dripped from the wound and a cut on her cheek.

Her eyes widened with fright as Biatta entered. She whimpered, then with a word, disappeared. The sound of buzzing told Biatta where to find her, but she was too late to react as the dragonfly flew through a small opening in the glass. She ran to the window, but the erratically flying woman was gone before she could stop her.

Not wanting any more surprises, Biatta checked the other rooms before returning to the living room. Jeremy had released his daughter from the chair and Daria helped him place her on the sofa next to the slumbering children. Jeremy knelt beside her, stroking her hair. Tears ran down his face as he apologized.

Biatta looked at Daria as she watched the man with his family. She was caught up in the moment, tears tracking down her face. Perhaps she was happy for the safe return of his family, but Biatta didn't think so. Too many of their students were outcasts, shunned by family and friends because they were different. Biatta understood. She had been one of them. Daria looked up and Biatta saw the truth in her eyes. She wanted to feel like family too.

Biatta moved to her and placed an arm around her shoulder. She pulled her in, but not too close or tight. Daria would reject what she thought was a pity hug. To ward off a rejection of her comforting gesture, Biatta said, "You did well, child."

Daria looked up through tear-filled eyes and gave a weak smile. "This was all my fault."

The comment surprised Biatta. Not the words, but because she was accepting responsibility. The girl was maturing fast; perhaps faster than was good for her, but in these troubled times, it was for the best. If Daria was expecting a denial, Biatta didn't sugarcoat her response.

"Yes, child, it was, but no one was harmed. Learn from your mistake and move on wiser from the ordeal."

She released her, not wanting to overdo her affection, and in truth feeling uncomfortable in the role.

"Jeremy."

The man was lost in his anguish at seeing his family held captive.

In a firmer tone, she repeated, "Jeremy."

This time, he looked up.

"We have to talk about all of this before your family wakes up."

He looked down at the sleeping forms, nodded, and stood up. He wiped his eyes as he approached.

"What do I tell my daughter when she comes to?"

Comes to? He thinks she fainted. That's for the best. "We need to discuss that."

"I mean, what do I say, since I don't understand any of it myself?"

"Come. Sit down here and we'll figure it all out."

With robotic steps, Jeremy sat in the same chair his daughter had been tied to.

"The less you say about any of this, the better. Let her think it was a home invasion. Nothing more. Do not tell her or anyone about what you witnessed in the woods. It will only make her worry."

He nodded. "I don't want that. She worries enough about me as it is." He wrung his hands as he spoke, then looked up abruptly. "But what did happen? I must know. Am I going crazy? Senile?"

Biatta smiled. "No. I doubt either of those terms apply to you. You've just witnessed some strange things that are difficult to explain but are all rational."

"Rational?" He glanced at the still frozen men. "How is this rational?"

She took his hand as she spoke. His wrist felt warm. "Some things are beyond explanation...at least for now." She put her long fingers inside the end of the cast and muttered something he didn't understand. "You won't need this anymore." The cast parted and fell away.

The look of surprise non his face amused her. She studied him. "You are an interesting man, Jeremy. I'd like the opportunity to learn more about you."

"Pe-Pop?"

CHAPTER FORTY

Stunned, they turned around to see Connor standing behind them. Jeremy stood fast, almost toppling the chair.

"Is the game over?"

"The game? What game, Connor?"

"The one with these funny men and the lady. They were being mean to Mommy."

"This shouldn't be possible," Biatta said stunned. "He shouldn't wake for hours, or unless I wake him." She turned an inquisitive glance at Daria.

"I didn't wake him. I don't know how."

"Yes. It's all over."

"Are they the good guys or the bad guys?" He pointed at Biatta and Daria.

"The good guys." He turned to look at Biatta. She could read the concern in his eyes that said he hoped so.

"Did we win?"

"Yes, Connor. We won."

He raised his arms and jumped. "Yeah! We are the champs."

Jeremy smiled and swept the boy into his arms lifting him from the floor.

"Pe-Pop! You're squeezing me too tight."

"It's a victory hug."

He kissed the boy's forehead and set him down.

"Are we keeping the men to play with later?"

"Ah…" He turned to Biatta. "What are we doing with them?"

"I'll handle it."

"Handle it? Like how?"

"Do not concern yourself. They will be removed and will not bother you again."

He thought he heard a whimper come from the standing man.

"You're not going to, uh…"

"Heavens, no. What do you take me for? You stay with your family and let Daria and me deal with them."

He gave a tentative nod and turned back to Connor. "Are you hungry?"

He nodded vigorously. "Yeah. I'll wake Mommy and Harper."

"No. Let them sleep. They're tired after playing the game. Let's have some man time."

"Cool. Man time."

Jeremy went to the fridge and pulled out sandwich items. Then he thought better of it and said, "How about hot dogs?"

His face lit up, then faded fast. "Mommy doesn't like us to eat hot dogs. She said it's bad meat."

"Well, let's not tell Mommy. Besides, it's okay to eat hot dogs once in a while. Just not all the time."

The boy glanced over his shoulder to make sure his mother wasn't watching, then gave a conspiratorial nod. Once Jeremy stepped back from the fridge, he noticed Daria, Biatta, and the two frozen guys were gone. Though he had a problem with killing them, he hoped whatever Biatta did at least caused them pain.

* * *

Biatta and Daria took the two still frozen men out back. The ground was flat for a distance, then began sloping downward into a valley. Houses sat up along the ridge and she went far enough to be out of sight. She set the men down. Both whimpered now in a steady stream of fear. They should be afraid, she thought. Though she wouldn't kill them, she would make sure they paid for their actions and could not be involved in such schemes in the future.

She took hold of their hands, closed her eyes, and released her darkest spell. In seconds, their hands began to blacken and wither. The two men screamed, though the sound was muffled. Once enough damage and pain had been inflicted, she released the bodies from the inert state and rolled them down the long slope. They bounced and bumped to the bottom, then got up and scampered away.

"So what happens now?"

"We have to deal with this, then return to the village."

"Are you going to wipe their memories?"

"No. That's not in my skill set. Besides, it appears Jeremy has a natural immunity. And perhaps Connor. I'd like to learn more about that," she said absently. "But we must get back. The others are well on their way by now. It will be dark by the time we arrive at the village. We'll stay the night there and start for the new camp in the morning."

"Is Jeremy coming too?"

Biatta thought. "It'd be nice to have him drive us back. Otherwise we'll be traveling through the woods in blackness."

"What about Connor? If he's immune to your magic, Jeremy will never leave him alone."

"Let's see if we can work out a plan."

They walked back to the house and entered through the patio door. Connor was excitedly munching on a hot dog. Jeremy told him to take small bites and chew well. Jeremy looked up and left Connor to his forbidden meal.

"I think it's time to answer some questions."

Biatta smiled. "Is it?" she said sarcastically.

"Yes. I want to know what's going on here. What have you got my family mixed up in?"

Biatta's eyes went hard. She neither liked nor appreciated his tone. "You got yourself mixed up in this when you followed Daria to our village. We didn't invite you. You just showed up. So before you go applying blame, make sure you start with yourself."

She felt a tug on her sleeve. Daria had a hold on it and looked concerned. Biatta looked at Jeremy and saw he had backed away and lost color in his cheeks. Without realizing she'd done it, she had drawn in energy for a spell. She had lost control of her anger and almost took it out on this man. With a flick of her wrists, she sent the energy from her body back to its natural state.

"I'm sorry. I did not mean to speak to you like that. I'm tired, and the stress of the day has taken its toll. That's no excuse for my outburst, but I am sorry."

They stood in awkward silence.

Connor interrupted, singing, "Lady in white. Lady in white," in a made-up melody.

They stared at him. He took another bite and chewed, suddenly aware of their gazes. "What?" he said through a mouthful.

"I have a lot of questions too," Biatta said. "We do need to talk."

Before she could say anything more, there was a loud knock on the patio door. In an instant, Biatta drew power, whirled, and crossed her hands in front of herself, ready to defend. Seeing the move, Daria followed suit, though slower and without having a clue what she would do.

A familiar face, Chase, stood at the door, motioning frantically for her to come. Biatta relaxed but did not release the energy. She opened the sliding door, stepped out, and closed it behind her.

"You are needed." His breathing was labored. She wondered if he ran the entire way from the village.

"What has happened?"

"The Harpy. Attacked. Mistress. Hurt bad. Needs your healing. Or..." He spoke in short gasps between sucking in gulps of air.

"Where? The village?"

He nodded and doubled over, putting his hands on his knees. Biatta whirled around, thinking how best to proceed. She stopped and faced the window, connecting with Jeremy.

"Okay, catch your breath." She stepped inside. "I have an emergency I must deal with. I know you've been through a lot already, but I need you to drive us back to the woods."

"But, ah, I...What about my family? I can't very well leave them here."

"They'll sleep for another few hours."

"But Connor's awake and doesn't seem to take to whatever form of hypnosis you used."

"Then bring him."

"What? No. I'm not putting him in danger."

"Jeremy. This is important. Someone I care about may die if I don't get back there as fast as possible. We came to aid your family. All I'm asking is you do the same for me. It won't be dangerous. Just drive us and drop us off. You can come right back and won't have to see us again."

Daria stepped forward and touched his arm. "Please, Jeremy."

He switched his gaze from Biatta to Daria and back again. "All right. Just this one last time."

"Oh, thank you, Jeremy." Daria threw her arms around him.

"Yes. Thank you," Biatta added.

"Is he coming too?"

"Yes," Biatta said.

"We won't all fit in my car. We'll have to take Chandra's. Besides, she has the car seats." He looked at the two sleepers. "You promise they'll be all right?"

"Yes. You have my word. Your house is protected."

"I don't know what that means, but you'd better be right."

He found Chandra's keys in her purse and led them outside. He locked the door and when he turned around, he saw Biatta waving her hand over her head like she was waving to a crowd.

"Is that some mumbo-jumbo to ward off evil spirits?"

"Precisely." Her serious expression and tone gave him pause.

CHAPTER FORTY-ONE

They arrived as close as they could and exited. Biatta leaned inside. "Thank you, Jeremy. I wish you and your family well."

"Does this mean I won't be seeing you again?"

"Yes. I think it's for the best. For you. For us. For your family." She closed the door and walked toward the trees. Her final words and the sight of her leaving saddened him.

A knock on the driver's side window caused him to jump. He found Daria there and lowered the window. "Thanks, Jeremy. I'm sorry I got you involved in all this, but if not for you, I'd be dead now. I'll never forget you." She planted a kiss on his cheek and started to leave, then stopped. She dug in her pocket and pulled out the cross. "Ah, I'm sorry for taking this." She handed it back.

Surprised, Jeremy glanced at the mirror, then remembered he wasn't in his car. He hadn't noticed it was missing when he went to collect his things from the wreckage. Jeremy reached for it, stopped, and glanced toward the heavens. As if receiving an answer, he nodded.

"It was my wife's. You keep it. I think she'd like you to have it. She'll watch over you."

"But if it was hers, you'll want it to remember her by."

"Oh Daria, I have so many memories and things to remind me of her. Besides, she's always looking out for me. She knows I need the help."

With tears flowing freely, she backed away from the car. In a burst, she ran after Biatta. Jeremy watched as they disappeared from view.

In the back, Connor sang.

"Lady in white. Lady in white."

* * *

They hurried through the darkening forest with a long journey still ahead. As they went, Chase filled them in on the battle with the Harpy and how Jerricka had somehow reached inside the creature and tore out its still-beating heart.

The news caused Biatta to gasp. Her legs went rubbery and Chase had to hold her to keep her from falling. Once stabilized, Biatta quickened the pace.

Jerricka, what have you done? Black magic? How could you?

Black magic had been banned for centuries. Those found practicing the evil art form were quickly terminated. The power and psychopathic tendencies that went hand in hand with black magic were deemed too dangerous a threat to the world to allow it to continue. The council of mages had long ago decreed practitioners of the black arts would be either stripped of their powers, memories, and skills to live a life as a mundane, or would be killed. The determination, being the damage one caused while using the banned magic.

Even if she saved Jerricka, she might still be put to death if word got out.

"Who else was present?"

"Jno and Neka," Chase said.

"The four of you took on the Harpy?" she asked, astonished.

"No. We had two others." He didn't need to say more.

The thought of so few, especially with only two wizards, taking on the most powerful and notorious Harpy ever known was madness. Was that why Jerricka felt it necessary to resort to such foul magic? The effects of the spell she conjured could be long-lasting.

She knew Jno was loyal to Jerricka, and Chase would do whatever Jno did. But Neka was always at odds with Jerricka. They seldom saw eye to eye on anything. Would Neka be so spiteful as to out Jerricka's decision? She'd like to believe she wouldn't, but in her heart, she feared for Jerricka.

They arrived at the village deep into the night. As she passed the threshold of the village limits, she did not feel the usual tug of the magical shield they'd erected to protect them. It was gone. They were exposed to whatever danger might come.

"Oh look," Daria said, pointing.

Though her mind was elsewhere, she followed the direction and saw the burnt shell of one of the girls' dorms. Daria had been assigned to it. Without comment, she hurried to Jerricka's cabin, the only one with a light showing, and ran up the stairs. Without a word, Jno pointed down the hall toward Jerricka's room.

When she opened the door, the smell alone told her something foul was dying. The room was lit by a small lantern. Neka sat on the bed on the far side, using a wet cloth to wash one of Jerricka's arms. To her complete shock, Biatta noticed it was blackened. Jerricka was in a fevered state; in and out of consciousness, bucking wildly.

"Biatta, she is dying."

Biatta noted her voice was remorseful. She cared. Maybe that meant if she could stop the plague raging within her, Jerricka would be safe from persecution.

Biatta sat on the opposite side and felt Jerricka's forehead. Her skin burned hot. Her eyes rolled back, showing the dull white orbs.

"She-she used black magic to kill Angwella. I know it was wrong, but if she hadn't, we'd all be dead." She was on the verge of tears.

"We'll discuss that later. She did what she must. It's over. I'm glad you're alive. I need your aid. What have you done so far?"

"Very little. I was never good with healing. What little I did had no obvious effect."

Biatta wanted to tell her she didn't know healing because her only focus for years had been offensive spells, but now wasn't the time. She had to rein in her anger and give complete attention to Jerricka or the woman would be swallowed by the evil now residing within her. In that case, they would be forced to put her down like a rabid dog.

"Go to my cabin and retrieve my medical bags. Bring them both. Hurry."

Neka stood and ran out. Biatta had everything packed for the trip when the commotion of Jeremy entering the village altered the plan.

She cleared her mind and began a low, steady chant. She held her palms over the writhing body and moved from head to toe. The magical scan showed where the plague had entered and was spreading. Ignoring the extremities for the moment, she concentrated on the organs. If they fell, hope was lost.

At this point, the liver and kidneys were infected, as well as half of one lung. The evil had not reached her heart or brain yet, but as her reserves and natural defenses weakened, the result was inevitable. The blackened arm was likely her greatest source of pain, but she would deal with that last. She might lose her arm, but better an arm than her life.

Biatta could not risk losing time on basic heals. They would buy some time, but their use would deplete her already low energy level and would not do anything to reverse the process. She stopped her hand over the highest point of infection, which was her lower right lung. Moving her arms to the sides, palms down, she began absorbing energy from the ground and the air. She wasn't full, but it was a start.

Placing one hand over the other and hovering them over the infected area, she began her incantation. Then, slowly she lowered her hands, feeling resistance from the malignant strain. They battled for several moments. Biatta increased her will and pushed harder. Whatever Jerricka had called into herself was powerful. This would be the weakest battle to be fought, and already she was wavering.

With renewed determination, she leaned over her hands and used the weight of her body to lower ever closer to the ribs. Her palm touched. The evil pushed back, lifting them again. This happened twice more before she was able to press her palms down and keep them in place. She chanted in low but strong tones, never ceasing or faltering. She felt the battle and the evil turn. Jerricka tried to sit up but Biatta held her down.

Jerricka spoke in deep, harsh demonic tones, roaring obscenities and flailing her legs and arms wildly. She grabbed Biatta's hair and ripped it to the side. A handful was yanked free, but Biatta would not release her. Fingers clawed at her face, furrowing the skin. Wetness crept down her cheek. A second effort was cut short as a hand snaked out and latched onto Jerricka's, keeping her from the attack. Jno had slipped into the room.

The struggle continued for another five minutes. Biatta felt her levels dropping too low to complete the removal process, her magical surgery, but she dare not let up for fear the blackness would return and take an even stronger foothold. On and on the battle raged until at long last, no sign of the evil showed in the lungs.

Biatta collapsed over the inert form, unable to raise her head.

Hands grabbed her from behind and gently lifted her. Someone strong carried her to a chair. She sat back, drained and unable to focus. She would have slept all night if left alone, but Neka's constant prodding brought her awake.

"Biatta. Please wake up."

Groggy, Biatta sat forward and leaned over her knees. She would have fallen head first if not for an outstretched hand catching her head and gently pushing it against the back of the chair.

"Biatta. What happened?" Neka asked. "Is she cured?"

Biatta shook her head. "No. Lot more to do."

She rocked back and forth a few times until she built enough forward momentum to stand. Once on her feet she staggered like a drunk but managed to catch her balance before doing harm.

"How is she? Any change?"

"She appears to be resting calmly for the moment," Neka said. "I-I brought your things."

Biatta thought she sounded rattled. That was unusual for her. Her norm was unflappable, aggressive, and straight ahead. There was nothing wrong with that. It worked for her. This was a side Biatta had never seen. Vulnerable. Scared.

"Come. I will need your help for the next part." She went to her bag and began pulling out vials of potions and jars and bags of strange exotic dried herbs and plants. Sorting through them, she found the combination she wanted and began blending them.

To Jno, she said, "Do you know where the patch of milkweed is?"

"Yes, Mis—Biatta."

He almost said Mistress. That gave her pause. My God. If Jerricka dies, as next in seniority she became the next Headmistress. Oh gods. No.

She looked at the man now. His pained expression showed his emotional tie to Jerricka and that he'd already worked out the ascension order. But was it a slip or a warning that he knew and would be watching her every move on Jerricka's behalf?

"Immediately beyond that is a plant that bears small round fruits. I need you to collect a handful and bring them here."

"But those plants are poisonous." He looked stunned. "You said so yourself. No one was to eat them." Then his facial expressions darkened and his gaze turned ice cold. "What is your intention?"

Biatta shot up in a flash and closed on him. With a sweep of her hand, his body was lifted and slammed against the wall. She met his gaze with one that flared.

"I intend to save the life of *the* Headmistress. Do not waste my time on your silly notions or stupid thoughts. Your job is to do what I say when I say it. Are we clear?"

What was clear was his extreme hatred for her.

Biatta tried another approach, one just as firm but less threatening.

"The pulp of those fruits if ingested in quantity is poisonous, but the oil is not. I need that oil for its viscosity. It is the only thing thick enough to combat the flow of deadly sludge moving up her arm. Yes, I am gambling with her life by using this oil instead of another, but no other oils are here now, since everything has been moved and we have little time to search for an alternative or waste time on this counterproductive debate."

She released him and he dropped to his feet. She noted his landing was in perfect balance and he had placed himself in a position to attack. She backed away a step but did not offer a defensive pose.

"Here are your choices. Do nothing and she dies. Get me what I want and she may still die, but at least there's a chance she won't."

She turned and walked back to her work.

CHAPTER FORTY-TWO

Montack made it to the portal, exhausted and in pain. She took on her normal form. Flying had been difficult with her wings torn. She would need to mend before setting off again. She had to report to Bradenbaugh that she had found the students. With a little more help she could capture some of them and get them to reveal where the others were hiding. She had to word her appeal just right to avoid his wrath for what he might deem a failed mission. But she hadn't failed. She had found a connection. She just needed another chance.

She made the gestures necessary to open the portal and stepped through. Once on the other side, she sealed it, making it invisible to the normal. She turned. The impact on her forehead was the last sensation she ever felt.

* * *

She did not pay Jno any further attention but heard the door close. When he returned carrying about a dozen oval-shaped purple fruits, she had everything ready for the next round of cleansing.

She stood and walked to him. She examined the fruits, picked out six.

"Take these and press them into a bowl or whatever you can find. Just make sure it's clean. Then remove as much of the pulp as possible and bring the rest to me."

Jerricka moaned.

"We are out of time. Hurry."

She collected what she would need and set everything on the table next to the bed. She absorbed energy and did a body scan. So far the poison had not returned to the lung. Jerricka squirmed. Her agony would make the next step more difficult unless she could keep her still. She didn't want to use another heal until necessary. The first one had drained her. To use another now meant she'd be too weak for the final battle.

They settled on either side of the bed again.

"You will need to hold her. Once the potion is ingested, her body will revolt violently. I must be free to direct it through her system, so keeping her in place will be up to you."

Neka nodded, but Biatta saw the doubt in her eyes.

The door opened and Jno hurried in. He offered her the small wooden bowl of thick oil. It had too much pulp, but she had little time to clean it.

"Find me a cloth."

"A cloth?"

"Yes. Like a t-shirt."

He scanned the room but had no idea where to find a t-shirt.

Biatta said, "Take yours off."

He paused but did as instructed.

"Cut away a section from the bottom."

He pulled a knife and held it upright for a second. Biatta imagined he would plunge the blade into her if Jerricka died. He cut a square and handed it to her.

"Take the bowl of oil and pour it into the cloth."

He did so and she held it over her prepared herbs and plants, squeezing the oil through the cloth. It landed in long, thick streams. She set the cloth aside and mixed the potion until it was a thick green paste.

"Jno, lift her head."

The man went to the other side of the bed and reached in front of Neka.

"She will fight. Hold her still."

Biatta pinched her chin and pulled her jaw down. She placed one wooden spoon sideways to prevent the mouth from closing, then spooned the mixture into her mouth.

"Get ready."

A glob of the paste fell into the back of Jerricka's throat. Within seconds, she began to buck and twist. Her eyes opened, revealing black irises. From somewhere deep within her core, an evil demonic voice rose. Biatta ignored the taunting voice and dropped spoonful after spoonful into her mouth until it was all gone. She tossed the bowl and spoon down, yanked the blocking spoon from her mouth, and clamped Jerricka's jaw shut. With one hand Biatta fought to keep her mouth closed while the other massaged her throat to ensure the concoction went down.

Even with three of them holding her they found it difficult to control her. Jerricka's eyes widened to the point of exploding. Her chest heaved. She kicked.

"Sit on her legs," Biatta told Neka.

The woman did and almost got kicked off. She tried again and managed to settle.

"Jno, control her arms. I'll handle her head."

"Chase!" she called. The door opened. "Rope. Cords. Anything to bind her with."

He returned a few minutes later with an assortment of bonds.

"Tie her legs together."

As Neka shifted her weight to allow the cord to be passed underneath Jerricka's legs, one broke free and kicked Chase under the chin. The force of the blow lifted him off his feet and to the floor. He stood shaken and bloody but continued his task until the legs were cinched tight.

"Now, tie off an arm to the headboard. Make sure it's secure."

Working with Jno, they tied the right arm, but the left came free and clawed furrows down Biatta's cheek.

"Ha!" the demon voice shouted. "I will do far worse soon. You cannot prevent me from taking over this woman's body. She is mine."

Biatta drove a fist into the face, shutting it up for a moment. With the left hand secured, controlling her body was easier, however, the constant thrashing did not cease.

Then she heard the demon voice chanting, "Lady in white. Lady in white. Trying hard to fight the blight. Lady in white. Lady in white. So much pain, such a delight."

Biatta was shaken the boy's words repeated in such a demonic voice. How could she the demon know about the boy?

They fought for the better part of an hour. As their strength waned, it became apparent something was occurring within Jerricka. Her aggressive posture had softened.

"One at a time, take a break. This isn't over yet. To finish, everyone will have to be at full strength," Biatta said.

With a nod from Jno, Neka climbed off and walked away, shaking out her arms and legs.

"What is happening?" Jno asked.

"Her body is fighting off the evil. If she is strong enough, she will pull through."

"And if she isn't?"

Biatta remained silent. Jerricka would have to be destroyed.

"We'll worry about that if and when the time comes."

She called up her power and scanned the body. She found the potion at a standstill in the stomach, being pushed back by the black mass. To be fully effective, the paste needed to be absorbed through the entire body. She concentrated on the mass, held her palm above the stomach, and began moving the paste in different directions. It was a long arduous process, but eventually she was able to move some of the paste around the blockage. As the body responded to the healing potion, Jerricka came alive again. This time the battle she waged was one of words.

"I know you," the demonic voice said. "I know who you are and what you're running from."

She was aware that Jno was now looking at her.

"They are still searching for you. I'm sending them a message to reveal your whereabouts. They are anxious to get their hands on you." She laughed. It had a bone-chilling effect. "Yes. They are coming for you and they will destroy any who stand with you."

Biatta tried hard not to react to the words. She could only deal with one crisis at a time. She lifted her hand, and with a twisting and closing motion, said, *"Silenzie."*

Jerricka went quiet. Her eyes flared and her head bobbed, but other than grunts no more sounds came forth.

Several minutes later, Jerricka convulsed. A scream was buried in her throat. She began kicking and bucking with renewed vigor. They bore down to hold her still, but just as suddenly as the convulsions began, they ceased completely. The woman's body slumped; head lulled, eyes rolled back in her skull. Then Jerricka did not move.

Jno leaped to his feet. "What? What just happened?" He looked at Biatta with pure hatred in his eyes. "Did you kill her?"

Good question. Biatta checked for vitals. To her relief, Jerricka was still breathing. "She is still alive, but barely. I hoped to get a better result from the potion." She lowered her head, reviewing what she had done and what else to try. She looked at Neka. "Get Daria."

Neka did not hesitate. She ran from the room. Seconds later, she returned dragging Daria by the hand.

"We are in the last stage now. We either succeed or fail. My strength has already been drained. I need you two to draw in as much energy as you can and take my hand. I will draw from you as needed. Neka, I'll start with you. When you feel depleted, put Daria's hand in mine and rest a few moments before drawing in more."

"But I don't have much capacity," Daria said.

"You will when this is over. Do the best you can, and do not try to stop me once I tap into your supplies."

"Everyone ready?"

She didn't wait for responses. Biatta absorbed as much of the energy as was possible, grabbed Neka's hand, and lowered her palm down over the infected areas. With extreme effort and concentration, Biatta began to force the evil from Jerricka's body. At first, the black mass refused to give way, but as Biatta drew from Neka, increasing her power, progress was made. She pushed the energy down and through Jerricka's body like an army on the march. She cleared the liver, then the kidney, but faltered there.

She released Neka's hand and held her ground until Daria was in place, then began again. True to her statement, Daria did not last long. She was forced to take Neka back, even though she had only replenished half her reserves.

The battle continued well into the evening, though none were aware. Most of the body had been cleared, but Neka and Daria no longer had anything left to give. Biatta tapped her reserves and forced the final evil to its last hold point: her reproductive organs. With one long burst of energy, Biatta made her final attack. As her levels depleted and her strength drained, Neka gasped.

"The bed. It's wet. And-and black."

A foul order arose, filling the room. Biatta ignored Neka's words and continued. With a final push, she evacuated the last of the black mass and collapsed over Jerricka.

"Is it done?" Neka asked.

"Almost. I need a sharp knife." One appeared before her face. Biatta followed the razor-sharp edge up the blade to the arm to Jno's eyes. He nodded. She took the knife and said, "Untie her right arm, but keep a tight hold on it."

She placed the tip of the blade at the top of the blackened arm and made an incision. She guided the blade down toward the wrist, careful not to make the cut too deep. When she reached the bottom of Jerricka's wrist, she dropped the knife and squeezed the skin together. Thick black blood ran from the cut. She began at the top and continued down the arm until the only fluid exiting was thin red blood. Once the arm had been cleared, she used the last of her strength to cast a heal to reclose the wound. In gasps, she gave her last instructions.

"Take the bed outside and burn it," she said to Jno. To Neka and Daria, she said, "Wash any black blood off Jerricka and wrap her in fresh blankets and watch over her. Be careful not to get any on yourselves."

Biatta fell to the floor.

CHAPTER FORTY-THREE

Bradenbaugh paced in front of the ancient stone fireplace, hands behind his back and head down, deep in thought. Something was wrong. He'd sent three teams through the portal and none had returned. All three had been reliable, faithful servants. Had something happened to them or had they not yet found their prey?

Perhaps he'd underestimated his enemy. Were they lying in wait on the other side of the portal dispatching his teams as they appeared? It was a good plan; something he'd do. Perhaps he needed to dispatch an army of his followers. If they came through the portal with overwhelming numbers and prepared in advance, he might be able to rid himself of the annoying gnats with one attack. Then he could place all his efforts on finding and eliminating Vandalue and his geriatric supporters.

A knock on the heavy wooden door drew his attention.

"Come."

A short squat man opened the door. "Your guest has arrived, my Lord."

Ah, it was about time. Now, he'd get some action.

"Send her in."

A tall light-brown-skinned woman entered. She was dressed in black, had raven-colored hair, and sported a dagger tattoo in the middle of her forehead. He liked the way she looked and her confident stride as she approached. He had a feeling this alliance would be beneficial.

"Lord Bradenbaugh, my masters send their regards."

She made no offer of her hand, nor did she bow or even nod. He filed that away. She would learn soon who her real master was, but for now, he would play nice. He studied her for a moment longer. Her eyes were cold and hard. Her body appeared to vibrate with raw power. He had no doubt she was a formidable adversary. That was something else he filed away. She was not to be underestimated.

"Your timing is perfect. I have a mission for you."

* * *

"Pe-Pop, Mommy's waking up."

Jeremy stood from the kitchen chair and walked to the sofa. Chandra opened her eyes and looked around, confused by what she saw.

"What's going on?"

"You fell asleep."

"Mommy snores," Connor said.

"I do not. Dad, where were you?" Her memory must have returned. She sat up and scanned the room. "Where are those...people?"

"What people?"

"You didn't see them? They tied me to a chair. They threatened the kids."

"What? What are you talking about?"

She gave him an inquisitive look that morphed into an angry glare.

"You know what people. What have you gotten into?" She stood, allowing her full anger to be exposed. "You got us kidnapped and threatened. These crazy people wanted to know something about kids from an art school. You better come clean or I swear, I'll take the kids and never see you again." If steam could have come from her ears, it would've.

"Are you sure it wasn't just a bad dream?"

She whirled on him, her fury in full force.

Connor came to her side and grabbed her arm. "It's okay, Mommy. We won the game. The bad people are gone."

"You remember them, don't you?"

"Of course. Pe-Pop's friends chased them away."

"Friends?" She looked back at her father.

He was going to deny knowing what Connor was talking about, but the boy said, "The lady in white and her helper."

"Who's the lady in white?"

"She's magic."

"Magic? What's he talking about, Dad?"

"Some friends stopped over. You and Harper were sleeping and we didn't want to disturb you."

She shook her head. "What are you not telling me? Where have you been all day?"

"At the village in the woods," Connor said.

Harper stirred, stretched, and opened her eyes.

Connor said, "Can we go see them, Mommy?"

"See who?"

"The lady in white and her friend."

"Somebody better tell me what's going on before I lose my mind."

"It's nothing. I met some friends. that's all."

"Did these friends have to do with us being abducted?"

"No. Of course not."

She gave him an exasperated look, then scooped up Harper in her arms.

"Come on, Connor. We're leaving"

"Now Chandra, don't be like that."

"Like what? Concerned for my family's welfare?"

"I think you need to be in a home. You're losing it."

"Hey! That's uncalled for."

"Oh, really? What's called for is some honesty. Who are these friends? I want to meet them. I've got some things to say to people who put children in danger."

"They didn't put them in danger. If anything, they saved you."

"So you say. Get them on the phone. I want to talk to them."

"Settle down."

"Oh, you don't want to say that to me right now."

"I don't have their number."

"How convenient. How do you get in touch with them?"

"I just sort of meet them."

"Where? Where, Dad? Take me there now, or I'm calling the police and filing a kidnapping report."

"Fine."

"Fine? Really? Let's go."

Without waiting to see what he would do, Chandra took both kids' hands and led them out to her van. She strapped each into their car seat, then got in and started the engine. When Jeremy still hadn't appeared, she laid on the horn.

Jeremy had to decide the best course of action. If he took her to the woods, they'd never find the village and would soon give up. She couldn't very well lug two kids for any great distance. Maybe it would mollify Chandra, at least for the present. He left the house and climbed into the passenger seat.

"Where to?"

"You're not going to be able to get there. It's a long walk. The kids won't be able to keep up."

"They'll do just fine. Where to?"

"It'll be dark before we get there."

"Where. To?"

He frowned and gave her directions. She fumed the entire trip, mumbling to herself, but not speaking to him. Twenty minutes later, they parked where he had before.

"This is the place?"

"Yes."

"Do they come to you, or what?"

"No. Each time I've found them by walking through the woods."

"Okay. Let's go."

"Chandra."

"Now, Dad."

Connor was ecstatic. "We're going to see the magic lady!"

Harper caught his contagious eagerness and she cheered, even though she had no idea what they were talking about.

They traipsed through the trees, staying close to the road. Nearly an hour later, neither Connor nor Harper thought much of the hike. Chandra too had calmed, more from the exertion of the walk than from not wanting to meet the kidnappers.

Jeremy stopped at the clearing.

"Where is this place?" Chandra asked without a hint of the anger she had displayed before.

"It's across the field and another half hour's walk."

"Okay. I'm done. You win. Let's go back."

They turned to make the trek back to the car.

Connor pointed and said, "Hey Pe-Pop, there's the bad guys."

They all turned to look. The two men from the house loped across the field.

"Oh my God. That *is* them," Chandra said. "Bring the kids."

She took off like a shot.

Chandra! Wait!" Jeremy called, but if she heard, she was ignoring him.

He scooped up Harper, but Connor dodged his efforts and took off after his mother. He tried to keep pace, but Chandra was driven by rage and Connor by youthful energy.

The two men disappeared into the trees across the field. Chandra reached the same place only minutes behind. By the time Jeremy reached the same spot, Chandra, Connor, and the two men were nowhere in sight.

Up ahead, he heard Connor call for his mother and followed his voice.

Then he heard, "Mommy, where'd the bad men go?"

"I don't know. They were right here."

"Chandra, enough. It's getting late. Let's get the kids back to the car."

Chandra spun, still searching for her prey but clearly in distress. She was worried about him, but she was the one close to losing it.

"Chandra. It's over.

CHAPTER FORTY-FOUR

Chandra lowered her head and released a long, slow breath. Tears welled in her eyes.

"I just want to understand, Dad. Can you explain it to me in a way that makes sense? Can you help me believe that you haven't gone over some deep mental cliff?" She wiped at one eye.

"I'm sorry, Chandra. Let's go home. We can talk there. There's nothing to see here."

"Yes, there is, Pe-Pop," Connor said.

Jeremy looked down at his grandson. An expression of joyful discovery shined from his young face. He lifted a hand and pointed.

"It's that way."

Jeremy tried to hide his surprise. "Wh-what's that way, Connor?"

"The people."

Chandra squatted next to her son and looked where he was pointing. "What people, Connor? I don't see anyone."

"They're through the trees. That way."

"Are you sure?"

"Yes, Mommy."

Jeremy's mind whirled. He knew the village existed and was indeed in that direction, but how did Connor know? Had he seen one of the villagers?

"Your mother's right, Connor. There's nothing there."

"Come on. I'll show you!"

Connor took off at a run.

"Connor!" Jeremy called.

"Connor, you come back here right now!" Chandra said.

But Connor did not stop, disappearing in the trees in seconds. Chandra sprinted after him. Jeremy scooped up Harper and hurried to keep up. In the distance, he heard Chandra call to Connor.

Connor's response was, "This way, Mommy!"

But Jeremy had lost sight of both of them.

A new fear struck him. The villagers had not been happy when he appeared and had been threatening to him. What would they do if they caught sight of Chandra and Connor? A knot of anxiety formed in his stomach. He pushed faster.

"Chandra, you must stop him!"

But he no longer heard them. Not their crashing through the undergrowth. Not their voices.

"Chandra!" he called louder.

Real fear engulfed him. If something happened to Connor or Chandra it would be all his fault.

"Connor!" he shouted.

"Pe-Pop! You're bouncing me too much," Harper said.

"Sorry, sweetie. I have to catch up to your brother before—"

"Before what, Pe-Pop?"

"Nothing. We just have to find them."

Twenty minutes later, worry had spread to dread. Still no sign of his family. His chest pounded. His steps faltered. Breathing became more difficult, but he could not stop. With a suddenness that startled him, he broke through the trees and stood on the edge of a clearing. It was the right clearing, but something had changed.

Several of the structures were now smoldering piles of charred wood. To the right was another heap, but it was not a building. It looked like the carcass of a massive turkey or some sort of animal he'd never seen before, like a creature out of Jules Verne's *Mysterious Island*.

Connor stood in the center with Chandra a few steps behind.

"See, Mommy? I told you there were people here."

"Where, honey? I don't see anyone."

"Right there. A man and a woman."

Chandra placed a hand to shade her eyes as she scanned the area. She shook her head, clearly frustrated. She turned as Jeremy approached. Harper reached for her.

"Pe-Pop bounced me too much."

Chandra took the girl but did not respond.

"I'm sorry, Connor, but I don't see anyone."

Connor stomped his foot.

"Are you fooling me?" He looked from her to Jeremy.
"You see them, don't you, Pe-Pop?"

Jeremy did indeed see them. He recognized the man called Jno. He stood perfectly still in front of a cabin with a woman he'd seen before but whose name he did not know. From their shocked expressions, they hadn't been expecting company; especially people who could see them. But the rest of the village had an abandoned feel. One of the buildings was now a blackened shell. Were they burning the place, or had some accident or battle happened here?

He waved at them and smiled at Connor.

"Of course I see them."

Chandra shot him a withering glare. "Don't encourage him. I don't need him to start seeing invisible friends." She reached down and snatched Connor's hand and pulled him back toward the trees. "That's all I need. Two crazies to deal with instead of one."

Connor turned and waved at the people. "I like your cabin," he said.

Jeremy waited for Chandra to enter the trees before saying, "Sorry. Is...is everything all right here?"

The two looked at each other. The woman spoke. "We'll be all right. Go, and never return here. It is far too dangerous for anyone to be here now."

Jeremy nodded. "Is Daria all right?"

The man whispered something to the woman. She frowned. "You should go. Now." She pivoted, walked up the stairs, and went inside.

Jno crossed his arms as if to say, 'You shall not pass.'

Jeremy turned and hurried after Chandra. What an extremely strange day this had been.

* * *

Still weak from her healing efforts, Biatta stood at the window watching the events outside. At first, she was stunned to realize the boy could see Jno and Neka. Then the woman came out and she recognized her at once. However, she did not see anyone other than the boy. Once Jeremy exited the woods, her curiosity was piqued to the max. She was tempted to go out and question them but did not want to make her presence known to the woman.

She thought about Jeremy and his grandson. Why were they able to see them when no one else could? There was something important there; something she needed to discover and understand. She needed time and a less stressful place to do a thorough interview and study of the man. She doubted his daughter would be cooperative and allow her to study her son. An idea formed. She turned from the window as Neka entered.

"Did you see?"

Biatta nodded.

"The boy saw us. I may not be the most powerful wizard in our group, but that spell I put up was strong. No one should have been able to break through it." She placed her hands on her face and dragged them downward. "I don't know. Perhaps in my haste I forgot a step."

"Don't beat yourself up, Neka. I'm sure the spell was fine. But there is something different...something special about Jeremy and his grandson. I want to know more about them."

"That may be, but we won't have to worry about them again. As soon as we leave, Jno will raze the village and erase evidence that we were ever here."

Biatta didn't answer. She nodded absently as she was busy refining her plan. She moved around the room, deep in thought.

"When will Jerricka be ready to move?"

"That depends on how she feels when she wakes. I'll check on her now."

She entered the bedroom and closed the door behind her. Daria jumped in her seat, bringing a smile to Biatta. The girl had been tasked with watching Jerricka in case she woke or displayed obvious problems. She had nodded off.

"Oh! I, uh...nothing has happened so far." She stammered in a hurry to cover her blunder. "I-I...she hasn't woken once."

"Relax, Daria. I'll watch her for a while. Go get something to eat."

Daria looked from Biatta to Jerricka, then back. She started toward the door, then hesitated.

"Yes?"

"I...ah, how did you know what to do?"

She understood the question. How did she know what spells and potions to use to cure Jerricka?

"It's all experience and training."

"But how do you learn to train to combat black magic?"

Biatta sighed. *For a time I was a black witch,* she thought, though she did not voice those words. Instead, she said, "You study your basics in school, but long after you graduate, you will still be studying. You will always learn new things. Some lessons will be out of curiosity. Others will be from necessity. Your education will never cease."

"But it was black magic, so how did you know how to exorcise the…ah, was that a demon inside her?"

"A long time ago in a different life, I had the occasion to learn a little about black magic. I studied and saved what I learned for just such a situation as this."

Daria inhaled, ready to ask another flurry of questions. Biatta interrupted.

"Go now, child. We may be leaving tonight. Get some food and some rest. We can talk more on our journey."

Daria nodded and left.

Biatta sat on the edge of the bed. She felt Jerricka's brow. It was no longer burning. Perhaps still a bit too high, but not dangerous. Drawing in her energy, she performed another internal full body scan. So far, the demonic black magic entity had not returned. The longer she kept Jerricka clear, the better her chance of a full recovery without any relapse.

She called upon another spell, then touched her finger to Jerricka's temple. An electric spark jumped from Biatta's finger and connected with her skin.

"Jerricka, I'm leaving you in the care of Neka and Jno. They will protect you and take you to the new camp. I will not be joining you at present. Something has come up that needs exploring and explanation. I will take Daria with me. I will report when I can. Until then, be safe, my friend."

She broke the connection. The message would deliver as soon as Jerricka woke from her recovery. She stood, placed her palm over her chest, and sent a minor heal through her to bolster her strength.

She left to put her plan into motion.

CHAPTER FORTY-FIVE

No one spoke on the drive home. The entire day had been an emotional drain on all of them. Both Harper and Connor were fast asleep by the time they turned up the driveway.

Jeremy reached for the door, but Chandra placed a hand on his arm.

"Please, Dad. I can't take anymore. Stay home. Stay out of trouble. For at least a day or two. Give me a chance to catch my breath."

Jeremy felt a heavy sadness settle over him. "I'm sorry, Chandra. I never meant to make you worry." He glanced in the back seat at the two snoozing kids. "Tell them I said goodnight."

She gave a tired smile. "Of course."

He got out, unlocked the front door, then turned to wave as Chandra drove away. He closed the door, walked into the kitchen and collapsed in a chair. He was exhausted. He was too old for all this intrigue and excitement. His stomach rumbled. When was the last time he'd eaten? He tried to remember but came up with a blank. He took out a can of chicken noodle soup out of a cupboard.

Miranda would cringe if she saw him eating canned soup. She always made her soups from scratch and they were the best. But he didn't have her skill in the kitchen or the motivation. He preferred his meals to be as simple as possible with the least amount of work. He poured the contents into a pot and turned on the burner. He stared into it for a moment, then went to another cupboard, took out a container of Italian seasoning, and sprinkled some in. He smiled to himself, feeling proud he had done something to alter the flavor, if only for Miranda.

After his simple meal, he cleaned up and went to bed, but his mind was too active for sleep. He replayed the day's events. What would Miranda make of what happened today? He laughed. If Miranda was still alive, she never would have let him get into all this trouble. Thoughts of Miranda calmed his mind, as they had always done when she was alive.

Sleep came quickly then.

* * *

"Come, child," Biatta said. "We must be away before first light."

The still sleepy Daria stumbled over the first tree root she came to upon entering the forest. She whined, "But I'm tired. The sun's not even up yet."

"Quiet, child. I don't want to wake the camp."

After she had roused Daria, they grabbed their packs. Though she'd snuck out of the cabin without disturbing anyone, she knew a guard was watching the perimeter. Chase confronted her before she got five feet from the cabin.

"I have a special task to undertake and must be there before the day begins. I have spoken with Jerricka and explained my plans. You can check with her when she wakes."

"The Headmistress spoke to you?" His voice was excited with a hint of disbelief.

Biatta noted the tone and cocked her head as if to challenge it. "She is well aware of my plan. We are leaving, now please step aside."

He eyed her with suspicion but had no reason to prevent her from leaving. He nodded and stepped from her path.

"Luck on your task."

She nodded and continued.

As they moved deeper into the woods, she snatched Daria's arm, squeezed, and pulled.

"Ow!"

"If you don't want it to hurt, then lift your feet and move. We have little time and much to do. I will not be delayed by a whiny child."

With sudden fury, Daria ripped her arm from Biatta's grasp and stood defiant.

"I am not a child! Stop calling me that."

Surprised at the abrupt change in the girl, Biatta eyed her with a slack jaw. "Then stop acting like one and move on your own with a sense of purpose."

She whirled and walked away, confident Daria would follow.

"That would be easier to do if I had a clue why we had to be up so early."

"You will be told in time. Now, keep up. If you fall behind, I will leave you here."

She heard the girl mutter, "If only it was that easy."

Biatta smiled.

They reached the first clearing as the sun hinted its awakening. Unsure of what dangers lurked in the woods, she coaxed Daria into a run until they reached the opposite side. As they walked, Biatta passed back a bottle of water and a roll.

"Can't we at least stop to enjoy this bountiful meal?"

"No. Be happy you have anything at all."

"I never knew how mean you were."

Biatta whirled. "I'm not mean, ch—*Daria*. I'm driven. I'm concerned. I'm—"

"Afraid?"

Biatta froze. She eyed the girl for a moment. "Yes. What I'm—what *we're* doing is important. It may make a great deal of difference to the outcome of the war we are facing. I will need your assistance to find that information. I see things in you that..." She searched for the right word.

"What? Remind you of yourself?"

The girl was astute. She was rude and had an attitude, but to be good with magic, it was almost a prerequisite.

"Heavens, no. You wouldn't have survived my upbringing. I was going to say potential. You have it in you to do great things if your attitude and laziness don't get in the way. I need you with me, not only for the assistance you can give, but so I can teach you things that hopefully will help you not only survive but contribute over the coming days."

Daria looked stunned. Her mouth worked, but for once no words came out.

"Can we continue now?"

She nodded and Biatta started at an increased pace. The second clearing came as the sun peeked over the treetops. They were making good time, but they had so much farther to go.

Halfway across the field, a disturbance in the air far to the left drew Biatta's attention. "Get down!"

She grabbed Daria and yanked her hard to the ground.

"What the—"

"Quiet. Your life—our lives may depend on what happens in the next few minutes. Stay still and do not speak."

Daria paled but lay flat.

Biatta had to know what was happening. She raised ever so slowly and peered over the tall grass and weeds. The blue, white, and black swirling entrance to the portal had just been activated. She watched, anxious to see if friend or foe stepped through. A minute later, a man dressed in a long black cloak stepped into the new world. He was tall and clean-shaven. His black hair glistened in the morning sunlight. She did not recognize him. He must be foe.

He took a long scan of the surroundings, stopping for an angst-filled moment and stared in her direction. Satisfied with whatever he had or hadn't seen, he turned and motioned into the portal. Three more men and a woman came through, all wearing similar garb. The woman raised a hand behind her and shut the portal down without a backwards glance.

This was not a friendly party. If Biatta had to guess, she'd believe Bradenbaugh had just sent in his A-team. They huddled for a moment. The woman looked around as the men focused on what the first man through was saying. He must be the leader. As the woman panned in Biatta's direction, she caught sight of her face and gasped. She ducked and covered her mouth. It couldn't be. Did they know where she was? Or was she just a part of Bradenbaugh's network?

The woman had a bright red tattoo on her forehead. Biatta didn't have to be close to know what the symbol was. The red dagger with a snake curled around the blade, its fangs prominent. Emblazoned on the golden hilt were the initials DS. Along the gold guard was the word Molatrese.

The Molatreseans had found her. The DS stood for Death Squad. The five members were highly-trained assassins in both magic and physical skills. They were an unstoppable team. As if by some immense magic spell, the clearing suddenly seemed devoid of air. Biatta's chest tightened and she rolled onto her back, gasping and staring in a panic at the sky.

Daria's eyes were wide with fear. "Wh-what did you see?"

Biatta was too frightened to reply. Daria's curiosity piqued and she lifted her head to glimpse whatever was out there. In a flash, Biatta's hand snaked out, snatching the neck of the girl's t-shirt and yanked her down. She rolled on top of the girl and pressed a finger to her lips.

When Daria calmed, Biatta raised again, but no one was there. With fresh panic squeezing the air from her lungs, she whipped her head side to side, catching a glimpse of the last man entering the trees to the left. They were heading toward the village. She had to warn them.

Jno had planned to have everyone up and gone by dawn, but that depended on Jerricka's condition. If this death squad found them, they would not be able to stop them. Fear clutched at her thoughts, dispersing them before she could form them into action.

She had to calm her racing heart. She had to think. Lives depended on what she did in the next few seconds. She willed her heart to slow its thumping. She had to go back but could not risk taking Daria with her. The girl would slow her down and wouldn't stand a chance against such a powerful force. She had to do it herself, and there was only one way to get there ahead of them.

Inside her cloak, she withdrew a small felt pouch. She opened it and dumped a small jewelry box into her palm. She lifted the lid, exposing a plain white gold ring. She ran her finger over the surface, feeling the finely etched image on its surface and traced the inscription on the inside of the band.

"Daria listen to me." She raised her gaze from the ring and locked eyes with Daria's. "This is extremely important. I must go back and warn the others. You need to keep going."

"What? No."

In a voice so harsh she didn't recognize as her own, Biatta said, "You will listen and do what I tell you. This is not a game or open to debate. If I tell you to do something, there's a good reason. The lives of the people in the village are at stake, and I don't have time to waste on your foolishness. Take my pack and go into those trees." She pointed behind her. "Continue walking. Go to Jeremy's house. You know how to find it?"

Daria nodded.

"Stay there until I return. You understand?"

She grabbed Daria's shoulders and held them tight. With a shake, she repeated the question.

"Do you understand?"

Daria nodded, but tears welled, ready to fall. She pulled the girl close and gave her an air-expelling embrace. Before releasing her, she lowered her voice and in strained words, said, "If I don't come back..."

Daria rebelled then, trying to pull from her grasp. Biatta held tighter.

"Listen to me." She squeezed even tighter. "If I don't make it back, stay with Jeremy. He's a good man and will look after you."

She pushed back but held onto Daria's shoulders.

"Promise me you'll stay there and won't come looking."

Tears streamed down her face. "You will come back for me, right?"

"Yes, child." But Biatta's words held no conviction. "I'll come back for you. Now, be strong. Be brave. Most importantly, be smart."

She stepped to the side, placed a hand on her back, and shoved her toward the trees. Daria moved with stiff steps, the burden of the extra pack making them uneven. She did not turn back. Biatta watched until she reached the tree line, then slipped the ring on her right ring finger. Instantly she felt the stored power surge through her.

She tilted her head to the morning sky and chanted words she hadn't spoken since arriving at the school all those years ago. The effects were both pleasing and painful. She repeated the phrase twice, then let out a cry as her body compressed, altered, and morphed into a great white owl.

With powerful beats of her massive wings, she took flight, soaring high above the trees and keeping well left of the death squad. As she gained altitude, she increased speed, feeling the raw power coursing through her. It felt wonderful to be airborne again, like reuniting with a friend she hadn't seen in years.

CHAPTER FORTY-SIX

Higher she rose, banking farther to the left. She swung out over the road beneath her. Her sharp eyes saw everything from people to small animals. Once beyond the next clearing, she veered right, crossing the treetops.

She sensed magic and dodged down and left as a lance of fire flashed overhead, singeing several of her magnificent feathers. She had been seen. That was bad. It took great skill to locate magic being used, especially from this distance. This team, or at least one of them, was extremely powerful. Since men rarely had the ability to use magic unless stored in an object with magical properties, she was sure it was the woman.

She dove below the trees and into the forest. With great care, she maneuvered through the upper canopy. The death squad would be moving at full speed now. She had little time to reach the village and warn them.

She broke from the trees. Below, Jno was helping Jerricka down the stairs. Neka and Chase wore large packs on their backs. They were moving, which was good, but they would still be too slow to escape determined hunters. Even weakened, Jerricka could sense her. Her head shot up and whatever she said made every head tilt up.

Biatta landed ten yards from the group. Neka stepped in front of Jerricka and prepared a spell. Jno handed Jerricka to Chase and stepped forward, a blade in each hand.

Biatta settled and countered her spell while still moving. Her body morphed into her own form. Relief flooded the group.

Before any could speak, she said, "You have a highly skilled team of hunters heading this way. You must be away now. I will try to delay them or lead them in a different direction, but they are very good. In time they will figure it out and track you. Take steps to hide where you are going and what you are doing."

Jno said, "Show me where. I'll help."

"No!" she shouted. "I'm sorry, but even your skills are no match for them. You must see Jerricka to safety. If they find you, you'll get your chance to protect her, but to do so now would be to throw your life away."

"Do as she says," Jerricka said, her voice weak.

"You know where I'll be," Biatta said.

Jerricka nodded. "I don't know why, but I trust you."

"Go. Now," Biatta said to Jno. She started running as she spoke the words. In a full sprint, Biatta's body changed. Her body lifted and in seconds was but a spot in the sky. She had no idea where the death squad was but had the feeling they'd make their presence known, and soon.

In owl form, Biatta had no magical offensive capabilities and few defensive. She had to rely on her cunning to avoid being turned into a burnt husk. She circled to the left trying to stay wide of the death squad. When they inevitably spotted her, she wanted to lead them to the east to buy enough time for the others to get some distance.

Aware of the striking capabilities of the wizard, Biatta kept her sharp eyes focused on the ground. She flew for the better part of a minute before the first signs appeared. Deep within the second forest, she spied a heat signature. It couldn't be the squad, because she only saw one, but it grew larger and stayed circular.

She knew exactly what was coming. Knowing she had missed with the narrower bolt of fire she sent skyward, the wizard was widening the path of destruction; this time sending up a ball of flame.

Biatta kept a close eye on the ever-growing fiery sphere, prepared to take evasive action like a fighter pilot. Then, it was sent skyward. Biatta banked left and beat her wings hard. A glance behind showed the ball of fire still coming, and with heart-chilling realization, gaining.

As the ball rose higher, it grew larger. Biatta was going to have trouble evading it. She rose higher, but the ball did not lose power to accelerate. With panic gripping her heart, Biatta pushed beyond any speed she'd attempted before. She rose, banked, dove, and rose again, trying desperately to shake the ball, but nothing worked. Was it her imagination, or could she feel the heat?

She crested a tree-covered hill. Beneath her, she spied a river. It wasn't wide or deep, but it gave her an idea. Perhaps her only chance of survival, she dove in a steep head first dive. Her wings pressed tight to her body to increase speed. Now there was no doubt. The fireball was heating her tail feathers. She raced ever closer to the water. She would only get one chance.

The smell of singed feathers reached her. The heat was growing to an intolerable point. The water was still fifty yards below. She screeched, the heat now unbearable. She screamed, the pain engulfing her mind as the fire would soon engulf her body.

She reached the water, feeling the cold brush against her breast. Then, in a spine-cracking move, she shot sharply straight up. The fireball struck the water at an explosive speed. The river erupted in a gout of water and hissing steam that rose above the surrounding trees.

She was still in pain. A quick rotation of her head showed her feathers were on fire. The pain intensified. If she continued to fly the flames would spread over her body and kill her. She dove again, this time splashing hard into the icy water. The force of her entry took her too deep. Her head slammed into the muddy, rock-filled bottom, stunning her.

She had an out-of-body sensation of floating. Her mind was fuzzy. All she knew was pain, then darkness.

* * *

Daria kept walking, her mind still reeling from what she'd seen. Of course, she wasn't going to keep going without looking, regardless of what Biatta had said. Once she reached the trees and felt she was out of sight, she ducked and crept back. What she saw left her stunned.

Her teacher had disappeared in a flash. What rose instead was a beautiful and majestic white owl. She stood and watched it fly away, mouth agape as she watched. How had she done that? Oh, she knew about lycanthropes and had heard about other shapeshifters, but to witness the change right before her eyes left her dumbfounded. She stood watching until the owl was lost in the high sky.

Alone, confused, and more than a little afraid, she started toward Jeremy's house. But what was she supposed to do there? What did she tell him? *"Oh. Biatta said you'd take care of me."* She could see that going over well. The real question was if she could even find his house.

She stopped for a moment and turned back. This was stupid. She should be with her people; her friends and classmates. They needed her help. An image of Biatta danced before her eyes. It wasn't a friendly picture or even a scolding one, but it had more power. It was the complete and utter terror displayed on her face when she saw whatever had come out of the portal. That look alone was enough to frighten Daria into turning right back around and head toward Jeremy's.

She hid Biatta's backpack, marking the tree with a small magic symbol she'd seen in one of her textbooks, then traveled for hours before reaching a residential area. It didn't look familiar. She walked back and forth on the street, trying to find a landmark to guide her. After a while, all the streets looked alike, so she picked one and hoped a sign would show her the way.

More than an hour later, she was lost. She sat on a curb and leaned her chin on her arms. What did she do now? She settled into a funk, staring into the street. A short time later, a car pulled to a stop and the window lowered.

Daria was unaware until the man said, "Are you all right?"

Startled, Daria stood fast and almost tripped over the curb. The man in the car was a policeman. He wore dark sunglasses that obscured much of his face.

"Are you lost?"

"Ah..." But instead of words, she nodded.

"Where are you trying to go?"

"To my friend Jeremy's house."

"Does Jeremy have a last name?"

That was a good question. If she heard it, she didn't remember it. "I-I don't know it."

The officer nodded, studying her. His gaze made her nervous. "How about a phone number?"

She shook her head.

"Where do you live?"

She couldn't very well say, *In the forest*, so she pointed towards the woods, but after all her walking they were no longer in view.

"Where are your parents?"

"Don't have any."

The cop frowned, and to her dismay, opened the door and unfolded his muscular frame from the car. With hands resting on his service belt, he came around the car and stood in front of her.

"So you don't know where you're going. You don't know your friend's last name or phone number, and you live somewhere over there. Do I have that right?"

"Yes."

He removed the glasses and hung them from his shirt pocket.

"Let's start with your name."

She hesitated. Her body swayed.

"You do have one, right?'

She nodded.

His mouth twitched. "You want to tell it to me?"

She wanted to say no, but said, "Daria."

"Daria, are you in trouble?"

Her first thought was yes, but she just shrugged.

"Is someone forcing you to be out here on this corner?'

The question confused her. She shook her head.

"You haven't been kidnapped or forced to do something you don't want to?"

This time she spoke.

"No." She was confused by his questions. She decided to take control.

"I'm supposed to stay with Jeremy until my, ah...aunt returns. I told her I knew where he lived, but..." She shrugged. "I guess I don't."

"Do you have any way to contact your aunt? Do you know her phone number? Do you have a phone?"

On her fingers, she counted off her responses. "No. No. And no."

"What's in the backpack?'

She'd forgotten she was wearing it. She glanced over her shoulder. "Clothes."

"Are you running away?"

How did he know? She shook her head.

"Is Jeremy a relation to you?"

"No."

"But you're bringing clothes to Jeremy's house and staying with him?"

"Yes."

"How long have you known Jeremy?"

"A few days."

That answer did not sit well with the officer. "Your aunt is having you stay with a man you just met? A complete stranger?"

Why did that bother him so much?

"He's not a complete stranger. We're friends. He saved my life."

"He saved your life?"

"These giant boars attacked me and he saved me."

"Boars? There are no boars around here."

"Better tell them that, 'cause they sure were chasing me."

He shook his head. "Daria, are you on something?"

She glanced down. "You mean like my feet?"

"No. I mean like drugs." His tone took on a harder edge.

She didn't understand what the man was trying to say. Daria had had enough of the questions. She'd just have to find Jeremy's house on her own. She turned and started away, but the officer grabbed her arm.

"Whoa! Hold on, there. Where do you think you're going?"

"I have to find Jeremy."

"How you gonna do that when you don't even know his full name?"

She shrugged. "I'll manage."

"No. I think you should come with me."

CHAPTER FORTY-SEVEN

That wasn't going to happen. She tried to break free from his grasp, but he tightened his hold and moved closer to control her. Feeling the panic rising and afraid of being taken away where Biatta would never find her, Daria slapped her hand on the man's arm.

"*Beestengich!*"

The officer shouted and released his hold. Daria turned to run, but he was too quick and caught her with his other hand. Daria rounded on him and kicked his shin. He howled and hopped on one foot. Still he held on. She kicked the other leg. Once free, she bolted down the side street.

He called after her. "Come back here!"

That was not an option. A glance back showed he was in pursuit but hobbling. She raced around a corner and sped down the street, but the backpack was a hindrance. Another look. To her surprise, he was not in sight. Then she heard the whoop of the siren.

Before the car came into view, she dodged up a driveway to the left and behind the house. She kept going until she reached a rear fence. The weight of the backpack made climbing unbalanced. She toppled over it. She ran across that rear yard and down the driveway.

She kept running until she could go no more. Then she saw the ravine and remembered there was one behind Jeremy's house. She slid down the bank, her foot catching a rock. She was pitched forward and tumbled down the slope to the bottom. With the wind knocked out of her and pain from multiple contusions, she lay face down and did not move.

As her breathing eased and she took stock of the fresh injuries, she pushed to her hands and knees and scanned the houses along the rim of the ravine. Her eyes stopped on one that looked familiar. Daria rose to her feet, but her ordeal and the weight of the back had her taking quick steps backward. She windmilled her arms for balance, but it was too late. She tumbled onto her bottom and stopped in a leaning position once the backpack hit the ground.

"That was fun," she said.

The second effort was successful, but the long climb up the far side of the ravine proved difficult. The backpack almost pulled her over backward twice more. Taking the climb slowly, she managed to reach the top and collapse on the ground behind the house she thought to be Jeremy's.

From between the houses, Daria saw the police car cruise by. He was still looking for her. She'd have to be careful. She got to her feet and walked to the rear door. The curtains had been drawn, obscuring any view to the inside. She tapped on the door. No answer. Was this even the right house? She wasn't positive but thought so. After knocking twice more with no answer, she decided to try the front.

She opened the gate, stepped through, and froze. The police car was driving back in the opposite direction. If he glanced her way, he'd see her in the open. She readied to run back through the gate, but to her relief, he was focusing on the other side of the street. She inched along the wall until she could peer around the corner. The police car was five houses down. She waited until he was at the end of the block before climbing the steps to the front door. She knocked loudly. On the second set of still louder knocks, the door opened and a surprised Jeremy stood in the doorway.

"Hi," she said. "Remember me? I've come for a visit."

Jeremy stood staring at her with wide-eyed astonishment.

"Ah...are you all right?" she asked.

"How—What—who...?"

"I'll answer all your questions, but can I come in? A policeman is cruising the area, kinda looking for me."

"Huh? Oh. Yes, of course."

He stepped aside to allow her entry, then scanned the street before closing the door. Daria entered the front room and removed her pack with instant relief.

"It feels good to be rid of that weight." She massaged her lower back then flopped down onto the sofa.

Jeremy walked in front of her and stared down.

"Why are you here?" His tone wasn't unfriendly, but not warm.

"I was told to come here as a place I'd be safe."

His eyebrows rose. "And who would have told you that?"

"Biatta."

"Biatta?"

"Yes. You know. The woman in white."

"Yes, I know who you were referring to, but why would she say that? We are strangers. Why would she assume I'd take you in? Why come here in the first place?"

Daria leaned forward. "Can I get some water? Please?"

Jeremy studied her for a moment, then went into the kitchen. She heard the water pouring. He came back with a glass of water and handed it to her. While she drank, he sat across from her in a lounge chair. She finished the drink in one long pull and offered the glass back.

"More. Please." She offered a smile.

He took the glass and set it on the coffee table.

"Why don't you answer the questions first?"

She paused, wishing Biatta was there to do the answering. She grew uncomfortable under his steady gaze.

"It'd be best if we waited for Biatta. She can give you better answers than I can."

"She's coming? Here?"

"Yes."

"Why? What's going on?"

Daria squirmed, unsure how much she was allowed to tell.

"There's been some trouble at the village."

"I saw that. What kind of trouble?"

"The kind you run from."

"So you're on the run and seeking shelter here?"

"Yes."

"Why didn't she come with you?"

"Something came up and she had to go back. She should be here soon," she added quickly. Then, to divert the next round of questions she could see forming behind his eyes, she said, "Can I have that water now?"

He frowned at her but rose to get the drink. When he sat down, he slid the glass to her.

"Tell me why the police are chasing you?"

"I got lost coming here. He stopped and asked me questions I couldn't answer, so I ran."

"Are the police who you're having trouble with at the village, or is it something else?"

"Oh, believe me, it's something else. Something way else."

Jeremy was silent for a moment and Daria was grateful for the reprieve. It didn't last long.

"What's in the pack?"

"Clothes."

"So you moved out?"

She nodded.

"But you didn't run away?"

That gave her pause.

"Well, I did. We couldn't stay there."

"So everyone left, not just you?"

"Yes. We didn't have much choice."

"Is it your intention to stay here?"

She didn't know what to say. Biatta hadn't divulged her long-term goals. She answered as vaguely as possible.

"I think so. At least for now. Is that all right?"

Again, he studied her before nodding.

"For now, or until I can speak with Biatta. Why don't you take your pack into the bedroom on the left and get settled in? Are you hungry?"

She gave a vigorous nod. At least that made him smile.

"All right. Go and wash up. You look like you've been rolling on the ground."

CHAPTER FORTY-EIGHT

Voices brought her awake.

"She went down someplace around here," a woman said. "Spread out and search."

Biatta pushed up from the ground, but her strength was gone and she fell back. She couldn't stay there and willed her body to move. She made it to her feet, staying in a squat and balancing against a small tree.

Rustling to her left told her where one pursuer was, but how many others were there? She had to escape. If they caught her, they would torture her in the most creative ways to make her give up what she knew. She wouldn't break; of that, she was sure. Others had tried but failed. She held no illusion that this would be less and would result in her demise.

She focused her will, trying to pull as much energy from the air as she could, but she was weak and the amount she needed fell far short. She tried again with the same result. Pain entered in equal proportions to the energy. She thought about using some of the precious power on a quick heal, not enough to fully recuperate her; just to help her focus. But she knew if she did, the woman would no doubt sense it and pinpoint her position. She would only get one chance, and it had to be good.

Biatta reached deep inside for her owl persona and found she could not touch it. That had never happened before. She feared it had been too severely damaged by the fireball to respond. She prayed she hadn't been destroyed, although that would explain her inability to tap into more power. That also meant in her current state, she would not fare well in a battle of magic with the female assassin. She had to escape by some other means.

She drew up to her full height, pushing aside the pain moving created and pressed against the tree. She needed to find the location of all the searchers to plot an escape route. Movement behind her and to the left showed where two of the team were, but that left three others. Maybe they had split their force and sent others to seek the village.

Her always white attire did not seem a great choice at the moment. Ahead of her, a black-clad man stepped through the thick underbrush and spied her immediately. He raised an arm and pointed a short stick that Biatta knew to be a wand. So these men had magical abilities, as well as being stone-cold killers.

Before he could use the wand, she muttered a quick word, swiped her arm across her body, and sent the man flying headlong into a tree. He dropped hard and loud. They would know where she was now. Without hesitation, she ran toward the fallen man and hurdled his body. She darted through the brush, hoping the thicket would conceal the noise she made.

"There!" the woman shouted.

The forest came alive all around her. She could not allow them to get in front of her or she would be blocked. As she ran, she tried in vain to reach her owl, but again found no connection. She gave up and concentrated on drawing power from the ground as she pounded over it and the air she disturbed in her path. She grabbed more than before, but still was not a full complement to her potential.

Something whizzed past her face and embedded in a tree to her left. She swept a glance to the right. A man keeping pace with her was now in view. She called up a spell and swept her arm toward the man, but he was too quick and had obvious experience dealing with wizards. He crossed his arms in front of himself without slowing. The spell was blocked in a bluish burst of crackling electricity. However, with his eyes focused on her, he ran into a tree, which stopped him for the moment.

Biatta veered in that direction, knowing she had a slim space to get past the man. More crashing came to her left. She caught sight of another man. This one, however, did not pace her. Instead, he burst through the growth in his path, his clear intention to get in front of her. She swept an arm at him and he disappeared from view, tripping and stumbling over branches that reached for him. Three down, two to go. But she knew the most formidable chaser was the woman.

A short prickly bush stood in her path. Without slowing, she hurdled it. As she left the ground, something hit her from behind, pitching her off balance. She landed, fell, and rolled, coming to a sudden painful stop at the base of a tree.

Though stunned, she retained the imperative of fleeing. Before she could rise, a man appeared, surprising her. He recited a word and pointed his wand. She was thrown back forcefully into the tree, knocking the air from her lungs.

Through the haze in her head, she forced her body to rise. An invisible hand swatted her back down. She gasped, momentarily losing consciousness, then tried to rise again.

"Oh, this is just too good to be true," the woman said.

Biatta shook her head, searching for visual clarity, but one eye remained blurred. She saw the woman. The wide smile on her dark tattooed face displayed her victory. She recognized her from years past, but the name eluded her.

"It's Biatta, right?"

Biatta sat in defeat, unable to defend, move, or speak. Blood trickled down her face. "Who are you?" she croaked.

The woman laughed. "Who I am is of no importance. You, however, are infamous. The guild will rejoice to know you have been finally captured and brought to justice. All our teams have been issued contracts to find and detain you. I think I'm about to get a big promotion."

Her arms were jerked roughly behind her and bound tightly enough to cut off circulation. Someone yanked her hair back. The fourth man held an assassin's blade and stood glaring down at her.

"It's a shame the contract is only to capture and not kill, but so be it. It's not for me to question the leadership. But now I have a dilemma. Do I turn you over to Bradenbaugh or take you directly to the guild?"

She appeared to ponder the question, but Biatta knew which it would be. She might be doing work for Bradenbaugh, but she belonged to the Molatreseans. That tie was blood and much stronger than any other allegiance.

"Of course, that's not a question. We'll find the ones we were sent to hunt. Bradenbaugh will be happy with whoever I bring back. But you. You have special value."

The other three men returned. The woman gave orders. "You two take her back. Do not let Bradenbaugh or his people see you with her. Contact the guild and ask where they want her delivered and go straight there. Do not botch this up, or it will mean your lives."

The two men nodded, each grabbing an arm and lifting Biatta to her feet.

"Just a second."

The woman came closer, uttered two words, and squeezed her fist closed. Biatta felt her lips pinch together. She was unable to part them, which meant she could not speak. The guild assassin was making sure Biatta could not evoke a spell and make an escape. She motioned with her chin for the men to go.

"Have fun rekindling your friendship with the guild."

Biatta was manhandled through the woods. With her mouth magically sealed and her hands bound, escape would not come easy. She did not doubt the skill of the two men escorting her. Even if she managed to get free, they would not be easy to overcome. She had to be patient; bide her time and plot. She would only get one chance.

As they approached the place where the portal had appeared, Biatta wondered how the men were going to open it. Unless one of them was a special creation enhanced with some magical ability, only a mage or wizard had the skill to work the spell it required.

They trudged through the field, each man still with a tight hold on her arms, and stopped midway across. The man on the left released her arm and the other man snaked an arm around her throat to keep her in place. The first man slid his hand into an interior pocket and removed a pale blue gemstone. He held it in his palm, waved the other hand over it, and recited a basic opening spell. The portal appeared.

Of course they would have had a way to open it, but it showed her neither man had magical skills. Otherwise, they wouldn't have needed an enhanced gemstone. That was good to know. If she could get her hands free, she had a chance to escape.

The man with the stone slid it back into his pocket, then in a mocking *After you* gesture, he bowed to Biatta. She refused to move, testing how far they'd go. Their reaction was immediate. The mocking man slapped her, moving with such speed that it happened before she knew it was coming. Her head snapped back, the pain spread like fire. The second man crouched and scooped her up, placing her over his shoulder.

The first man came up behind her. "We've been ordered to bring you to the masters alive. We weren't told how alive you had to be, so as long as you're breathing, we can administer as much pain as we desire."

He grabbed her cheek and pinched. When she didn't give him the satisfaction of a cry of pain, he twisted. His face reddened with anger. Finally, she gave him what he wanted, if only to get him away from her. An evil smile spread across his tattooed face. He slid a finger under her eye, wiped a tear, and placed the finger in his mouth.

"Such sweetness. You should test me again. This was such fun."

He led through the portal. From entry to exit only took seconds. Once through, the lead man turned to close it. A buzzing sound like an extremely angry hornet whizzed past her face. The man's head disappeared in a spray of red and grey. He dropped. The man carrying her was turned the other way and did not see the death blow but heard the body fall. He turned to see what had happened and his head also erupted.

He fell forward. Biatta dropped on top of him, rolled, and darted for the portal. In her haste and awkwardness, she tripped over the first man as another angry hornet whizzed past her ear. She dropped halfway into the still-open portal. Not able to use her hands, she scampered forward with her legs to push off, her chin dragging across the ground. She toppled and felt a fiery pain in her thigh. Though her mouth was sealed, it could not contain the cry of agony. She kept her feet moving and heard another buzz, but this time it was not accompanied by pain.

Seconds later, she emerged on the opposite side, stunned and bleeding.

CHAPTER FORTY-NINE

Rowan Vandalue was stunned. "Excuse me. Did I hear you right?"

"You did, sir," Tarney said. "The man we tasked with making contact with the academy staff and students has reported someone is guarding the portal."

"Bradenbaugh?"

"I think not."

Tarney walked to the bar and helped himself unbidden to a stiff pour of brandy. Rowan watched but did not reprimand his boldness.

"How so?"

To Rowan's dismay, Tarney swallowed half the drink in one draw. One did not gulp such fine and expensive liquor like a shot of whiskey at the local pub. It added to his already annoyed demeanor.

"Well, for one, the guards are highly-trained snipers. They were wearing military camo."

He swallowed the rest. He reached for the bottle again, and Rowan was about to speak but saw the tremor a bit before setting it down. Rowan was shocked. The usually unflappable Tarney was scared.

"And two?"

"The victims are not our people."

The statement brought both relief and confusion. "Not ours? Then who?"

"They appear to be Bradenbaugh's people."

Rowan was too dumbfounded to speak. His mind raced for meaning. He had to have heard wrong, or the man they sent was mistaken. His eyes swung toward the bar. Or drunk.

"And our man. He's sure?"

"Very, sir. Said they had the look of military. If not current, then former. Two of them. As he approached the portal, keeping a stealthy eye out, he saw that it had been engaged. Two men were exiting, but before they could take more than a few steps out they were both shot. Headshots, at that. Made quite a mess, he says."

"Did he come to any conclusion?"

"He stayed for a few minutes to see what happened next."

Rowan grew more agitated at Tarney's lack of narration.

"Out with it, man. What else?"

His harsh tone snapped Tarney from the fugue that had settled in his usually clear and brilliant brain. "A black van pulled up. Four men exited and picked up the bodies. They cleaned the area and took the bodies away."

"So it's a full assassin team and cleanup crew."

"Exactly. But who is commanding them is the question."

"Did he see any rank or insignias on the uniforms?"

"None that he could see, but then he admits he wasn't that close."

"What does this mean?"

"There's a third player in this game that we have yet to meet."

Rowan nodded, having come to the same conclusion.

"There's more, sir."

"More?"

Rowan went to the bar and poured himself a drink. He was about to set the bottle down when he decided Tarney needed another. He refilled the glass and handed it to him. Tarney took it but did not drink. His eyes had a glassy, faraway look. Rowan took a sip and allowed the burn to travel down his esophagus.

"Tell me."

"One of the men who came out of the portal was carrying someone over his shoulder."

Rowan felt the hard knot form and feared the brandy was about to revolt.

"It was a woman. Though her clothes were ragged and soiled, he could see they were all white."

Making the quick connection, Rowan's jaw fell open. His stomach roiled against the burning liquor.

"He was sure it was Biatta."

The news was too much to bear. Rowan lifted the glass and downed the entire contents. He set it down and placed both hands on the bar for support.

"And?"

"Unknown. She appeared to be bound and possibly unconscious. However, when the cleanup crew arrived, our man was positive only two bodies were picked up."

"She somehow made it back through?"

"That was his thinking. However, three more shots were fired at the portal. She may have been hit. We won't know until we can send someone through. But to do that, the snipers will have to be dealt with."

Too many questions and fears assaulted him to allow focus on any one thing. He released his hold on the bar and paced on rubbery legs. At any moment he thought he would either fall or vomit; perhaps both. His mind traveled back in time to the day a young and distraught Biatta had first drawn his attention. She was being chased by some unseen pursuer, but the fear she displayed was no act. He hid her with a simple spell, then watched her for the next few days before approaching her. He had seen great things in that child, and to both of their credits, that potential had been reached and surpassed. He beamed with the pride of a father when she graduated from the academy. She'd done nothing but swell that pride further since joining the staff.

Was she still alive? Were any of them alive?

He turned to Tarney, who stood in shock, still holding the full glass of brandy.

"We have to know what happened. Somehow we have to get one of our people through."

"There is only one way to deal with the snipers. Are you willing to take that step?"

Rowan looked at his old friend. They had been through so much together. Had saved each other's lives on countless occasions. He understood what Tarney was asking. Once that line was crossed, there was no going back.

"I'll take whatever steps are necessary to ensure the continued safety of our staff and students."

Tarney did not move or speak for several moments. He finally set the still undrunk glass down. "Then I'd best be getting started." He pivoted and moved toward the door. "I know you don't want to know the details. Just leave it to me. Decide who you want to send through the portal and have them report to me."

"It might be beneficial to talk with the snipers. I'd very much like to know who they work for."

"As do I. Have no fear. I'll get what we need."

Rowan felt the shiver creep up his spine and tried not to show it. He knew exactly how Tarney would retrieve the information they needed—and that *was* something to fear.

"Tarney. Nedford. Do be careful."

The man paused, nodded, and exited.

"They have to be all right, don't they?"

Tarney stopped with his hand on the door. Without replying, he exited.

Rowan returned to the bar to pour another drink, than thought better of it. He had to keep a clear head. There was much to do. Much to plan. He did a quick mental review of the entire staff and student body, picturing each in his mind's eye. The images depressed him. They had to be all right. Were all right. He would not think them dead until he knew for certain one way or the other.

But.

He swore if even one of those precious people had been harmed, he would declare all-out war on those who had perpetrated such action.

He turned to walk back to his desk, but stopped, pivoted, and snatched up Tarney's glass.

CHAPTER FIFTY

Daria stood at the front window and scanned the street. She'd been in that position on and off for the better part of three hours.

"Daria. Come here. Dinner's ready."

"Something's wrong. She should've been here by now."

"I'm sure she's all right. She'll be here when she can. She wouldn't want you to worry or starve."

He pulled a chair out at the table and stood behind it, waiting for her. With a roll of her eyes and a grunt, she went and sat.

Jeremy was not great around the kitchen. That had always been Miranda's domain and she ruled it well. He knew a few basics; one, being spaghetti, which was on the table now. Though she continued to crane her neck to see out the window, the appeal of a hot meal was strong enough to keep her seated. He delighted in her slurping and the globs of sauce that dotted her face.

"So while we eat, let's talk."

Without lifting her head from the plate, her eyes found his and showed fear.

"Look, Daria. You're asking a lot of an old man, and I remind you that we only just met. If you expect to stay here, I need to know what's going on. I don't think that's too much to ask."

She slurped, swallowed, and set her fork down. She turned as far as she could to see out the window.

"Daria. I'm not an ogre. I'm not going to throw you out, but it's only fair that I know what I'm getting myself into. Please. Talk to me."

"I-I don't know what to say."

"Just start with the facts and the truth."

"I'd feel better if Biatta was here to explain things. I'm not sure what, ah—"

"—you're allowed to say?" He finished for her.

Her face reddened, telling him he'd hit the nail on the head.

"What can be so bad you can't talk about it? Are you and your friends on the run from the law?"

"Ah...well, not the law."

"But you are running from someone."

She nodded.

"I saw and heard things that make me think you're not exactly from around here. Did you come from a foreign country?"

She nodded again and turned her face down to concentrate on the food. Jeremy let her take a few more bites before continuing.

"Don't you go to school?"

"Yes."

"How do you do that when you live so far away and in the forest?"

"We're ah...homeschooled."

"I see. Are the other adults parents of the other kids?"

"No. They're our teachers."

"Teachers? Is this some kind of a cult or something?"

She gave it a moment's thought while she slurped in another strand of pasta, then shook her head. She finished quickly and took the plate to the sink. She rinsed, washed, and dried the plate and utensils. She looked at the cupboards as if deciding where they went by trying to look through the doors.

"Just leave them there. I'll put them away."

"Okay." She walked toward the front room. She stopped halfway and turned. "Thank you for dinner. It was really good."

He smiled. "You're welcome."

While she kept her vigil, he cleaned up the kitchen. By the time he was done, Daria had taken to pacing. She whirled on him as he entered the room. Fingers were in her mouth and she was ripping at a fingernail.

"We have to go look for her. She could be in serious trouble."

He paused to study her. "Explain what serious trouble means."

"Something bad had come to-to do something to the people still in the village. She went back to warn them."

"Something like those two creatures that chased you?" He didn't add *and me*.

"Something far worse. I'd never seen Biatta afraid before, but when she saw those people, her face went whiter than her dress."

"Are you and your…ah…people selling illegal drugs?"

"Huh? What? No. We're not criminals."

He eyed her, trying to read her reaction. "If you are, I won't let you stay here."

"Jeremy, please. Help me find her. I'm really worried."

He could see she was not just worried but scared as well. He thought about his promise to Chandra, but this was different. A life may be at stake. He didn't want to consider that life might be his own.

"Okay. Let me get a few things first."

"Thank you. Thank you. Thank you."

He collected two flashlights, some warm jackets in case they were out late, and a large pocket knife his father had given him when he was a boy. The blade wasn't as sharp as it should've been and rust made opening it a chore, but it was concealable. He didn't want Daria to see he was armed. Not that he could or would stab someone, but having it made him feel better.

As they drove out of the garage, the sun was well into its decline.

"We won't have daylight for much longer. Help me narrow down the search area. If we have to walk all the way back to the village, it's going to be dark long before we get there."

"I don't know where else to tell you to go. That's where she was heading when she changed into—I mean, when she left."

Jeremy drove farther down the road than he had before, hoping to cut some of the walking distance. He parked along the side of the road and they got out.

"Test your flashlight."

She did and both of them lit. He'd brought extra batteries just in case. They stepped over a guard rail and in seconds were swallowed by the forest. They kept a fast, steady pace without wasting breath on talk.

By the time they reached the first clearing, only a reddish haze remained in the western sky to offer any light. Halfway across, Daria grabbed his arm.

"What?'

"Shh!"

Jeremy Kline & the Invisible Village 438

She squatted, pulling him with her.

"I saw something move over there."

Jeremy rose slightly to get a look. It was too dark to see for any distance and he dared not use the flashlight. He strained, his old eyes cursing him for ever getting old. Then he did see something. A ghostlike figure moved in the shadows, either drunk or in trouble, because they were staggering. At one point the figure fell. Jeremy wondered if the person was now hiding from them.

They waited in strained silence. His hand slid into his jacket pocket and wrapped around the knife. Minutes later, the figure rose again. it was coming closer but at an angle heading into the trees to their right.

"Oh no," Daria said. "I-I think it's Biatta."

"What?" Jeremy lifted his head higher for a better look. "Are you sure?"

"No, not completely, but look at what she's wearing. It's a dirty white dress."

He hadn't noticed.

"She's moving strangely. Like her arms are broken or something."

"Or like they're tied behind her back. Stay here."

He started to rise.

"No."

Annoyed, Jeremy glanced down at the girl, but she was already up and moving.

"Biatta."

Jeremy hurried to keep up, but the girl was fast. The figure stopped, the dress billowing around her, giving her the look of a spectre. What he'd seen over the past few days made him believe anything was possible. Fearing for Daria, he pulled the knife and opened the blade as he ran.

The woman faced Daria and made strange, garbled sounds, further convincing Jeremy that he was looking at was a spirit. Daria continued until she reached the being. She stopped for a moment, then embraced the figure. Jeremy half expected her to pass right through the body. Instead, the contact knocked both of them to the ground.

Jeremy ran up, out of breath and unable to speak.

Daria said, "I'm so sorry, Biatta. Are you all right?"

Knife still in hand, he bent for a closer look. The bruised and mud-smeared face was difficult to recognize in the dark. He hoped Daria had the identification correct.

Daria stood and offered a hand, but Biatta did not reach for it. Instead, she made muffled noises.

"There's something wrong with her." A worried note crept into her voice.

Jeremy stepped forward.

"Let me."

He squatted behind Biatta and used the knife to sever the rope. Biatta swung her hands in front of her face and sucked in air like she'd run a marathon.

"Oh, thank goodness you found me," she gasped.

"What happened?" Daria asked, helping Biatta up.

"I'll explain later. We should go."

"I think you have a lot of explaining to do," Jeremy said.

She eyed him for a moment.

"Yes, I do. A lot."

CHAPTER FIFTY-ONE

Jeremy drove into the garage, parked, and remoted the door closed. Biatta and Daria sat huddled close in the back seat. Biatta looked exhausted. She caught his eyes in the mirror once, but never looked there again.

He exited and came around to assist Biatta out. In the garage light, he could see the mud was mixed with blood. He made no mention of it, but clearly she'd been through an ordeal. He placed a hand under her elbow for support while Daria took her other side and opened the door.

"I know you have a lot of questions, Jeremy. I promise I'll answer them, but I would like to get cleaned up first."

"Of course."

"Daria, do you have my pack?"

"Ah...no. It was too heavy to carry both, so I hid it in the forest. I thought you'd be back early enough to go back and get it."

Biatta sighed.

"I'm sorry."

"Don't fret, child. I'll make do. But I have important...ah, items in there. I hope you can find it again."

"I will. I promise."

"Daria, why don't you take Biatta to the bathroom while I gather some things for her?"

Jeremy opened the linen closet and withdrew a towel and a washcloth. He shut the door, thought again, and reopened it, taking out a second towel. Turning around in the hall, he rapped lightly on the bathroom door.

"I have towels for you. Soap and shampoo are already there."

"Thank you, Jeremy."

He set the towels on the floor in front of the door. As he bent, he could hear whispering through the door. Biatta was instructing Daria. Daria was not as quiet. Some of her words and exclamations came through.

"Oh my God! Is everyone all right?"

"Shh!" Biatta hissed.

"Sure"

Whisper.

"I can do that."

Whisper.

"Okay. Now?"

Whisper.

Jeremy heard movement and moved from the door. He entered his bedroom as the bathroom door opened. Daria walked past his room into the one she had claimed for herself. Moments later, she exited and went back into the bathroom. He couldn't see if she was carrying anything.

He rummaged through the closet in search of anything of Miranda's that might fit Biatta. He found pants and a pullover sweater. It may not be the style she liked, but it would serve its purpose until she could retrieve her pack.

He returned to the bathroom as the shower began running. The door opened a second later and Daria stepped out.

"I found these. See if she wants to wear them."

Daria gazed at the clothes. Her face scrunched in disapproval, but she took them and entered the bathroom, closing the door behind her. Jeremy wanted to eavesdrop again but thought better of it. He didn't want to be discovered snooping.

He went into the kitchen and put water on the stove for tea, then leaned against the counter. He didn't mind helping them, but he was not going to be used or taken advantage of. If he didn't get the answers he wanted, he'd ask them to leave in the morning.

Daria came out and looked toward the kitchen. Seeing Jeremy, she opted for the bedroom. She closed the door. That was fine. Biatta was who he needed to speak with anyway. Depending on how the conversation went, he preferred Daria stayed in the bedroom.

He opened the refrigerator and took out some sliced turkey breast, mayo, and swiss cheese. He made a sandwich, placed it on a plate, and set it on the kitchen table. Thirty minutes later, the bathroom door opened and Biatta stepped out. A towel was wrapped around her head. She wore Miranda's pants and a t-shirt that must have been Daria's.

She flashed a soft smile at Jeremy, then walked toward him. "Thank you for coming for me and letting us stay here."

He nodded, then pointed at the sandwich.

"I made you something to eat."

"Oh, that's wonderful. I'm famished."

"Tea?"

"Yes. Thank you."

He poured the tea and set the mug in front of her along with a small carton of low-fat milk and a bowl of sugar. He watched as she added milk and sugar to the tea and took a bite of the sandwich. She chewed delicately and rolled her eyes in mock enjoyment.

So good. Thank you again."

He let her get a few bites into the sandwich before starting his questions.

"Why are you here?"

She paused for a fraction before continuing chewing, then daintily patted before speaking.

"Why Jeremy, don't you want us here?"

The question for a question tactic annoyed him.

"Answer the question, please."

The smile faded from her eyes. She set the sandwich down, took a sip of tea, and leaned forward as if ready to divulge top-secret information. Her face was hard-lined, as was her tone.

"You need to understand something. Dangerous forces are hunting us. We are very protective of our people. The more I tell you, the more danger you're in, which means the more danger we're in."

Jeremy watched her face as she spoke, searching for lies or tells. He was no expert, but if they were there, he couldn't see them.

"If that's the case, you've already placed me and my family in danger. That is not going to go away. I need to know what you've gotten me into so I can be prepared to deal with whatever comes."

Now she studied him. Behind her pale blue eyes, he could see the wheels turning through the thought process that would lead to her response. He was determined to hear it all, or they had to go. She broke eye contact, glanced at her sandwich, then lifted her head.

"First, let me say I'm sorry that you ever got involved in this."

He started to speak, but she cut him off with the wave of her hand.

"It was not our intention. We wanted to stay hidden for as long as possible without interacting with the locals. That being said, I believe there was a reason we came in contact. I'm here because...well, we needed someplace to hide for a while, but more importantly, to determine what that reason is."

Jeremy absorbed that.

"Go on."

Biatta glanced away as if to regroup her thoughts.

"My people are very good at hiding. You should never have been able to find the village. You saw right through the veil placed over it. When we discovered you, your memory of us was erased. The person who did the mind wipe is an expert. You never should have had an inkling of what happened, let alone been able to find your way back. Somehow, our abilities do not affect you."

She made no mention of his grandson being able to see them, but it was too soon to bring him up.

"Explain these abilities."

"I'm not sure I can. At least not in a way you'd believe."

"Try me."

"The women of our people are born with an innate ability to perform...let's call it magic."

She waited for his response. When none came, she continued.

"Each of us trains in what we call the arts. We all have a special talent, and once it's discovered, we are given more specific training in that field."

"For example?"

"I'm considered a healer. I have other abilities, but my strength is in healing."

"What about Daria?"

"She is too young to know what her specialty art will be. She is a first-year student at our academy. She receives basic training that will intensify each year she progresses. As she attains the next level, she is given a broader spectrum until a match is made. In her final year, she will declare that skill and train and study to become accomplished in her chosen field."

He nodded but held his words.

"What more can I tell you?"

"I'm sure a lot more. Go back to what brought you here."

She slipped the tip of her tongue out and licked at the corner of her lip.

"If you think what I've told you so far is far-fetched, this next part will challenge your belief system."

CHAPTER FIFTY-TWO

Nedford Tarney was a dog. He was good at a lot of things. Over his near century of life, he'd learned more skills than he could ever impart to his students. But then, some should never be taught. He had come from a different world than the new breed of students. He didn't learn his skills at some school. He'd never attended school. He received his education on the streets running with various gangs and studying whatever tomes he could find or steal.

One of the skills that had served him well was the ability to alter his appearance to become something he wasn't, basically something less threatening. It wasn't shape-shifting, but more an illusion cast over himself that projected the image of whatever form he chose. He kept an inventory of twenty-three different guises from humans to animals. The success of this type of spell was in the details, something he excelled at studying and developing. His talent allowed him to get close to his prey or target. This day, he chose the form of a mangy dog sniffing at the street in search of his next meal. Over his lifetime, he ate from the street, if only to maintain his obscurity.

If another mage was vigilant, they might have been able to detect the magical residue used to not only achieve the appearance but maintain it, as well. That had happened once and was the reason he had a slight limp. His opponent was smart and fast but did not have the skill or devious mind of Tarney to survive in a dangerous world. He'd killed the man after a lengthy battle that involved magic, weapons, and physical prowess.

Older now, his physical abilities had eroded, but his mind was still strong and his thoughts fleet. His first task was to locate the shooters. He scanned the area for a lie that offered a clear line of sight at the portal's entrance. It would be high ground and a distance away. It took him all of two minutes to find the location and zero in on the two-man sniper team on the roof of a ten-story apartment building a little less than half a mile away.

Under the guise of the dog, he made his way to the rear of the building. Behind a dumpster, he allowed the spell to fade, revealing his human form. The only way up to the roof was an old rusty fire escape; its lower extension two floors up. With the sweep of his hand, the ladder descended. He gripped it, and with enough effort to make him resolve to lose some weight, he began the long climb to the roof.

He paused several times to catch his breath. He *was* getting old. By the time he reached the roof, he needed a longer break to ensure he had the energy to accomplish his mission.

He reached the top and peeked over. Neither man was in sight. With care he slid over the rooftop ledge and scurried behind a series of air conditioning units. He called up the mental image of what he'd seen from the ground. The two men were near the left side of the roof and about twenty feet apart. Their blinds were professional and well hidden from any casual observers from the ground or any windows of the buildings facing it. However, if anyone knew what to look for, which he did, the façade melted away to reveal what lay underneath.

He circled to the left. There were two rows or three massive units each. He moved to the inside of the last one. In front of him at the roof edge, he saw one of the shooters stretched out scanning through his scope. The second shooter should be to the right of him. He crept toward the front unit and crouched. He glanced down at the tarred gravel roof to ensure nothing was in his path to give him away. From an inner pocket, he removed a short dark brown wand. He could cast a spell, but he liked to have the wand as a backup in case of emergency.

As he readied to move, he realized that he should be able to see the second shooter by now. Warning bells went off in his head. He whirled, but no longer possessed the speed of his adventurous youth.

As the blade sliced through his stout belly, his killer grinned.

"Big mistake coming up here, old man."

Despite the pain ripping through his body, Tarney smiled. It created a confused look on the man's face.

"Guess we both made mistakes today. *Expeliatous*," he said.

The wand, which was trapped between them but angled upward, shot an energy beam that caught the man under his chin, snapping his neck back. His body flew up and back, slamming hard into one of the air conditioners. His body bent over the top and a loud snap sounded as his spine broke.

He glanced down. The spell had worked with such speed and force that the killer's hand was torn from the knife, leaving it embedded in his gut. No time for that now. He turned and ducked as a shot whizzed past him.

The jolt of landing on the abrasive surface sent a new wave of pain through him. He moved so as not to impale the blade farther into any life-ending organ. The shooter advanced.

Tarney had little time to move. He wanted to keep one of them alive for interrogation, but with his life flowing out of him at a rapid rate, he might have to alter his plan.

The man whipped around the unit and targeted Tarney, but before he could pull the trigger, something crushed his torso in an invisible vice. The man squealed. The rifle discharged, the bullet flying harmlessly overhead. Tarney had a closed fist lifted in front of him. He lifted the man, then slammed him into the unit, once, twice. As his head lolled to the side, he struck once more to ensure the man was no longer a threat before releasing the body. It fell limply to the roof.

Tarney scooted back and propped against the unit. He reached into his pocket and removed a small glass cube. He blew across the top and a panel slid back. A large queen bee emerged and hovered in front of him.

"Rowan, things didn't go quite as planned. Could use some assistance. ASAP. My friend will show you the way. If you don't make it in time, best wishes."

He waved his hand and the bee flew away. He looked at the combat knife with its wicked blade and wished he was better at the healing arts. He did what he could, then settled back to wait. He hoped his friend arrived in time, but then, with what lay ahead for them, maybe he didn't.

CHAPTER FIFTY-THREE

"We come from another place and another time."

She paused to see his reaction. His eyebrows rose a fraction, but otherwise showed no indication of disbelief. "We live in another dimension. We passed through a portal created by our headmaster. From what I've gathered of your world, our time might be equivalent to your Nineteen Fifties.

"Our people have special abilities. We stay hidden from your world as best we can. To make our presence known and what we can do would be to invite persecution. People fear what they don't understand and move in haste to eliminate what they perceive as a threat. Throughout our history, there have been documented times when we have been hunted and exterminated like a plague. Much like the witch hunts of your Salem."

She stirred her tea but did not drink it.

Jeremy spoke for the first time since she started talking.

"Is that why you're running? Because people found out?"

"No. We've become quite sophisticated in our approach to the general population. We keep to ourselves and train our students well. They are never to use their magic unless necessary to protect another's life or their own."

"If not them, then who?"

"As with any group of people, there will always be those who disagree with how things are managed. With us, it's an evil lord who believes our kind should rule over the others and not be ashamed of what we are. Many agree with him. I understand the viewpoint. But where I would choose to educate and assist and live in harmony, Lord Bradenbaugh wants to dominate and make the normal our slaves. We cannot have that. It's...well, it's just wrong. No one should be forced into service of another."

She did not mention Bradenbaugh's efforts to raise the Dark One. It was already too much for Jeremy to comprehend. She didn't want to overload his mind or cause him to stop listening because her story was beyond belief.

"Why not just make a stand and work to nullify what they are attempting? It's all politics. It's no different in this country."

"Because instead of discussions and debates, he attacked the school. Our school is very well protected, not only from the normal population of our world, but from other mages as well. They should not have found us. Many of our students were either killed or taken prisoner. My guess is because he wants to bend them to his will. The rest of us fled until we could escape through the portal to this world."

"How long have you been here?"

"Four months."

"In the meantime, you've left the other dimension for this Bradenbaugh to conquer?"

"No. We're but a small fraction of those who support our ways. Our task is to keep the students safe. Others are fighting the battles in our world."

Jeremy watched her thoughtfully.

"Something's changed. What?"

Biatta smiled. He was smart. She liked that about him.

"Yes. Bradenbaugh discovered the portal and has sent his people through to hunt us. Again, the portal should have been undiscoverable, yet they have found us. Something is happening here that is still unknown. How they have been able to locate us is something we must find out, or we will never be safe."

"If you were as protected as you say, the only way I can see for this Bradenbaugh to find you is if he has someone on the inside feeding him information."

Biatta worked her jaw from side to side, her eyes penetrating his.

"The thought has entered my mind. I'd like to believe our staff is loyal and would never sell out the students, but in truth, I can see no other choice."

"Could it be a student?"

"Doubtful. None of the students would be privy to our inner workings and do not have the skill needed to counter the spells used to protect us. Some senior-level students do have great potential, but even after they graduate, none of our defenses are ever disclosed."

"Could a student be more than they seem?"

Biatta cocked her head.

"Explain."

"What if a more experienced...ah, mage who was actually a spy working for this Bradenbaugh posed as a student?"

Biatta rolled the idea around. A minute later, she shook her head.

"No. I don't see it. We vet the students to the extreme. We wouldn't enroll someone who could be a danger to our way of life, the school, or those attending."

"But that's the ideal, the goal. Not every plan works perfectly. I see in your eyes you give the idea some credence."

She sighed. "Yes. I'll admit it could be possible. Not likely, but you've given me something to digest." She picked up the mug, sipped, and tried not to display her dislike of the taste. "At this point, it's more important to keep the students safe and far away from whatever Bradenbaugh sends through the portal to find us."

"Like those boars and the people who came to my house?"

"Yes. Again, I'm sorry about getting you involved. I'm afraid that now that they know you have a connection to us, they may return. That's one of the reasons I'm here. To watch and protect over you."

"But you admitted that what you do mostly is heal. So are you here to protect me or heal me after I've been attacked?"

"I promise to do both to the best of my abilities."

"And what about Daria? You said she's a student."

"I'm afraid Daria will have to grow up faster than intended. Her survival may depend on it."

He thought for a moment and she took another sip of her now cool tea.

Jeremy stood, took the mug from her hands, and placed it in the microwave. While it heated, he said, "You told me one of the reasons you're here. What're the others?"

She pursed her lips. "As you saw, the village was almost deserted. In fact, by now it surely is. We were discovered and forced to flee. We have established a new base camp, but some of our people were scattered. Daria and I were forced to leave sooner than expected and we missed departing with our group. We had nowhere else to go. Since you're one of the few inhabitants of this world we've had any contact with, we chose to come here." Hastily, she added. "I know it's an imposition. If you want us to leave, I'll understand. I don't want to burden you with our troubles. But please give us a couple of days to learn the area and get established before you send us on our way."

She didn't mention her desire to study him. That was something she wanted to do in secret without putting him off the defensive.

He didn't answer right away, which made her nervous. She'd hoped to appeal to his kind nature and big heart. After all, he had saved them twice and almost died—twice. But she hadn't played that part well. She spoke in an unemotional narration sans the feeling she needed to pull at his heartstrings. It was too late now. Other than pleading, which she refused to do, the choice was his.

"I'll let you stay for two days. We can see where we go after that."

She beamed.

"Oh, Jeremy," she gushed. "Thank you so much. This means a lot to us. I promise we won't be much trouble. We'll stay out of your way as much as we can. Besides, I'll be spending a lot of time tutoring Daria."

He nodded, but the expression on his face was far from happy. The microwave beeped. He turned, removed the now steaming mug, and set it before her. She picked it up, blew across the rim, and sipped. This time there was no expression. She finished her sandwich in large bites and washed it down with the tea. She thanked him again and stood to wash the dishes.

"That's all right. I'll take care of those."

"Okay."

"I guess I'll turn in, then. It's been an extremely exhausting day. Goodnight."

He offered a weak smile. "Goodnight."

She walked down the hall and entered Daria's room. It hadn't been a resounding victory, but she had bought them two days. A lot could be done in that amount of time.

Daria was laying on the bed staring at the ceiling. She bolted upright when Biatta entered.

"Is he going to let us stay?"

"Hush, child. Your exuberance causes your voice to carry. You must learn to control your emotions. Starting tomorrow we'll work on that and much more."

Daria lowered her voice to just above a whisper. "Is he letting us stay?"

"Yes. For now. We have two days to either learn all we can before moving on or convince him to let us stay longer. You'll play a big part in that effort. I sense he likes you. He sees you as a daughter. We mustn't alter his normal routine, at least as little as possible. That means on top of the lessons I will be giving you, you will also have chores to do around here that help him."

She frowned.

"Oh, please. It's no different than being at the school. You had your studies and chores there too."

"Yeah, but no one was trying to kill me."

Biatta wrapped her arms around Daria and drew her close.

True, she thought.

CHAPTER FIFTY-FOUR

Rowan Vandalue rushed across the rooftop and slid to a stop on the graveled top, dropping to his knees as he reached the unmoving body of his longtime friend. The escalating fear he'd felt deep in his core upon receiving the magical message ratcheted to a full-blown panic attack.

"Tarney. Oh, please still be alive."

He scooped the man up, cradled his head, and felt for a pulse. None. He was too late.

Wait. There was one very faint throb. Extremely faint. Reaching into an inside jacket pocket, he withdrew a small vial. He popped the cork stopper with his teeth, wedged the vial between the unconscious man's lips and tipped it up. Then he prayed the fortifying potion would keep him stable long enough to receive proper care.

The two men he'd brought with him checked the bodies of the two shooters. One caught his attention and shook his head. They'd get no information here. He held his friend, wishing he had better control over his healing magic. He'd use it if necessary, but he might cause more damage than he would heal. He'd wait to see if the potion had an effect first.

Rowan didn't want to admit it, but the skills that had made him perhaps the most formidable male mage in the land had been on the decline over the past few months. Ever since the attack on the academy, he suspected Bradenbaugh had created some new magic to drain his power. Either that, or he'd been poisoned. But if that was the case, the poisoner was someone on the inside; someone he knew. He preferred it to be magic he had yet to discover rather than find he'd been betrayed by someone he trusted.

He set Tarney's head down. A bloody combat knife lay next to Tarney. Was it his own or the weapon used to take him down?

"Help me check his wounds and bind them. The potion will lose its effectiveness if he bleeds out."

The taller of the two men squatted and used a knife to cut away the shirt where the bloodstain was most prominent. In a steady fluid motion, the trained medic exposed, examined, cleaned, and bandaged the wound.

"Deep knife wound. Possible internal injuries. He'll need medical care fast."

Rowan nodded, then placed Tarney's head back in his lap.

"Sir, we'll have to get him down from here. That will not be easy."

Rowan hadn't thought about getting Tarney off the roof. He'd been more concerned with keeping him alive. He couldn't deal with this.

"Make whatever arrangements you deem necessary."

The tall man nodded and stood, giving directions to the other man.

A minute later, Tarney emitted a sound. His chest appeared to be rising and falling with more strength. A minute after that, his eyes fluttered open.

"Tarney? Nedford, can you hear me?"

He coughed, blood tinged spittle flying out in a fine mist. He closed his eyes and tried to hold back his hacking. Soon Rowan's hand and jacket were coated in blood.

Eyes still closed, Tarney said, "Are we lovers now, with my head in your lap?"

Rowan said, "No. Still just friends, but all bets are off if you die. I will do horrible things to your corpse."

"I truly believe that."

"Be quiet, now. We have bandaged you and are working to get you off this roof. Save your strength."

A hand rose and gripped his arm with surprising force.

"You must listen, Rowan. The danger is more profound than we thought."

"Tell me later. After you recover."

"No time." His voice became coarser; the effort to speak more severe.

"Hush, now."

The hand released his arm and he thought his friend would rest, but it closed around his jacket and pulled him close to his face. The intensity in his eyes was enough to keep Rowan from speaking.

"There are other forces in play here like you thought." He coughed. Rowan felt the blood dots land on his face. "A new evil is coming from the normals. I questioned one of the snipers. Before he perished, he told me he was hired through a corporation called Dominate Domain Industries. It's a front, I'm sure, but supposedly deals with people who want to protect their homes with high-tech systems. It sounds like a residential defense system."

More coughing. More blood. Rowan ignored it, as did Tarney.

"Whoever is in charge knows about us...knows what we can do. They want to rid the world of our kind."

"They're not connected to Bradenbaugh?"

"Unknown. It's possible. But whoever is in charge is powerful and determined."

"No idea who?"

"The inconsiderate man died before I could get that far. But this changes things. We are now fighting a war on two fronts against two different very motivated and deadly foes."

They heard the sound of a rotor in the distance. The tall man ran up.

"I have a medical evac coming."

"We need to hide those bodies before they catch sight. Explaining this will be difficult enough without them seeing a military corpse."

The man nodded, motioning to his partner, and they went to take care of the problem.

Tarney lay still. For a moment, Rowan feared he had passed. Then he saw the chest rise and fall, though not with the same cadence as before. The potion was already wearing off. That meant the internal damage was more involved than he'd hoped.

With his eyes closed, Tarney whispered, "You must strip my body of all devices and objects that might raise questions and compromise me."

With Tarney, you never knew where the man might hide something or what might be a device, so Rowan took it all and secreted the items inside his abundant jacket pockets.

By the time the chopper landed, all on the rooftop and Tarney were ready. The door opened and a man and woman darted out. Explanations would happen later. He'd have time to prepare a statement. Now, they just needed to know the extent of the injury. He told them. They asked a few questions about Tarney and his medical history as they went to work with quick and efficient skill.

Five minutes later, the somewhat more stable Tarney was hoisted onto the helicopter and lifted away. Rowan stood and watched until the medivac was but a dark dot in the blue sky.

"Sir," the tall man said. "We should go. You've been up here entirely too long. With unknown forces rallying against us, it will be harder to keep you protected."

"Any clues on the bodies?"

"Nothing to lead us to who sent them, but I did find markings on the air conditioning unit. Two sets; one with the initial R, and the other, K. Beneath each were scratches I'm assuming were tabulations. It appears they have been here a while. They scored five kills."

"But no way to know who?"

"No sir."

They descended the fire escape while Rowan mulled over the idea that five people had died. They knew two of them were Bradenbaugh's minions, but who were the other three? Had Jerricka sent messengers through the portal, only to have them killed?

This was troubling news. If the new player was aware of the portal, how could they continue to use it safely? One thing was certain; if they had regular check-in times, someone would be sent to discover what happened.

"Keep someone posted here to observe what happens. I want to know the minute a replacement has been set up."

"Do you wish them dispatched or interrogated?"

"We need information. Then you can dispatch them. We have to get word to Jerricka not to use the portal until further notice. Send two of your best men and an escorting mage. Jerricka is smart. If she feels their position has been compromised, she will move them. It will be difficult to locate her again. The mage will be necessary."

They reached the street and took a circuitous route back. The tall man led, his partner following a discreet distance behind. Along the way, they picked up two more of their team, both mages. Both female and highly skilled.

Rowan walked on, lost deep in thought and relying on his protectors to stay vigilant. Too many unanswered questions rumbled through his brain. Who was this new group? What was their goal? Was Bradenbaugh involved? Made sense yet didn't feel right. For that matter, what was Bradenbaugh up to? He'd been quiet for a while.

He rubbed his temple. He could feel a headache coming on. For the first time since the primary attack, Rowan Vandalue had doubts about the outcome of this war, that now

apparently involved normals.

CHAPTER FIFTY-FIVE

Jeremy was awakened the next morning by the sound of clattering. His eyes popped open and he listened. Someone was moving around inside the house. A glance at the alarm clock showed the time to be six forty-two. He stood, slipped on a robe and slippers, and crept to the door. He cracked it open to listen. It was logical that his two guests were up and moving around, but it was early and others had snuck into his house before.

He looked around the room for a weapon. Intruders were not something he was prepared for, which was an oversight he vowed to correct.

"Like this, Daria."

The tension flooded away as he recognized the voice. It was Biatta, and she did not sound under duress. He opened the door and stepped out. He was halfway across the front room before Daria noticed.

"I think we woke him."

Biatta turned. She was dressed in the same clothes she had gone to bed in. A bright, broad smile lit her face.

"Well, good morning, Jeremy. I hope we didn't wake you."

"It's not even seven."

"I'm sorry. We're used to getting up early. We thought we'd make you breakfast today to show how much we appreciate your letting us stay here."

Jeremy thought, *You're trying to bribe me—with my own food*, but he smiled and said, "That's considerate of you. I'll get dressed and be right back."

He went to his room, closed the door, and leaned against it. He still wasn't sure he trusted them. It had been obvious Biatta was holding something back that was important. He'd have to watch her closely.

Then a new thought entered his already overworked brain. Would they poison him? That way they could stay as long as they wanted. He ran the idea through his mind before letting it go. He didn't think so. Besides, Biatta was smart. She knew Chandra would eventually show up. Exhaling a long breath, he thought this new living situation was going to take some getting used.

A short time later, they were all seated around the table eating their meal of ham, eggs, and cheese with pancakes. He had to admit, however Biatta had prepared the meal was more enjoyable than his own cooking.

And the pancakes. Wow! They had a very unique, almost addictive taste. Once the thought had entered his mind, he gazed at the plate with suspicion. Had she laced them with something to make him pliable to her commands? He glanced at her as she chewed her pancake. Could she be that devious, or was it just his imagination creating a problem where one didn't exist?

She caught his gaze and smiled. Her eyes twinkled. He'd have to watch what went into the food from now on.

He picked up his coffee mug and sipped. Even the coffee tasted better. He decided to probe.

"What did you use for coffee?"

She tilted her head as if confused by the question.

"Whatever you had in the cupboard. Is something wrong with it? Did I not make it the way you like?"

"No. No, it's not that. It's just that it tastes so much better than when I make it. Did you add something to it?"

She visibly relaxed and smiled.

"No. No additives. Just some major subtractions."

"Huh?"

"Your coffee pot was filthy. I gave it a thorough scrubbing and all the residue came off. Now you're tasting fresh coffee." She laughed. "I don't know how you drank that coffee before."

Daria finished her food and eyed the table for more.

"That's all there is, child. You're going to have to learn to control your appetite."

Daria frowned.

"Now clear the table and start on the dishes, please."

Her frown deepened, but she got up without a word and collected the plates.

Jeremy said, "I didn't touch my other pancake if you want it. I'm full."

She dropped into her chair so fast that she almost dropped the plates she was holding. They clattered down on the table and she glanced up at Biatta with a sorrowful look.

"Slow down," Biatta said.

Jeremy slid his plate to Daria, thinking she'd put it on her plate, but she snagged a fork that may or may not have been hers and dug in like she hadn't already eaten a meal. Amused, he watched the girl eat, aware that Biatta was watching him. As Daria shoveled the remaining bites into her mouth, he shifted his eyes and gazed at Biatta over the rim of his mug. She returned the gaze. He tried to read her expression. Her eyes still twinkled, her expression giving away nothing.

Daria stood next to the sink, getting ready to wash the dishes. Jeremy opened his mouth to speak but was interrupted by a knock on the door. Surprised, he set the mug down and shot an inquisitive look at Biatta. She shook her head. She wasn't expecting anyone.

Jeremy walked to the door. Behind him, he heard a chair scrape across the linoleum and knew Biatta had stood. He glanced out the peephole and spied Chandra.

"Uh-oh," he muttered.

He hadn't wanted this confrontation yet. He wanted time to decide whether to allow his two guests to stay. If they had left, he could've avoided the scene about to play out. He opened the door, thinking to block her from entering.

"Good morning, Dad. I'm glad you're awake." She was past him before he could move. She carried a bag of takeout. "I brought breakfast. It's sort of a peace offering. I said some horrible things to you yesterday."

She halted at the kitchen and froze. Even from behind, Jeremy knew his daughter well enough to see the mood change. She swung from happy and bubbly to boiling mad in seconds.

"What are you doing here?"

She set the bag down with no thought to jostling the containers and made a threatening step forward. Jeremy rushed to intercede. He grabbed her by the shoulders and spun her to face him.

"Now, Chandra. It would be impolite to throttle my guests."

"Guests? These people are invaders, as far as I'm concerned. What trouble are they going to get you into next?" She whirled, breaking free of Jeremy, and pointed at Biatta. "I don't know what your game is, but you and your daughter need to leave now or I'm calling the police."

"Maybe if you settled down we could discuss this." Biatta's tone was calm but her body language said otherwise. She was prepared to meet Chandra's attack head-on.

"Calm down?" Chandra's voice escalated. "There's nothing to discuss. You leave my father alone. I don't know what you're holding over him, but you need to withdraw your talons and fly away. Preferably far, far away."

She reached into her purse and pulled out the cell phone. She punched in what Jeremy assumed was 911, but before she could place the call, Jeremy grabbed her arm and removed the phone.

"Hey!"

"Chandra, you need to listen. Biatta and Daria are my guests. They will be staying here for the time being until other arrangements can be made."

"No. That's crazy."

"It's what I'm doing, crazy or not. This is still my home. I decide what I do or don't do here. I've decided they are staying. Now either accept it or leave."

Chandra's expression went from hostile to questioning to hurt, then back to angry in seconds. She snatched the phone from his hand and stormed out of the house. Jeremy followed and watched as she squealed the tires and sped away.

"That's just great."

"I'm sorry, Jeremy," Biatta said from behind him.

He hadn't heard her approach. The sound of her voice so close startled him. He turned and stared hard into her eyes.

"This had better not be a mistake. You just came between me and my daughter and if I know her, which I do, she'll stay mad for quite a while."

He went to his bedroom, closing the door behind him. He stretched out on the bed. He had a lot of thinking to do. Things were moving too fast for his normal leisurely lifestyle. He glanced at the picture of Miranda on the nightstand and reached for it. His hand bumped the frame, knocking it off. It crashed to the floor, the glass shattering. He stared down at the broken frame, Miranda's face under shards of glass. In his mind, he imagined her now scowling at him.

"Guess you're mad at me too."

He picked up the frame, careful to keep the glass from spilling onto the floor and tipped it over the trash can in the bathroom. Some fell, but most he had to pull from the frame. One of the last pieces was stubborn. He pulled harder. It released and his hand slid across the frame, slicing his finger on the jagged glass.

He flinched at the sudden pain. Blood welled into a small bead. He reached for a tissue to blot it, but something stopped him. He stared into the blood bead and an image formed. An image of an old and familiar man. His grandfather. His face sharpened and the details came into view. Fear. His grandfather was afraid of something.

The scene was dark. A heavy mist rose from the ground, enveloping them. With one arm, his grandfather pushed him behind and blocked his view from whatever had caused the terror. Words were exchanged, though none he could understand. Then, sudden motion and cries of pain came from several different sources.

His grandfather staggered back as if pushed by someone. His arm came back and wrapped around Jeremy, protecting him and keeping him from falling.

"No!" he shouted. "You shall not have the boy."

He crouched and stretched both arms forward, speaking in a language Jeremy did not know.

White crackling light and blazing orange flame met in a ground-shaking boom. Then in another flash, a horrifying scream faded into a deathly silence. His grandfather bent forward and dropped to one knee. His breath was raspy and pained.

Jeremy could feel his fear escalate as he worried for his grandfather. He touched the man's back and he turned to face him, meeting his eyes.

"It's okay, boy. We're safe. I won't let them take you."

But the beads and dots and spray of blood that coated his grandfather's face gave Jeremy the impression of being anything but safe.

The vision faded, leaving him gasping for air and staring into the mirror at a face that looked so much older than the one he'd stared at on his birthday a few days ago. He barely recognized his reflection.

He staggered back, touching his face. But when he looked again, all was back to normal. What had he just seen? Was he hallucinating? Again, he wondered if Biatta had slipped something into his food or coffee. She professed to be a healer, but wouldn't she also understand how to cause harm?

He pressed his hands on the countertop and stared into the mirror seeking answers. A thread had unraveled. A distant memory stirred. The vision, if that's what it was, had been terrifying, yet somehow the scene was familiar. Had it been a daydream or something from a movie?

He felt it was more than that. It had a basis in reality. But whose reality?

He splashed cold water on his face and let the drops fall on their own. His eyes lowered and found the smiling face of his dear wife in the damaged frame. For the first time since her death, the picture failed to soothe him.

What was going on inside his head? Threads and images wove through the synapses of his brain searching for like entries and trying to make connections. There was something hidden deep within long-buried recesses just out of reach. The effort to bring them forward was exhausting. He closed his eyes, shook his head, and tried again, but whatever had been lurking beneath the surface had vanished.

He gave up after several failed attempts. The threads were gone. Once more, he stared at the image of himself.

"Well, you old fart, what have you gotten yourself into?" He frowned. What could possibly come next?

ABOUT THE AUTHOR

Ray Wenck taught elementary school for 35 years. He was also the chef/owner of DeSimone's Italian restaurant for more than 25 years. After retiring, he became a lead cook for Hollywood Casinos and then the kitchen manager for the Toledo Mud Hens AAA baseball team. Now he spends most of his time writing, doing book tours and meeting old and new fans and friends around the country.

Ray is the author of thirty-Nine novels including the Amazon Top 20 post-apocalyptic *Random Survival* series; the paranormal thriller, *Ghost of a Chance*; the mystery/suspense *Danny Roth* series; and the ever popular choose your own adventure, *Pick-A-Path: Apocalypse*. A list of his other novels can be viewed at raywenck.com.

His hobbies include reading, hiking, cooking, baseball and playing the harmonica with any band brave enough to allow him to sit in.

You can find his books on all your favorite book purchasing sites.

You can reach Ray or sign up for his newsletter at raywenck.com or authorraywenck on Facebook.

Other Titles

Random Survival Series

Random Survival

The Long Search for Home

The Endless Struggle

A Journey to Normal

Then There'll Be None

In Defense of Home

Danny Roth Series

Teammates

Teamwork

Home Team

Stealing Home

Group Therapy

Double Play

Playing Through Errors

The Dead Series

Tower of the Dead

Island of the Dead

Escaping the Dead

Pick-A-Path Series

Pick-A-Path: Apocalypse 1

Pick-A-Path: Apocalypse 2

Pick-A-Path: Apocalypse 3

Stand Alone Titles

Warriors of the Court

Live to Die Again

The Eliminator

Reclamation

Ghost of a Chance

Mischief Magic

Twins in Time

Short Stories

The Con   *Short Stop: A Danny Roth short*   *Super Me*

Super Me, Too

Co-authored with Jason J. Nugent

Escape: The Seam Travelers Book 1

Capture: The Seam Travelers Book 2

Conquest: The Seam Travelers Book 3

The Historian Series

The Historian: Life Before and After

The Historian: The Wilds

The Historian: Invasion

Jeremy Kline

The Invisible Village

Ray Wenck

Bridget Conroy Mystery Series

A Second Chance at Death

Traveling Trouble (Coming Soon)

Ray Wenck